THE SKI DREAM

James P. Warner

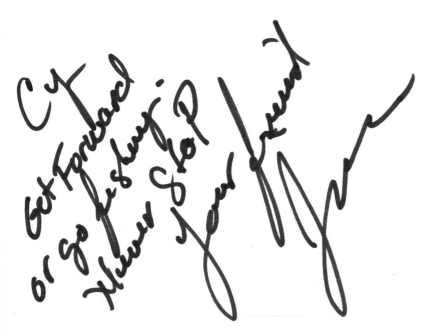

ISBNs
Paperback: 978-0-9863855-0-6
Cloth: 978-0-9863855-1-3
eBook: 978-0-9863855-2-0

Foreword

WHAT YOU ARE ABOUT TO read is just a story. It is not intended to and does not depict any actual events. It's just a story told by the author for the amusement of you, the reader.

I would like to dedicate this book first to my hero—and the person who believed in me the most—my father Major George Howard Warner, and secondly, to my brother who tragically lost his life following his dreams, Daniel Jay Warner.

This book wouldn't have been possible without the love and support of my family, which allowed me to face challenges and follow my dreams.

I would also like to recognize the kindness and wonderful accomplishments of Margaux Hemingway. The world is a lesser place without her.

James P. Warner

The Ski Dream

PEOPLE FIND INSPIRATION IN MANY ways. This is a story of a magical time in a boy's life. With the support of his family, one boy and his best friend learn about a passion in life. They are driven by the grandeur of the mountains, the exhilaration of speed and the appeal of the decadence of ski towns.

Sunny, a boy from Glen Ridge, New Jersey, with a speech impediment and learning disabilities, was not your average kid. Skiing motivated him to discover the world on his terms and find success in life. Sunny and Carl, both from New Jersey, team up with a unique, unlikely group of ski bums and create a Ski Dream.

To a dedicated skier, ski bumming means to love skiing more than anything. Once, ski town employees were a valuable commodity. To most people the term *bum* would be a derogatory word, but in the ski world at one time, it was a term which carried pride and dedication. Employers would offer room, board, and lift passes to anyone who would come to their ski town and work for the season; hence the birth of the ski bum. Ski towns were filled with people who came solely for the love of skiing, eating, and sleeping. Ski bumming was more than just a pastime, it was a lifestyle. To someone who had a true passion for skiing, ski bumming became their identity. It was who they were, and being a ski bum shaped how they saw the world and how the world saw them. A ski bum woke up thinking about where, when, and how they were going to ski. On every run, on every turn, they wanted to find a way to learn, to improve. Learning to ski better was the passion. People that just skied down a mountain just didn't get it. You had to ski harder, faster, longer and take more risks. It was a hunger. The harder, faster, longer you skied and the more risks you took and got away with, the better you felt. Yes, it was all about the adrenaline. The problem was that ski bumming was to be short-lived and the lifestyle was in jeopardy. As skiing and ski towns grew, professional waiters and waitresses came and ski bums became a dying breed. In every ski town the never-ending question still remained: Who is the best, who is the king of the mountain? Who is the fastest, who will ski harder, longer and take the biggest risk and get away with it? This is a story of one boy's dream to be The King of the Mountain during the last days of the ski bums.

To tell the story of Sunny's pursuit to be the King of the Ski Bums or the King of the Mountain, one would have to go back and see how a ski bum is made. It wasn't so easy. So the story starts with growing up in, of all places, New Jersey.

Growing Up in New Jersey

NEW JERSEY IS A WONDERFUL place that is unique, actually having four balanced seasons. 1958 was a magical time when the economy was rebuilding after a recession, post-World War II. Sunny lived in a small town named Glen Ridge about 15 miles outside of New York City. The town was 2 miles long and a half a mile wide. The Memorial Day Parade was attended by everybody and led by Sunny's father, a true World War II hero and also his hero. The main road that went from one end of town to the other was lined with beautiful shaded trees and gas lamps. There were gas lamps throughout the entire town. In the fall when the trees turned colors, the town looked like something out of a Norman Rockwell painting. When the leaves fell, people could rake them into the street and burn them. It was wonderful that you could smell the leaves burning throughout the town. Everybody went to the town football games and Sunny could hear the high school band playing from his bedroom window. It was a time of innocence. Cars were made of metal. Families ate dinner together every night. Most houses only had one phone on the wall and nobody dared to answer it during dinner. There were no school buses in Glen Ridge; children walked to school. Sunny's grade school, Forest Avenue School, didn't even have a cafeteria. At lunchtime the students were dismissed and they went home for lunch. He walked home by himself about a block and a half on Forest Avenue. Nobody thought that children shouldn't be able to walk home by themselves in the 50s. Glen Ridge was close to a commuter train, which went into New York. Many businessmen were able to walk directly to the train station. New Jersey was a great place to grow up, but it wasn't the place that was known for its ski industry—yet it did have a fair amount of snow each winter. For Sunny, at the age of eight, each season seemed a year long and something to look forward to, while winter seemed the severest of them all. Bad weather meant staying in the house after school, or sometimes even to stay in on a Saturday. Now, New Jersey isn't known for its snowfall. But when someone is only 4 feet tall, 10 inches of snow is overwhelming. No one in New Jersey really *prepared* for snow.

When the snow fell, people just stayed put until things got cleared up. At least the adults did. It was every New Jersey kid's dream to have the streets covered with snow and also have the day off from school. Mothers bundled their children up in snowsuits which provided them with enough padding and insulation to survive any winter assault. In Sunny's family, wrapping eight kids up was nothing short of an art form. From the oldest down, there was Gus, then Gary, the twins Gillian and Georgia, Jody and Sunny, Jeff, and the youngest, Danny. There were six boys and two girls in all. Sunny's family was a blended family of yours, mine and ours before its time. Sunny's father remarried, and Sunny's step-mother had four children, Gus, Gary and the twin girls Gillian and Georgia. In Sunny's family, there was his oldest brother Jody, younger brother Jeff, and then came Danny who tied the two families together.

This undertaking was no small task. Managing a household of eight children took courage and discipline. Sunny's father had gotten custody of him and his two brothers, so marrying a woman with four children was an act of kindness, love—or well, we'll just leave it at that. His father, George Warner, made a career as a military man. He had attended Valley Forge Military Academy as a youth and upon graduation, found himself smack dab in the middle of the European Theater during World War II in a battle called the Battle of the Bulge. If there was a time you wanted to be an officer, this probably wasn't it. He stayed in the military reserves after World War II to complete a 20-year career. It's no wonder that the household had discipline and structure.

Sunny was a boy of his own mind—happy, athletic, and energetic with a passion to dream. In 1955 when Sunny started school, terms such as dyslexia and Attention Deficit Disorder didn't exist. There was no special education for people like Sunny. And you weren't special, but rather an inconvenience for the teacher. For Sunny, he quickly understood he was different and was subjected to daily insults and accused of being nothing short of retarded. Fortunately for Sunny, his father had an unwavering belief in him. And the 6 foot something, red-headed principal Mrs. Gardner PhD would not let him give up. She would see Sunny standing in the hall after disrupting the class, look down and say, *"Sunny I know you're smart. I know you can do this."* So Sunny learned at an early age that he had to figure things out or face failure, the former being a skill that would eventually serve him well.

For Sunny, being in a large family meant a lot of things. First, having eight kids always meant having someone to play with, but it also exemplified all his difficulties and meant that the focus was not always on him. When the snow came, the older crew seized the opportunity to pick up extra cash by shoveling walks. Everybody knew where the older people and single women lived; that was a sure thing. Of course, nobody went anywhere until their own home was done first. All the steep streets were impassable by car, and therefore skillfully packed for toboganing and sledding. However, Sunny quickly found tobogganing lacking a demand for skill and he became curious for something else. That particular year, the snow had come early. So his request to learn to ski sparked his father's idea for a Christmas present.

When you have such a large family, you learn not to expect large expensive gifts. Sunny's family wasn't wealthy, but they weren't poor either. Christmas presents took up at least two rooms in the house. Needless to say with a family of eight, secretive Christmas shopping was impossible. There simply was no time when his parents could move within a 100 mile area without bumping into at least one kid. The best that could be done was to wrap things up and not tell which box went to which child.

One Saturday, Sunny had chosen to spend the day with his dad. His task was to move some Christmas presents to his grandparents' house, as their own home could not hold any more gifts and still be functional. So he and his dad went around loading the family station wagon. The reason they took the family station wagon was that U-Haul wasn't in business yet. Sunny couldn't help inquiring about this one item. It was too long and thin. Sunny had to ask,

"What's this?" Much to his surprise, his father replied, "Oh that's yours. It's a pogo stick."

Now being his age, Sunny did not question his father but he was curious about the size. If someone had not seen a pair of skis wrapped up, it could have looked like a pogo stick. So Sunny didn't give it a second thought. He trusted his dad. Still, he was excited and it felt good that his dad had confided in him. He planned to act surprised when opening the present so he wouldn't ruin the surprise his mother expected.

On Christmas, all the children spent the night up in their sisters' room on the third floor. After all, if you were going to listen for Santa, you had to get as close to the roof as possible. All the children grabbed their blankets, pillows, and found a spot to wait for the sound of sleigh bells. It was a night filled with anticipation. With this many kids waiting for Santa, there were enough butter cookies left out to give Santa hardening of the arteries before he left the house.

The problem with all the children sleeping in the same room—with visions of sugar plums dancing in their heads—is that when one woke up to see what Santa had left, all of them would soon follow.

First stop, the tree on the first floor. If the descent down two flights of stairs did not wake the parents, the kids jumping on their bed did! In later years, the family had a "no opening presents until 5 o'clock in the morning" rule because Sunny's parents had spent so much time providing the moment; all the children would open one gift at a time so all could share the surprise.

When it came time for Sunny to unwrap his "pogo stick," the size and shape drew everybody's curiosity. Needless to say, Sunny was overwhelmed when he discovered his pogo stick had turned into a pair of skis. All his brothers and sisters were delighted and anxious to see how they worked. Watching this awe from their children, his parents must have known they had created a land-slide interest in a family sport.

Fortunately, it was a white Christmas and the nearest hill was one block away. It wasn't a ski hill, but it was a hill. Actually it was a snow covered street, but that day it was a ski hill. So Sunny's dad grabbed his skis and Sunny as well, and off to the hill they went, neither of them having a clue what to do. They spent most of the time on their butts. Eventually they learned how to snowplow, but still, using their butt for a brake seemed the most effective way to stop.

Now remember, they had several hazards to encounter. The first, being a street with curbs, trees, and houses on either side. The second, they weren't alone. Every kid on the block who had received a sled, toboggan or dish was utilizing the same thoroughfare. Sunny was the only one with skis besides his dad. This was both good and bad. It was good that they did not have more kids flying down the street out of control, and bad that Sunny had no one else to provide him with an example of what to do. Still, he loved it.

Moving Up

BY THE FOLLOWING YEAR, SUNNY was anxious for something more challenging. The next available terrain which provided some shelter from traffic was the local golf course. Not exactly the Alps, but it was a step up and he could walk there. To his amazement, other people were there with their skis. At this point, he didn't really understand the concept of mountains or ski lifts.

To Sunny's surprise, two or three other people besides his dad had the same ambition to learn skiing. It was nice not to be alone in the world and now they had someone else's direction on what to do. Turning was a challenge, as that portion of the course which provided enough terrain was still very short. To be able to stop was an increased necessity as they progressed. Their whole skiing experience was much like ski jumping. They started out straight down, looking for a bump to provide additional excitement. The ultimate thrill was to stop before hitting a tree, fence, or street with oncoming traffic. To them, skiing at the Glen Ridge Country Club provided dreams that would eventually become a motivator and lead to a career in the industry.

Now it had been a while since he had received his skis. As previously mentioned, New Jersey does not get all that much snow. Sunny had made many trips to neighboring golf courses and by this time, had actually mastered some skills. Sunny had, at least, not broken anything on himself or on anyone else.

One Saturday his father, while driving by one of the golf courses, stopped to watch him. To his amazement, he found Sunny's attempts at skiing somewhat inspiring and his dad decided to organize an actual ski trip. Ski areas had come to Northern New Jersey as early as 1937, but Sunny's father decided to try a ski area just up along the Hudson River in New York State some two hours away. There was no way his father was going to experience this adventure with only one child of such a large family. This was going to be a full-blown family adventure.

Now to organize eight kids in order to get up and be on the road at 5 in the morning was a feat in itself. Sunny's dad, having come from a long military career, had everything organized to the greatest detail. He systematically packed skis, boots, poles, etc. in the car the night before and had all the children lay out their clothing for inspection. They did everything short of sleeping in the ski clothes.

They all woke promptly up at 5 a.m. with great anticipation of what was yet to come. They dressed and stood for a final inspection—then climbed in the car and fell asleep. With eight kids and equipment in one car, sleeping on top of each other was expected and they must have looked like puppies in a box. Sunny always sat up front, as he was extremely susceptible to motion sickness. They had been on many family trips before so they all knew the travel routine. When they arrived and got their first look at a ski area, Sunny was so amazed by how much snow and how big the mountain was. There was more mountain than Sunny had ever imagined. The idea of lifts and prepared skiing areas was unbelievable.

Sunny had been involved in athletics for a while. He started, as the whole family did, swimming at an early age and managed to advance his skills to an AAU (Amateur Athletics Union) competition level. Sunny didn't really have the skill or interest, but he would go train three nights a week rather than do homework. He was older now and wanted something more social.

As a result of Sunny's swimming accomplishments and tenacity, his family thought he was an okay athlete. Not knowing any better, he excelled—because if they believed he could, so did he. If you really believe you can do something, you probably will. And believing in yourself is the most important part of succeeding. Anyway, even with all the excitement, Sunny was a little overwhelmed and challenged. Always enjoying a challenge, Sunny took to skiing as his family expected him to and did alright. In some ways, if you have the support from your family and you can find that special passion, you begin to believe in yourself. That one thing you can use to *drive yourself to succeed*, past the obstacles of a learning disability. You can use it to succeed in a sport that is not germane to your environment, and your goal to become a professional skier and coach becomes much clearer. So Sunny's father took him skiing, and it began.

Sunny's father wasn't poor; he also wasn't stupid. He took one look at the cost of skiing lessons, realizing the family had to have some, and decided to take a quick one hour private lesson and disseminate the knowledge down through the ranks (that would be all the children). The ski equipment that sat in the basement, his dad had received as a child too. When his instructor looked at what Sunny's father was trying to put on, he first proceeded with an explanation of equipment, and then did what he could, teaching him with what he had to work with. By now, it was lunch time and all the family needed a break from the rope tow. Besides, one had lace-up boots in need of tightening. After lunch, the family started in a group lesson taught by the new substitute ski instructor, Sunny's father. Sunny could not believe his rising levels of ambition and tenacity; he was sure he had reached his maximum of those great qualities already. After a long day, he and his brothers and sisters slept on the way back home again, a box of tired little puppies. Sunny's ski dreams had just begun. That was the first of many ski trips, and with each trip, Sunny improved and became hungry for more.

Magog, Canada

IF SOMEONE HAS NOT BEEN bitten by the ski bug, they do not know how skiing can change their life. Family ski trips became a regular routine and were an exciting part of family life. There was the excitement of the trip the night before, anticipating the challenges of the next day, but it was even more than that. It was being together. It was being in the car together, laughing together, skiing together, and eating lunch together. Driving in the car and watching the miles go by, the endless games of making words out of letters of license plates from other cars—laughing at jokes and falling asleep against whoever was sitting next to you; all of this was memorable. The ski trips were in the family station wagon, the last seat facing backwards. If you were unfortunate enough to have to sit in the back, you got a great view of where you had been.

The family even learned how to take turns helping their dad stay awake while driving. By the way, Sunny's mother never took an interest in skiing. With eight kids, it's possible she enjoyed her time alone when everyone was gone.

Every Christmas or birthday, ski equipment became a common gift in Sunny's family. One year, Sunny's dad decided, for God knows what reason, that Canada was the place they should spend their Christmas vacation (maybe it was the exchange rate). So they ventured north, ten hours or more to Magog, Canada. Sunny couldn't imagine paying for all those lift tickets, much less the motel rooms. The trip started out excitingly, early in the morning as everybody was just waking up and anticipating a long week off—to not only a new ski area, but *in a different country*. To avoid spending a lot of money, the car was packed with snacks and lunches. The only stops were for bathroom breaks and coffee. It was an exciting time to watch the road go by mile after mile. As the car ventured further north, the trees became more covered with snow. It increased everybody's anticipation. Some kids were able to read books and keep themselves busy. Sunny always got car sick, so he sat up front and just daydreamed. Ski trips like this brought the family closer, yet they weren't without their challenges. On the first trip, Sunny's mother drove—only to have the family station wagon drop its transmission, leaving them stranded. This is where all the structure paid off. Each member of the family knew what their part was, and pulled together to make things easier. There was no complaining about snow; there was only seeing how you could help. Both Sunny's parents were somewhat survivalists, so with a nine hour layover in New York State, they finally made it to their destination.

Canada was colder than anything Sunny or his family could have imagined. The cold would have been unnerving to almost anyone else. But to Sunny, it was surprising to know that he could see forever, and at night he could see more stars and sky than he could imagine. The snow was so dry. And it crunched when you stepped, and your nose hairs stuck together when you breathed. To Sunny, there was snow everywhere; and atop a big mountain, the sky was like something he had never seen before. Despite the cold, they skied avidly. This time, the family had private lessons and their instructor was a wonderful skier named Mario; he will never be forgotten. Actually, the Warner family didn't sign up for private lessons; the family just took up the entire class. Sunny skied on the tails of Mario's skis every chance he could, emulating his every move. Not the best performance, but by now it was evident that Sunny had more courage and balls than anyone.

Ever since then, Sunny had the passion to learn and the drive to ski better at each turn. Sunny had the love to ski faster, harder, and take more risks.

Staying in the motel, meeting new people, and skiing with Mario and his family left a big impression on him. The effort Sunny's parents put into overcoming obstacles and providing such a wonderful family trip created a memory that would last him a lifetime.

After skiing in Canada, Sunny couldn't wait to practice his new skills at any opportunity. Sunny's abilities grew with every turn on every trail on every ski trip. It became the one thing in which he was able to find some success. If he was unable to talk his dad into taking him skiing, he was able to hitch a ride with one of the other families in town who also skied. The ski community was kind of a close knit group. Everybody who skied knew each other. It was something you had in common. Sunny realized that he could be known for something other than his struggles in school. He enjoyed hanging out with his friends, but didn't seem to get caught up with the same big social changes that were going on in the world.

In 1964, the Beatles and the British Invasion hit and the world had gone from Eisenhower to experiencing Kennedy's assassination to the Vietnam War and Lyndon Johnson. There were antiwar protests and the Civil Rights Movement and even shorter dresses on women. In Sunny's world, school continued to be very difficult and the only explanation was that he must be lazy. Rather than focusing on what he couldn't do, Sunny focused on what he could do, and that was skiing.

Fall 1965

After such an experience, Christmas ski presents didn't cut it anymore. Sunny was now looking for some performance in his equipment. He had actually graduated to a buckle boot, and now it was time for some better skis. That fall, Sunny and his dad went to ski movies by Barrymore or John Jay, which were magical, and they read ski magazines. The movies were shown in the Montclair High School Auditorium. Sunny saw so much great skiing and so many other people who skied in his area. It was clear that his ambitions and his equipment weren't keeping pace. He knew it was time for an upgrade. When it was time to pick out some skis, Sunny knew what he wanted. Howard Head had the best line of skis, and Sunny had decided on metal intermediate skis named the Head Master. Standing in the ski shop with his dad on a Saturday, Sunny's father pointed out,

"Sunny, these skis represent a large investment. This will take all your savings."

"Yes, I know! But I want to try racing this season," Sunny replied.

Sunny couldn't imagine that his dad didn't have any idea he wanted to move on to racing. Still, Sunny seemed to take him by surprise with this news and his father looked with concern and said,

"Well, we'll have to talk about that."

Sensing disapproval, Sunny looked up at his dad with a bit of panic in his voice. "I think I'm good enough to beat some of the kids we saw racing in Canada," Sunny confidently said, turning into a salesman himself.

"Do you think these will be okay for racing?" Sunny asked a salesman, pointing out his choice.

The salesman could see Sunny's passion. "They'll be plenty good enough to start with," the salesman assured him.

Sunny's father could also see Sunny's drive. "I guess this is inevitable," he said. "Go ahead and pick out some bindings." Just like that—a race career was born.

Sunny's excitement showed on his face. He had a smile from ear to ear. It was like a *dream come true*. He brought the skis home and would not let his parents take them from his room until winter. Every day, he would look at his skis *and dream of racing*.

Two areas in New Jersey had opened, making weekend skiing more accessible. Sunny also joined the Ussa (United States Ski and Snowboard Association) and got his card enabling him to race. School dances, football games, etc., had taken precedence over Saturday or Sunday ski trips, as far as his brothers and sisters were concerned. So many times, it was just his dad and Sunny on those trips. It was a good season, and Sunny managed to get in some early skiing; now he felt ready to race.

Sunny really didn't know anything about the racing world. He picked the first race from the Ussa Race Schedule that was closest and correlated with school. It was a downhill race, and that seemed perfectly logical to him as it was the fastest of the three disciplines. And if you didn't know anything about ski racing, it seemed to be the simplest—yet Sunny would learn a big lesson.

Alpine Ski Racing consisted of three disciplines: slalom, giant slalom, and downhill. A slalom race is a series of shorter radius turns, more controlled turns, down the mountain through a series of gates designed to test the skier's skills. A giant slalom course provides more open higher-speed turns with a larger radius and a longer course. The downhill is the longest race, which has relatively fewer turns, but goes at a very high speed with jumps.

Sunny wasn't worried about the speed, and he didn't want something he had to think too much about. This, to him, was more balls than brains. What he didn't know was it was the most difficult and dangerous. Fortunately, his dad didn't know he had picked a downhill. The race was at Bellayre Mountain in New York State. Sunny sent his registration card in early, and soon enough, they both went up to the race.

19

Now today, a downhill race requires two days of training. Many of the other kids had taken time off from school to go up and train on the course. You would think Sunny would have jumped at the opportunity to do that, but he had not. When Sunny and his father arrived, Sunny asked around and found the registration. The boy who directed him took Sunny under his wing more or less. Sunny guessed it was obvious that he didn't have a clue. His name was Herman. Herman and Sunny went on to become good friends.

Sunny had seen people with race bibs and was anxious to identify with the other racers. Sunny quickly figured out that when your race bib is in the high double digits, you are in trouble. Nevertheless, he was assigned his bib number, and he was proud to be in the race.

Herman and his dad accompanied him in course inspection. They allowed themselves plenty of time before the start. If Sunny had been his dad, he would have yanked himself out of the race right then and there. It was clear that he was in over his head. Sunny's first observation was that his skis were too short. Still, he was determined to start and hopefully, finish.

The race started. Sunny watched several racers fly by on the course. It looked easy enough; at least those first racers made it look easy. When he proceeded to the starting line, all he could think was, if they could do it, so could he; they were people just like he was. His dad came to the start with him, wished him good luck and even surprised him with his favorite sweater from Austria. His father then proceeded down to the waiting area on the course to watch. To this day, Sunny still has and wears that sweater. Sunny was last to start, which did not bother him, other than being almost frozen. It was getting dark when his number was called. He climbed onto the start, scared to death. The countdown: 10 seconds...... 3, 2, 1. His adrenaline was pumping at an unbelievable pace, the starter yelled "GO," and he was off.

In his strategy, he had never planned to take it easy, but just try to make it to the finish line—even though that wasn't his style. So within 100 yards, he was tucking hard and going faster than he had ever gone before, and the steep part was still yet to come. Fortunately, his willingness to take risks was bigger than his brains, so he just pointed his skis downhill and went for it. He was all over the place turn after turn.

Luckily, his tuck wasn't bad, but enough to slow him down some. Sunny would never forget the series of big bumps. He hit the first with absolutely no preparation and flew. He could actually hear the crowd gasp. Somehow he landed upright and flew even further on the second bump. Again, the crowd gasped. As he touched down, he could see the finish line. He was still standing and heading for the third bump. For some unknown reason, Sunny believed he could do it. He hit the third bump, heart in throat, off balance, and pulled it off—grabbing in a tuck in a last effort for speed, and headed for the finish line. He finished!

Sunny couldn't describe that feeling. His dad and the other racers were more amazed than he was that he made it. To the other racers, he just showed up out of the blue, with the wrong equipment, no training or prior experience, still managed to finish and avoided coming in last. Sunny made a lot of friends that day, Herman being one. He was impressed, his dad relieved. The experience of being there—having his father there, feeling a part of a race community, the adrenaline and finishing—would set the standard for not only his lifetime ahead, but a step closer to becoming a professional skier.

Summer 1967

Sunny went to a few other races with his dad, but no more downhill. They decided to try some slalom and giant slalom. Reducing speeds and focusing on increasing his skill level might be a good strategy. For what little knowledge and preparation he had about racing, he did okay. But it was clear that he needed some instructions in tactics and technique if he was going to continue. Sunny was relying on his skill to figure things out, but it wasn't enough. He had a thirst to learn, and he was motivated to listen.

Herman and Sunny had become pretty good friends, so he had gone up to Great George, New Jersey's biggest ski area, and skied with him as much as possible. Herman lived up there with his family, so Sunny was able to stay overnight and enjoyed the lifestyle of skiing every day. The season ended, but his ambitions did not.

Unfortunately, the civil unrest in the country had grown worse. The war in Vietnam had escalated and the peace rallies were growing. Israel had gone to war with Syria and Egypt in a Six-Day War and riots had broken out in Detroit; and on July 12, 1967, riots broke out in Newark, New Jersey. Glen Ridge was only a mile outside of Newark. Sunny was never considered a golden boy. More often than not, he was drawn to trouble. Sunny was a far better skier than he was a student. The only things Sunny ever read were ski magazines and his father's *Playboy* when he wasn't looking—which oddly enough, turned out to be an appropriate reading list for his upcoming career. One day while reading the spring issue of one of the ski magazines, Sunny came across an ad for a summer race camp. Sunny could not believe you could actually ski in the United States in the summer, so he brought the ad to his dad to ask if it was true. His dad wasn't sure, but if it were true, it might pose as a perfect opportunity to get him out of New Jersey for a little while.

Sunny hardly believed his father would allow him to go as far as Oregon by himself, but it was clear that Sunny was going to ski race. And if Sunny was going to continue with any success, race camp would provide the formal training he so badly needed. The deal was that Sunny would split the cost of the airfare with his dad and dad would pay for camp. Sunny worked very hard to save enough money, which also served to keep him out of trouble. Turns out, parents can be pretty clever.

Not being a very mature kid and not having traveled much, going to Oregon seemed like going halfway across the world. Sunny's older brother Jody had been attending private school in New Hampshire, and he was a pretty good skier himself. Sunny's skis were alright, but Jody's were the latest model and faster. Jody, being an older brother, was sympathetic to Sunny's enthusiasm and consented to lending him his skis. God, two miracles were happening; it was too good to be true. Sunny packed and off he went.

Summer Race Camp in Oregon

TO BE SURE HE WOULDN'T get flustered and lose his way, his dad wrote the instructions on Sunny's arm. A good idea at the time; however, after Sunny got on the plane, he discovered his dad had written the directions, including the plane changes, to where he could read it, right side up. But it was upside down and backwards to Sunny. Yes, Sunny was dyslexic, but it didn't help. Sunny wound up standing in the bathroom reading in the mirror, and asking the stewardesses where he was supposed to go. (No, the stewardesses were not in the bathroom at the time.)

Sunny made it to Oregon and caught the bus to Mount Hood by doing what he did best—he figured it out. First stop, Government Camp, a little stop on the mountain road up to Mount Hood. Sunny had never seen anything like it. It was like driving through an enchanted rain forest. It was miles of giant trees and a never-ending forest. As Sunny waited at the small general store for the bus to Mt. Hood, the smell of the area was clean and exciting. He couldn't help but think how much further up the lodge was, and about what he had gotten himself into. He was a long way from New Jersey and on his own. When the bus finally got to the lodge after a long trip, he got off and found himself standing in a *dream*, in front of what looked like an updated medieval castle. The lodge was a WPA (Work Projects Administration) project designed by President Roosevelt during the Great Depression, intended to provide work for the unemployed. It was built of stone and had magnificent hand-crafted woodwork.

During the winter, there was skiing available below the lodge for the general public. During the summer, approximately a mile above the lodge, there was a glacier and snowfield perfect for advanced skiing and race training. A chair lift went up from the lodge, but not far enough. The racers were then transported in snow cats, which are like small bus cabs on treads, kind of like a tank. They were slow, but they got skiers to where training was optimum.

Mount Hood is a semi-volcanic mountain as well; the whole scene was something Sunny had never imagined.

The camp was an International Race Camp made up of top racers from all over the world and Sunny had no idea how he was going to be accepted. Maybe it was because he had sent his application in so early that they didn't feel like rejecting his admission fees. It seemed like a good idea, but he stood out like a sore thumb, and he was obviously the least-skilled skier there.

New Jersey never seemed to offer much when Sunny was young, although it had given him something invaluable: survival. Living in New Jersey seemed to be one survival test after another, so one learned those techniques along with tenacity as a primary way of life.

Basically, if you could make it in New Jersey, Oregon was a cake walk. Meeting his roommates was no more difficult than, say, his first day of school.

For Sunny, there was a lot to learn and he was anxious to learn everything they could teach him about racing. The guy he shared a bunk with was a Canadian who attended a New England private school. His school was known for having a really good coach named Warren Witheral. His bunk mate's name was Jim. He seemed unsure of Sunny at first, but soon took a liking to him. Why he liked Sunny was puzzling. Maybe it was because Sunny was a refreshing change from the usual racers he had been exposed to. Anyway, Jim was one of the best racers there; his acceptance of Sunny was a real advantage in Sunny getting to know the other racers.

Sunny was naïve to his new surroundings. He knew nothing of who's who in the ski circles. This being the case, all the racers were the same in his eyes—which meant they were all better than him. As for the coaches, they were all internationally famous. For those of you who remember, they were Canada's National coaches: Earnie McCulla, Loren O'Conner, Adrian

Duvallard, Pepi Gramshammer, Pepi Steigler, and Rene Allard, as well as a local girl, Dedi.

The star of the camp was a young Canadian, Betsy Clifford. She was the youngest girl ever to be on the Canadian Team. Sunny's friend Jim had introduced him to Betsy. She too had taken a liking to Sunny, and this really brought him up in overall acceptance.

It never occurred to him that there was a social ladder in ski racing. To Sunny, all the racers were equal. However, the social ladder became more than evident as training started. Although Sunny was on the first rung of the ladder, he was still able to handle things, including having fun. The same courage and tenacity which had made him so many friends at other races managed to earn him respect and friends at camp.

Now skiing didn't represent all of Sunny's interests; he had not gone through life without noticing girls. Sunny began to focus any free time he had toward the female athletes. After New Jersey women, it was easier to date a Russian. Sunny quickly learned that the girls in New Jersey were a tough breed. Being in control was part of a Jersey girl's training, and being able to tell somebody to screw off was as natural as brushing her teeth. He was almost shocked to find out that a girl would actually smile and talk to you without telling you to go fuck yourself. Girls from the American Alpine environments were a pleasant change.

It wasn't long before Sunny had spotted one of the female racers and was anxious to meet and spend time with her. Becky was from Crystal Mountain, Washington. She was exceedingly pretty, kind, and by the way, a great kisser. Sunny soon found out at a dance they only had until the end of the season for any hope of a relationship. Sunny had his first experience of how emotionally devastating a romance could be at that age.

Sunny

Born with a speech impediment that caused him to slur his "S's", life presented its challenges for Sunny. One morning, Becky and Sunny were riding the lift, and Sunny remarked what a sunny day it was. Becky quickly became aware of his inability to enunciate. After laughing and telling him how cute it was, and from that moment, he had earned the name "Sunny." The name stuck with him for many years.

Sunny went back to training; however, he wasn't a good racer …yet. Sunny had only finished a few of the training courses a handful of times. Sunny never had the formal training in skills to execute the short turns and strategies in the slalom course. His coaches were very patient. At the end of four days of slalom training, there was to be a slalom race, followed by four days of giant slalom. Giant slalom was better suited to Sunny, as he enjoyed the speed and it allowed him time to negotiate turns. Sunny fell in the slalom race and didn't finish, and he came in last in the giant slalom race. There were still two more days of camp reserved for downhill training. Sunny still had no fear of speed, so he felt that downhill was something he could excel in.

All at home were anxious to hear the results of the races, thus after the giant slalom race, Sunny called home and told them what had happened. He also said that he felt he was getting better and begged to be able to stay for the next ten day session. Sunny felt that he was just catching on and wanted to stay. Sunny's father, pleased he had taken such a strong interest in something positive in his life—and since he was out there and the riots were still going on in New Jersey—felt that ten more days just might be okay. Sunny did more skiing in those ten days than he had done all year.

Downhill is a discipline which takes extensive training. Sunny enjoyed skiing fast, but he still didn't have the technical skills to execute high speed turns. Since the racers could only spend two days on it, the best the coaches could hope for was an introduction of the basics. The first day of training, the racers climbed up the mountain to the crater and looked down inside at the steaming sulfur coming out of the mouth. Sunny had seen some mountains in the east and he had seen some mountains that he thought were big; but Mount Hood was something he couldn't even imagine. It was this towering peak of jagged rock that went up to an elevation that—well, Sunny never truly understood a mountain could be so high. In the middle was an open crater with sulfuric fumes coming out. The sulfur smelled like rotten eggs. Mount Hood was a semi-volcanic mountain. The thought of having snow even in the summer was something beyond Sunny's wildest imagination, never mind his understanding of what a volcanic mountain was. Being able to hike such a mountain was more than exciting. It was an adventure—something that he was going to be able to tell everyone back home. The thought of taking each step through the snow, and being able to see for hundreds of miles around you with the sun beating down on you in July, captured every bit of Sunny's imagination. Many people would've been intimidated, yet Sunny was empowered and motivated.

The group then skied over to the top of an extremely steep rock face. When covered by the moonlight, that steep face seemed illuminated; hence its name, Illumination Rock. The racers called it Elimination Rock as there wasn't too much room on the top to stand, and it was also straight down for 50 yards. The plan was to start with several turns and grab a tuck, practicing the basics, the tucks, body position and getting used to fast skiing. One by one, the group started down Elimination Rock. Sunny was still anxious to show what a funny talking kid from New Jersey could do. Turning on such a steep face was tricky, so he kicked off and skipped those turns and headed straight for the tuck.

Sunny was with a coach, Adrian Duvillard, one of France's best racers who skied in the 1956 and 60 Olympics. Adrian took off directly in front of him and he was determined to try to keep up. After skipping the initial turns, Sunny managed to minimize making any high speed turns, simply because he didn't know how. It wasn't long before Sunny was completely out of control. Since he didn't know how to stop without killing himself, and to stand erect and slow down would show he was scared, he thought, 'What the hell, I'll stay behind Adrian and ride it out.'

Sunny skied on for a while, which seemed like an eternity to him, and then Adrian stood up and slid to a stop. Sunny didn't possess that valuable skill of stopping, so still in a tuck—keeping up was a goal in itself—he flew past Adrian. Sunny then hit a sun cup, which is a hole in the snow caused by direct sunlight. One leg stayed and the rest of him proceeded through the most spectacular fall anybody had seen. Not willing to give in to embarrassment and defeat, Sunny did his best to pull himself together. A little shaken, he managed to ski to the lodge.

Feeling he had failed his last attempt, Sunny went straight to his room. In a matter of minutes, his right knee was swollen like a balloon and he was in pain. Actually, it scared him more than he was hurt, so off to the hospital he went.

The next phone call his dad received was from the lodge owner and camp director, Mr. Comstand, a really nice man. Somehow, both of them managed to talk Sunny's dad into letting Sunny stay. There were a few days between camps, and he felt sure his knee would get better. Sunny didn't want to go home having done so badly. Sunny still believed he could do it, given more time. All the years of ignoring people's opinions and relying on sheer tenacity was paying off.

Through good coaching and encouragement, Sunny had learned a lot and felt sure the results would show up in time. At the awards banquet before camp ended, Sunny received honorable mention for "Most Determined" and the "Best Crash!"

Sunny hated staying off the mountain between camp sessions because he really wanted to practice, and he just flat-out loved racing. The next camp started, so he wrapped his knee and went up for practice. Sunny came to the mountain early the first couple of days and still managed to train some. By the third day, he was back to fourth gear. Big Balls Sunny was determined as ever. By the end of the fourth day and the slalom race, he had managed to pull off being 20th out of 100 racers. By the end of the giant slalom race, he managed to be moved up to 13th out of 100. Thanks to the coaching and Betsy, who spent every free minute helping him, Sunny had shown real progress.

It was time for downhill again. This time Sunny had advanced his skills to where he was sure he could at least stop without a wipeout—never mind that his high speed turns were still pretty bad.

A Frenchman on the National team had heard of Sunny's determination and crash, and offered him his downhill suit. His name was Jean-Claude Killy. Sunny was in awe of him. He had no idea how well he skied the next two days. During those 23 days, Sunny had made great friends, learned how to ski and race, and was awarded "Most Improved" at the banquet.

It was the experience of Mr. Comstand, Betsy, and all the coaches, Becky Morrison, whom Sunny will never forget—but most important, thanks to his family who made it all possible, especially to his dad for believing in him. Sunny really came home a winner!

Moving on in Education

SUNNY CONTINUED TO STRUGGLE AS a student. Later Sunny learned through formal diagnosis it was due to a form of dyslexia and a little thing called Attention Deficit Disorder. There was no explanation or understanding in the 60s for academic struggles. In Sunny's case, the school couldn't understand why he would not turn in his homework, why he would forget his homework, or wouldn't be able to follow the lesson in class. To Sunny's teachers, he was simply lazy and he required more discipline. It was either his parents' fault, or he was just a bad kid. Sunny's father was a very well-respected man in the community, so it couldn't have been a product of his upbringing. It must have been that he was just one of those kids who were incorrigible.

In Glen Ridge High School, some administrative genius decided that there should be a three track system. Track one being for the advanced academically gifted children, track two being for the average student, and track three for the less academically gifted, or challenged, student. During the day, somebody from the front office would make announcements for track one—to please report to your respective classrooms, at which time all the track one students would move into the hall. Next, track two would get their announcement, and lastly, the announcement that "track three students should please report to...." and all the track three students would then proceed to their respective classes. The thought of how the students felt being identified in a class system had escaped the administration. It didn't escape the students. It certainly didn't escape Sunny in his daily struggle to be like the other kids. Sunny wasn't lazy; he was actually working harder than the other kids, but didn't learn the same way and was reminded of it daily. By the age of 16, it did not matter to the New Jersey School System. The vice principal was tired of finding him at the wrong time in the wrong place, so on his 16th birthday in Glen Ridge, The Principal seized the opportunity to remind Sunny that he was now eligible for permanent dismissal—and remembered to wish him a Happy Birthday.

During one of the study halls, Sunny actually did some research. This time, he researched private schools. Sunny went through the book of listed private schools, picked out about ten, and applied. Sunny's transcripts did not reflect the sort of promising prospect the private schools were looking for. His first choice was to go to Kimball Union to be with his older brother, Jody.

His younger brother Jeff attended a different school in Connecticut which was okay, but it did not have any skiing. Sunny had gone up to Jody's school in New Hampshire to interview. His interviewing skills were about as impressive as his transcripts.

While Sunny was in Oregon, his father took the opportunity to attend several interviews without him. Sunny was sure his father felt more confident that he could stress the positive side of his son without him being there. The Stowe School was one of the schools Sunny had expressed interest in, and so had his dad. It was a small New England private school, located just a few miles from the best skiing in the east. Fighting for survival, Sunny believed his father's ability to pay the tuition was the strong point in his interview.

The Stowe School had given the acceptance he had hoped for. It wasn't Sunny's first choice, but then again, he didn't have a choice. It was the only acceptance he had received, and the school was okay. It was also a traditional New England private school. Sunny was bound to an education as a "preppie." Besides, if you had to have a kid in a private school, Stowe, Vermont was a very good place to have a kid in one.

When he returned from Oregon, Sunny received the news. He really had no idea how his dad did it, but he was excited. Now being excited did not mean he didn't have reservations. Sunny loved his family and friends, and skiing with Herman and the gang in New Jersey would also be tough to give up. But come fall, he was off to Vermont.

The drive up was long and Sunny was nervous. To ease his tension, his father had wisely planned ahead. They left a day early so they could spend some time together. It was fall, the trees were turning colors, and the air was getting colder and crisper. Sunny knew he would miss being in Glen Ridge for the fall, which was one of his most favorite times with football games and the smell of burning leaves. Nevertheless, Sunny felt special to be able to spend time with his dad. In one respect, it felt like one of their usual ski trips. But he knew in the back of his mind that he wasn't going back. Sunny's dad didn't take much time off from work; and for his dad to take this time off to drive all the way up to Stowe was something special. It was a long drive. It felt like he was driving all the way to Canada, like when the family went on that Christmas vacation years ago. Sunny was a little surprised as to how far the school was from home. Everything he owned was packed in the car.

On the first day of school, Sunny and his Dad got up early and drove to the mountain. Sunny's first look at it left him breathless. This was a reaction his father was counting on. Mount Mansfield was the biggest mountain in Vermont. Standing at the base of the mountain, Sunny looked at the beautiful wooden lodge and the ascending chairlifts in awe.

Sunny's father could see the excitement on his son's face and quietly looked at him and said, "Look up Sunny. You can see what they call the Nose Dive; it's the trail to the right."

"Why did they call it the Nose Dive?" Sunny asked.

His dad showed him a brochure and said,

"Look here. If you look up, the mountain looks like a sleeping giant. That is the nose, forehead and a chin."

The mountain did look like a sleeping giant just waiting for Sunny to awaken it. School and being away from his family didn't excite him, but the mountain certainly managed to capture Sunny's heart. Realizing it was an opportunity of a lifetime, like everything else Sunny ventured into, he went for it. His dad would provide Sunny transportation every chance he got to go home, as he really missed everyone in New Jersey.

Stowe, Vermont

A PRIVATE SCHOOL EDUCATION WAS very different from a public school education. The Stowe School was actually an old hotel converted into a private school. Sunny and the other students lived upstairs, while they attended classes downstairs and in some of the other buildings. At New England private schools and at The Stowe School students wore a jacket and tie, and they ate breakfast, lunch, and dinner together. Your day was scheduled by your school. Sunny didn't have a chance to miss anyone. The Stowe School had decided each student should start their educational experience with participation in Outward Bound. Outward Bound was a relatively new program which was designed to challenge individuals physically and mentally through developing survival skills. The Outward Bound program would push people out of their comfort zones by having them hike, rappel, rock climb, and learn leadership skills and survival techniques. This was a custom fit for Sunny—a chance to rely on his physical abilities, as well as his skills to figure things out—along with the tenacity he had always banked on to get him through. The Survival Course served to strengthen Sunny physically and build confidence. His final challenge was to hike seven peaks in seven days, starting in the White Mountains, including three days alone.

The New England snow soon fell, and Sunny couldn't wait to ski. Sunny had climbed the mountain half a dozen times, dreaming of what it would look like covered in snow. When the time came, Sunny hit the mountain hard. There were a lot of good skiers in the school, but he still managed to make the ski team. Sunny had a lot to learn; his slalom and giant slalom were okay, but to be on the ski team, he had to try cross country and jumping. Sunny ran at a little track in New Jersey, so cross country was fun, but ski jumping was a perfect discipline for a certified adrenaline junkie like him.

The Stowe School tried hard to instill discipline in something other than his athletics. Unfortunately, Sunny's academics didn't reflect his efforts. Thus, he tried hard to compensate by being a five event man.

The following year, Sunny was the best skier at Stowe's school in slalom, giant slalom, downhill, cross country, and last but certainly not least, jumping. Sunny had no experience in ski jumping before he got to The Stowe School, but he took to it quickly. Ski jumping was an exhilarating sport to Sunny. The school had built a small fifteen meter ski jump for practice right next to the school. This was great for Sunny to practice on. When someone ski jumps, they look down a very steep incline on very large, very wide skis—only attached by their toe, so that their heel can be loose. At the end of the runway, skiers lunge forward off an even steeper hill, falling away beneath them, to eventually finish out the run. Most people wouldn't consider launching themselves off the top of the ski jump to what they believed would be the abyss. Sunny found ski jumping to be the perfect sport for him. He loved the speed, the steepness of the hill, the exhilaration of the flight, and had no problem with the balance and landing. Sunny's only challenge was to find a bigger ski jump. Of all the events, cross country was the worst because he always ran until he threw up. The other schools had kids that specialized, which didn't give him much of a chance. Each day the mountain was open, Sunny hitchhiked up, skied four of the steepest trails with hip-high moguls nonstop, skied three miles down the toll road, crossed the street, and hit the back trails to school. As quickly as possible, grabbing his jump skis, he ran to the hill for as many jumps as he could get in before dark. After dinner and study hall, if the moon was bright, Sunny would get permission to run cross country until bedtime.

The snowflakes sparkled from the moonlight on a cold New England night, and by a fall moon you could see everything. At night, there is no color; the whole world shows in black and white. Sunny continued to struggle with his academics. However, he found runs like this helped him cope and keep trying.

The Matterhorn Bar

To Sunny's delight, there was a bar across the street from school. It looked like a small inn sitting on a stream with a bar and some lunch tables. The bar sat right next to the road, on the right-hand side on the way down the mountain. It was in a perfect spot to stop for an après-ski drink. The bar was a kind of a sore spot for the school's administration. In other words, it was off limits to all students. Faculty members were expected to present an example and abstain as much as possible. You couldn't help but look across the street and see the bar absolutely packed.

Sunny couldn't help himself, he was drawn to the excitement like a moth to a flame. It was not only that there were people over there partying; it was that they were all skiers, too. They were talking about the day on the mountain, and the bar was filled with women who had just come down from skiing. Sunny had to see what they looked like. He started by sneaking over and grabbing a Coke, a sandwich, or whatever he could afford during lunch when it wasn't crowded. The atmosphere was great. Sunny got to know the bartender, Maureen. Then one day, Sunny was sitting out in front of his school looking at the Matterhorn.

The music was loud and people were stumbling in and out after a hard day of skiing. The Matterhorn bar reflected the entire town's decadence. Hell, it was great! Although skiing had commanded Sunny's top priorities in life, women and fun were right up there too. One day, he noticed that The Matterhorn was particularly crazy. He had been over there many times, but always during the late morning or early afternoon hours when nobody was there. This particular day was St. Patrick's Day, New England's most celebrated day next to Christmas. The excitement got the best of Sunny, so he ventured forth to the decadence. Sunny managed to slip past the bouncer at the door, and made it to the bar before being discovered and getting the boot.

There were people everywhere! They were hanging from the rafters, standing on the bar, dancing. As he got to the bar there was a nude girl, painted green, laying on the bar with a man drinking out of her belly button with a straw. Sunny looked on in amazement; he didn't know a belly button held enough to drink from. Anyway, he looked around and thought this was the life for him.

Sunny had been in the bar from about 10 a.m, until it got busy, around 2:30 p.m. At this time The Matterhorn served lunch, so when he was stuck or had time between classes, he would sneak over to The Matterhorn or "The Horn" and have a Coke and talk to the bartender, Maureen. She didn't ski, so Maureen worked the day shift. She was about five feet eight, had short dark hair, a fair build, and a great sense of humor. Maureen was part Indian, or so she said. She always wore a short dress, no underwear, and could drink any grown man clear under the table before taking him home.

One day, Sunny had gone over to the bar and Maureen asked him how come he was in there instead of being on the mountain. She knew there was always a town race on Monday, and that he always stopped in after the race to announce the results. Maureen asked Sunny, "What are you doing over here instead of up at the race?" Sunny replied,

"No money this week. I just don't have the entrance fee."

Maureen was quick to respond in disgust, "That's ridiculous! How much?" When Maureen asked a question, one was wise to answer; so Sunny did. "10 bucks."

To Sunny's surprise, Maureen looked at him and said,

"Here." She handed him 10 dollars.

Sunny knew he couldn't pay her back, so as much as he wanted the money he had to say, "Nope, I can't pay you back." Bad move, saying no to Maureen was *not* the thing to do. Maureen quickly said,

"Okay, listen. You always do pretty well, so take the 10 dollars and race for The Matterhorn and we'll call it advertising." Saying 'no' was not an answer for Sunny, and he looked at Maureen to simply say,

"Really? Okay, I'll kick ass!"

Sunny did just that, too. He registered for The Matterhorn and won. When the results got presented, none of the other bars really knew him; they thought The Matterhorn had picked up a ringer for the prestige. They didn't correlate Sunny with the Stowe School.

The following week, two other bars entered their employees and the ski bum race had its birth once again. By the end of the season, the bars and restaurants had gotten together and organized teams and rules. Four men and one woman were the minimum per team. It grew so popular that the mountain moved the ski bum teams to Wednesday. If it weren't for that pantyless bar maid and the young kid, the ski bum races may never have evolved.

Maureen was like a big sister to Sunny, always watching out for him and always taking an interest in what was happening in his life.

Herman and His Friends

IN THE YEARS OF 1967-68, the time of national unrest, Sunny had spent his second summer at Mount Hood, Oregon. His racing skills were becoming greatly refined since his first look at that Timberline Lodge, the base lodge at the bottom of the mountain. To pay for his skiing education, Sunny worked in the shipping department for his father in New York City.

Surfing was Sunny's second love, and every summer weekend he snuck out of work early and—with whomever would take him—headed for the beach. Herman was a good surfer as well; they spent as much time as possible cutting up waves. Sunny and Herman were excited about the oncoming season and now that Sunny was located in Vermont, the season looked even more promising.

Returning to school in September, Sunny wouldn't get a break until Christmas vacation. This meant spending Thanksgiving at school.

That season, the snow had come on schedule and the mountain was going to open Thanksgiving Day. Herman and three of his friends couldn't stand the thought of all that good skiing done without them. The day before Thanksgiving, Sunny received a call that some friends were there to see him.

The national unrest had moved to The Stowe School, which had adopted a more liberal, progressive direction defined by a school named Summerhill in England. This meant no more ties and jackets, longer hair, more town and skiing privileges, and best of all, the adoption of a pass/fail system instead of grades. To Herman and his friends, this only meant that they would be able to sneak in and stay with Sunny days at a time. Many of the students attending the school lived close enough to home, took the day off and went home for turkey dinner.

For the rest of the group, Thanksgiving Day came and Herman, the rest of the crew, and Sunny headed for the mountain. Watching a group of young aspiring racers cutting up a mountain was a sight to see. The snow wasn't great and the only part of the mountain that was open was the Gondola area, an advanced intermediate area. It wasn't long before all of them were sitting on top of the Gondola in a restaurant, looking for something more challenging.

The most challenging portion of the mountain was closed, and it was separated from the open parts by a large ravine. They could see across the ravine, and the thought of all that snow being over there and the group being here was unbearable. The mountain behind them proceeded straight up to the top where it was possible to hike over the top of the Nose Dive, the famous downhill trail. Sunny had hiked that portion of the mountain several times before, without snow, and it only took about 45 minutes. So, what the hell! Sunny turned to the group with a big smile and declared,

"I know a way to get over there." Herman quickly responded,

"Sure, by helicopter."

"No, look up in back of us. There's a trail about five to seven hundred yards to the top. From there, you can see how far it is. We could do it in no time," Sunny explained to the group.

One of the guys who Sunny didn't know yet spoke up and pointed out, "Look guys, we didn't come all this way to sit here. Let's go."

By general consensus, they decided to go for it. Skis on their shoulders, they started off. The trail to the top of the mountain was really steep. It wasn't long before a couple of the guys started becoming concerned and dropped out. By the time they got to the top, only two of them were left: Sunny and the guy who had spoken up down at the lodge. Sunny turned to the only member of the group brave enough or crazy enough to follow him and say,

"You're Carl, right?"

"Yeah, why?" Carl replied. Sunny looked at him for a moment.

"Two reasons. I just wanted to be sure who's as crazy as I am. Second, look at that weather front. If we are going to try to make it, I want to know who I'm going to die with."

41

They looked over the back side of the mountain; there was a huge storm front coming in. They were stuck. Going up was a lot easier than going down; besides, going down would be admitting defeat. Carl looked at Sunny with a smile of reassurance.

"Don't worry, I'm on a ski patrol. You aren't going to kick off with me around. Besides, I'm not going to die up here with some hippie named Sunshine." For some reason, Sunny knew he liked this guy even if he couldn't get his name straight. He had balls as big as he did. Sunny couldn't help but to stop smiling at Carl and say,

"It's Sunny, not Sunshine. Well let's go, Dr. Switzer, before that storm catches us."

They didn't get far before the storm front did catch up with them and visibility became zero. To be honest, neither of them knew what the hell they were doing, but they pretended to. Carl was up ahead. Sunny yelled to Carl, "Carl, DON'T Move!"

Carl stopped dead in his tracks. Carl did not want to take orders, yet replied,

"What for? O-o-h shit!"

Just then, the clouds parted and Carl was standing inches from the lip of a cliff that led straight down to the ravine. Carl looked briefly over at Sunny and said,

"I thought you knew where you were going?"

With a half-smile, Sunny looked at Carl and said, "Well, I know where I am now."

They turned to head off to solid ground when Sunny stepped in a hole and banged his knee and yelled in pain, "Oh shit!" Carl looked at him, concerned and asked,

"You alright?"

"Wait, it hurts," replied Sunny.

Trying to utilize his training, Carl looked at Sunny and instructed,

"Don't move."

With his classic New Jersey humor, Sunny was quick to respond to Carl's statement with: "Where am I going to go? I think I'm okay."

Carl looked at Sunny with a sigh of relief. "Good!" "I don't know much about knees."

"I thought you were ski patrol?" Sunny inquired.

"I am! If you break your leg, I'll get a toboggan and haul you out of here. Sunny, why don't you call room service while you're at it?"

"First we've got to get out of here before you can save me. I think I'm okay; it just scared me."

Sunny and Carl finally made it all the way across, making wise cracks about each other's pretentious abilities. Standing on top of Nose Dive, they embraced, jumping up and down in their victory. They had just been through a pretty hairy ordeal. Now ready for the fun of being the first ones to ski the mountain for the season, they snapped on their skis and headed down. The snow was about knee deep and as wet and heavy as it could possibly be. It was lousy skiing at best.

When they made it to the bottom, the ski patrol greeted them with a lecture about how dangerous it was and how stupid they were. They both knew the patrol was right, but they had made it nonetheless. One more thing Sunny knew was that he had made a friend up there—someone who thought like him, a friend for a long time to come. When Sunny and Carl returned to school, Herman and the others shared Thanksgiving dinner. Sunny truly had something to be thankful for. One, he was there. Two, he had made a new friend; true friends are a rare commodity. Herman, Carl, and the crew headed back to New Jersey and the rest of the year proceeded as usual. On his Christmas vacation, Sunny looked Carl up and they spent time cutting up the New Jersey hills, telling the story over and over again. The word had gotten out, and they had become local heroes in New Jersey. They were a team!

Carl

CARL AND SUNNY HAD BECOME good friends; Sunny's father entrusted Sunny to Carl. Sunny didn't know whether his dad really trusted them together or just wanted to get rid of them. Either way, it meant staying a few days in a motel in Stowe.

Carl was a self-taught musician. He played the guitar and sang with as much natural talent as anyone Sunny had ever heard. When they got to Stowe, they conjured up a plan to put his talents to work to provide enough money for lift tickets. The people at The Matterhorn knew Sunny, but they didn't know Carl.

When Sunny and Carl went into The Horn for lunch, Carl brought his guitar and Sunny introduced him around. By this time, everyone was curious about his guitar case. They just had to heighten everyone's interest in order to make money. Sunny gave the nod to Carl and he hit the head. Sunny then greeted Maureen, and told her Carl was really good—that he had been playing professionally, but he promised not to ask him to play because they were on vacation. It worked like a charm. As soon as Carl came back out, Maureen came over.

"Can you play that?" she asked. Carl could only look at Sunny and answered,

"Yes, but I asked Sunny to not tell." Maureen wasn't one to not get what she wanted or take no for an answer, which was something Sunny was counting on.

Sunny looked at Carl with a quick request: "Maureen is a good friend, so let's hear one." Maureen seconded the request, which by now had a lot of interest from the other people.

"Come on, Carl. Let's hear one."

The set up was done and Carl replied, "Okay, okay…" and grabbed his guitar.

Carl sat up on the table and tuned his guitar with flair. By this time, anyone who hadn't noticed him before was now awaiting a show. Carl proceeded to belt out one of his best performances. Following the song, everyone applauded and Carl stopped. The crowd was not about to let it go after that, and urged Carl to play more. After that, in order to make extra money, Sunny made a deal to collect fifty cents at the door, plus lunch, drinks, and tips. Carl did three sets, and by that time, they had enough money to ski. They also had some company for their lodging, too. Sunny and Carl used this scam to travel and ski many times more. Between skiing and surfing, the two best friends had enough adventures to fill a book.

Graduation

CARL AND SUNNY LEARNED TO be long distance friends. Sunny continued school and constantly made new friends across the street at The Horn. The Horn was bought by some construction guys from Boston, and was being managed by some guy out of Boston College whose specialty was sailing. Through Maureen, Sunny became good friends with those guys.

The manager was Richard, and his friends were Duke and Sammy. In the morning, Sunny would get out of class, suit up for skiing, and run across the street, climb up the roof, crawl in through the window and wake up Dick, Duke, and whoever else was there to go skiing. Dick had previously been an All-American football player, and Duke was his teammate at that time; both were good athletes. It was really easy to teach them how to ski. Sammy was good, but lacked the guts Dick and Duke had. Duke really preferred to sleep and wait for their return. Sunny became The Horn's official ski pro.

One morning, one of the students in Sunny's school ran into his room. With a sense of urgency Sunny heard, "Wake up, wake up! The Horn burned down last night!" Sunny jumped up and ran to see the fire trucks across the street hosing down the rubble of The Matterhorn. He was devastated. Sunny ran over and saw Richard. He looked green and asked,

"You okay? Was anybody hurt? What happened?"

Richard looked back, coughing. "I'm okay and glad to see you. I didn't know where you were; we weren't sure if you had left last night. I can't believe you slept through it."

Sunny replied, "When I got to the school, I was pretty drunk."

Richard started wheezing. Sunny looked at Richard and without a second thought said, "Come on; let's get you to the hospital. You can tell me about it on the way."

They jumped in his truck and Richard proceeded to tell Sunny how the owner felt hungry at 3 in the morning and decided to cook eggs. What he cooked was The Matterhorn!

Everyone got out okay, but Duke and Dick lost everything: all their clothing, skis, etc. Fortunately the insurance could replace most things. Dick and Duke finished that year by staying with a girl from Sunny's hometown whose parents had a place in Stowe.

A young local who had just finished his studies from Dartmouth and Pratt in architecture drew plans to rebuild The Horn. The architect's name was Cam—tall, blonde, intelligent and incredibly good-looking as far as the bar scene went; he was the king of the ski bums. Sunny and Cam became good friends. The Horn went under construction and was quickly rebuilt in the following months.

Graduation was soon approaching for Sunny. Maureen and Richard really wanted the best for Sunny, but they knew about his lack of academic ability, and by this time, they knew he had dyslexia. Determined to do the right thing, Richard, Sam, Maureen, and Cam filled out enough college applications to get Sunny accepted to a junior college in Massachusetts. Everyone really wanted Sunny to stay and attend a local college, but they knew if skiing and the decadence of Stowe was too accessible, his chances of getting any studying done were slim to none.

With the new Horn being constructed, Sunny said goodbye and headed for New York City to earn money and surf the New Jersey Shore before going back to school.

Carl and Sunny lived pretty close. Every weekend, Carl, Herman, and Sunny went to the shore for surf, sun, and women, in that order. They took the beach by storm, and between Carl's music and their stories, they had a great summer.

Sunny Goes to College

ALL THINGS MUST COME TO an end, and so Sunny was off to school again. There was nothing wrong with his intelligence; he wasn't stupid, he was just bad at school. When Sunny started, he was determined to knuckle down and do well. The campus was small and fortunately close to town. After living in Vermont, Sunny wanted to try something more urban. He actually started out okay and made friends easily.

Somehow Sunny managed to get a dorm room to himself, and was quickly drawn to anything athletic like soccer, touch football, etc.—nothing that inhibited his studying, of course. There was one little weakness left, though—women. A girl named Kathy was by far the prettiest girl in school and was in Sunny's accounting class. Kathy had long, dark, curly hair so Sunny called her Raq, short for Raquel Welch. Raq had a boyfriend who lived down the hall. Every day in accounting, Sunny would talk to Raq and then see her later in the dorm. Sunny's intentions were soon obvious.

One day on her way out, Sunny caught her eye and motioned for her to come over. When she did, Sunny pulled her into his room so they wouldn't be noticed by Boy Wonder, her boyfriend. They talked for quite a while; until the next morning. They then had to get dressed and get to class.

Fall was beautiful in Massachusetts, and winter was approaching. Sunny was doing his utmost to fight his instincts to start skiing again, and he was determined to stick it out. He really missed The Horn and his friends, on one hand. He missed Carl and New Jersey on the other. Then it happened; the snow came, and so did Carl.

One day Sunny was in his room having that familiar conversation with

Raq, when he heard Carl coming down the hall; he just couldn't believe it. Sunny jumped up, put some pants on, and ran out to see if it was true. Raq didn't think much of the timing.

It was true; Carl was coming down the hall yelling: "Sunny! Which room is Sunny Warner's?" When Carl saw him, he ran and jumped into his arms. Carl wasn't much for boundaries and couldn't wait to tell Sunny, "I did it!" They went into the room, and by this time Raq had managed to get on a blouse and panties. Sunny introduced Carl to Kathy.

With his usual New Jersey humor, Carl looked at Kathy and said, "Do you always dress so fashionably?"

Kathy, a Long Island girl, was just as quick to reply,

"Generally, but usually with less clothes on. Today was an exception."

Kathy was beautiful and alluring, half-dressed and provocative. Carl's only response could be,

"Sunny, are there any more like this?"

He was quick to see that Carl was fishing.

"Yes, but I got the best," Sunny replied.

"You usually do," said Carl. It was time to get past the usual banter. Carl was a long way from home, and he wouldn't have come to Northampton, Massachusetts without a reason.

Sunny asked Carl,

"So what are you doing up here?"

Carl began to explain. "Well, I was down at Vernon Valley and they decided to start a Nastar Program, a racing program for the general public. They were looking for two instructors who could get handicapped and be their pros, so I volunteered us."

Sunny had been trying his best to resist running off to the ski industry, but he wanted to be a professional skier more than anything. He was struggling with his academics. He was getting by, but feared failure. Sunny felt this opportunity might not come around again. Still he was a little surprised Carl had "volunteered" him.

"What do you mean?"

Carl explained, "$300 per week, skis, room, board, and…"

Sunny had to ask. "What?!"

Carl explained further and mentioned the all-expense paid trip to the Pro Handicap Races in New Hampshire. Sunny stated the obvious.

"Carl, I have school."

Sunny had looked at Raq, then to Carl who had a contract in his bag that was already signed by the owner of the mountain. Sunny was clearly overwhelmed as he looked at Carl, but needed a moment to think without Carl's bantering about the whole thing.

"Will you cool it a minute? Let me think. How long do I have?"

Carl smiled and said,

"Take your time… two hours."

Sunny had a panicked looked on his face.

"What?!" screamed Sunny.

Raq was looking at Sunny in disbelief. She had known his interest in racing and walked over to give him a hug. Sunny was visibly shaken.

"What was that for?" asked Sunny. Kathy looked at Sunny with a smile and simply stated,

"Do it."

Sunny couldn't believe what he was hearing.

"What? Do you know what this means? Besides, I don't have any equipment." Sunny replied in a panic hoping to put an end to the discussion. Carl was quick to answer, "Not true, oh foolish one. Come here."

They walked to the end of the hall to the steps where Sunny could see a red 911 Porsche with a ski rack and skis. Sunny looked in amazement and looked at Carl.

"No way, that really isn't really yours?"

Carl smiled, "Yup, but that pair of skis on the passenger side is yours, brand new K2s."

Sunny looked at Carl realizing he had been set up and asked,

"Boots?" Without hesitation, Carl replied, "In the back. I stopped at your parents' house to borrow some clothes; they're in the back, too."

Even though Carl was offering Sunny the opportunity to fulfill a dream, he resented the manipulation. Sunny looked at Carl and said,

"Carl, you can't come here with everything set, thinking you know me, and I'll drop everything and run. I'm a responsible student and I have Raq and a college career ahead of me. I WON'T do it."

Sunny turned and looked at Raq. She had a big smile; not from his speech, but from Carl's prospect that seemed more than exciting. Raq knew Sunny wanted to go. Again, she hugged him with a kiss and whispered to do it, that he would not lose her; although inside both knew he probably would. Carl looked at Sunny, not fazed by his rant and said,

"Do you feel better?"

Sunny looked at Carl, smiled and said, "Yeah, I just had to say that for my dad's benefit. Let me call him." After a long phone call with him, his dad supported his decision with some reluctance. Sunny looked at Kathy and then looked at Carl. He kissed Kathy, turned to Carl and simply stated,

"Let's go."

Before Sunny knew it, they were headed north to Waterville Valley for the Nastar Pro Handicap Races in his best friend's Porsche. The excitement was unbelievable, their first Pro race. Sunny couldn't help but think he had finally turned his first love, skiing, into dollars—thanks to Carl, even if he did it without asking and at the expense of his college education.

Still apprehensive as to what his father had talked to him about, Sunny called him when they got to Waterville Valley. Sunny explained the situation about his feelings.

Much to his surprise, Sunny's dad supported him and told him to "go get them." This was the same support Sunny could count on since his first race in New York some years ago. Sunny only wished his dad could be there to see him at his first pro race. One thing was for sure, with that endorsement, not much could stop Sunny from his usual flat-out effort.

The Nastar Program had many sponsors, one being Bonnie Bell Cosmetics, which meant the Bonnie Bell Girls would be there. They were a group of skiing salesgirls. What a bonus. Sunny and Carl didn't get much sleep between their conversations with some of the girls and the excitement of the races. One of Sunny's twin sisters, Georgia, had gotten a job as a Bonnie Bell sales rep, so Sunny and Carl were able to have dinner with and meet the whole sales team.

It was early in the season and they hadn't had a chance to do any skiing, much less race training. Neither Carl nor Sunny had skied at Waterville Valley before. The race hill was steep, well groomed, and the other pros were really good. Individually, it might have been difficult, but together

Sunny and Carl were hard to intimidate. If one couldn't figure out how to get something done, the other one could. They watched the other skiers who took a few runs, and in no time, they were back in race form pushing each other to go faster.

They were tired the next morning and they had to take seven runs through the course, average five best times, and handicap themselves against the best pro. Carl and Sunny skied with all their hearts and the conviction of champions. Sunny wasn't going to let his father down and Carl wasn't going to let Sunny beat him. They weren't the best, but nonetheless, they did great. Sunny and Carl's handicaps were identical.

Carl had no formal training in ski racing, but possessed as much natural talent for it as he did with his music. Sunny was less talented, but compensated for it with his formal training at Mount Hood, courage, and perseverance. When it was over, the time came to return to North Hampton to finish the semester—then head to New Jersey for work.

On the way out of town, they broke a fan belt in Carl's 911. One of the Austrian racers stopped and showed them a trick using a ladies pantyhose. It worked, but every 50-60 miles, Sunny and Carl had to stop to talk some waitresses out of their pantyhose, with hilarious results.

When Sunny returned to school, Raq was glad to see him. Sunny and Kathy finished the semester and vowed to stay in touch. It was difficult to say goodbye, especially because Sunny knew they would probably be in touch less often and she did mean a lot to him at that time.

On the other hand, school remained difficult for Sunny and he couldn't help but feel an enormous elation when it was over. Skiing was something he knew, and if he was going to have success at anything, skiing would present the greatest likelihood.

Sunny arrived in New Jersey just in time for the Christmas rush. When people buy or give ski equipment for a Christmas present, they rarely hold it back if skiing is possible before that time; they were showing up a week or so before Christmas to try out their Christmas presents.

That particular season, the weather had decided to only partially cooperate. It didn't snow, but it was cold enough to make snow. New Jersey didn't get much snow so Vernon Valley and Great Gorge, the two New Jersey neighboring ski areas, represented the latest in snow-making technology.

It presented a most unusual sight; everything was brown, except for the few trails where the areas had decided to make snow for skiing.

Working as a full time instructor meant showing for lineup at 10 am, 12 noon, 2 pm and 6 pm. Having man-made snow presents instructors with a very different working arrangement. Man-made snow represents such a large expense that the management constantly tried to maximize efficiency and search for the most profitable use of snow. It was difficult to find appropriate terrain to teach on, as the instructors were expected to teach as large a class as possible. It was not at all unusual to have a class of 15 or more.

More devastating to Sunny was that employees were expected to minimize time on their own free skiing, not to mention the impossibility of setting a course and running gates for training. When people think of being a ski instructor, they think of this cheerful, Nordic-looking man having this great teaching experience. For New Jersey instructors, it was an impersonal mass production where one could teach some 100 or more students in a single day. As each day passed, Sunny prayed for natural snow.

Leaving Carl and Sunny alone with all these skiing women was like leaving a mad dog in charge of a meat house. Carl and Sunny took every opportunity to acquaint themselves with any or all females needing assistance and some not needing any help. Part of the contract did provide housing; and they made sure to get maximum utilization out of that facility.

As time passed, even such a deluge of women couldn't disguise the fact that Sunny wasn't skiing. After all, he didn't take the job to get dates. Sunny wanted to ski, or more precisely, *race*. Awakening early one morning, Sunny just couldn't stand it anymore; he had to train. He thought if he got up early enough, no one would mind a little training. The whole scene was depressing him and he became determined to train on his own.

Sunny arrived around seven that morning at the mountain with the brown and white stripes, a far cry from the towering snow-covered Vermont mountain. Nonetheless, it was skiing. After tramping through the mud-covered parking lot and base area, he got to the lifts just as the operators were doing their final checks. He snapped on his skis, excited about some personal training time, then the chair lift operator stopped him. He jumped out of the lift house, looked at Sunny and yelled,

"Hey, where do you think you're going?"

Sunny was excited to ski yet looked at the lift operator and said,

"Good morning. I thought I'd get some skiing in before work."

Sunny knew better than to mention anything about training. With disappointment, the lift operator dismissed Sunny's enthusiasm to ski and responded,

"Sorry, Bud. The area rules clearly say that all employees shall abstain from or minimize personal skiing during marginal snow." Sunny hoped to reason with him.

"Hey, wait, I'm one of the racing pros and have to inspect some of that hill for the Nastar Race today."

The lift operator was clearly more interested in winning his turf war.

"Sorry. Not before 10 a.m. It says no employees besides lift operators and ski patrol, and since you aren't either, hit the road."

That was it. Sunny wasn't going to sit around and argue with this idiot any longer. So, he proceeded to tell him where he could put his rules and informed him that any effort to keep him from skiing might result in physical injury. Sunny went on the lift and proceeded to train. He also proceeded to get himself fired. Sunny had had enough of pimping as a ski instructor, trying to squeeze every nickel out of every unsuspecting skier. It wasn't his style and furthermore, he was there to race. As soon as Carl heard, he found Sunny.

When Carl caught up to Sunny he couldn't help asking, "What the hell happened? I heard you punched out some unsuspecting lift operator and demanded training time." Sunny looked at Carl seriously.

"Not quite. I grabbed him, threw him on the lift and told him to take me to the top." Sunny smiled.

Carl asked again, "Be serious. What happened?" Sunny looked a bit more pensive this time.

"Nothing, really. I just tried to get some training in early, and that short dip shit on Chair 1 tried reading me Regulation 646 Sub Section 102-6. I told him where to stick it and went up."

Carl, with his usual solution-focus determination said,

"Come on, we'll talk to Bill, the head of the ski school. They need us." Sunny looked at Carl for a long moment.

"No, they don't and I don't need them. Carl, I want to race. This isn't skiing; this is walking around in a fucking ski instructor's sweater and faking it."

Carl didn't say anything. He knew Sunny was right. One thing about Sunny and Carl was that they couldn't bullshit each other when it got down to brass tacks. Carl knew this wasn't easy for Sunny. Sunny had quit school to start a ski career and felt like he had fucked it up. Carl just looked at Sunny and asked,

"What are you going to do?"

Sunny paused and looked back; it was breaking up a team and as good as it felt to stand up for his values, he didn't have a plan.

"I don't know. This late in the season, it's going to be hard to get in anywhere. I guess I'll go back to Vermont. Maybe I can work at The Horn."

Carl was silent as Sunny continued,

"Maybe we can do our entertainment scam? What do you think?"

There was a long moment of silence. Carl looked at Sunny. They both knew Carl was the one who made the deal and Sunny didn't have a plan. Carl knew he had to say,

"No, I've got to stick it out."

Sunny knew he was right. After all, he was the one who had got himself fired, not Carl. Sunny would miss him, and the thought of being out on his own without his best friend was scary, but they both knew Sunny would have a better chance at The Horn as a solo. Sunny also knew he would never lose Carl as his best friend.

Without phoning ahead, Sunny packed up his VW and headed north, wondering that whole seven hour drive how the ski town would receive him. Ski town people came and went without the town missing a beat; maybe they had forgotten him.

Sunny started his drive in the morning. It was a long drive, and he was unsure about what happened and whether he was doing the right thing. He had everything he owned in his car, and he was heading back to uncertain future. It was a clear winter day, and there was snow on the road. He was on the road north from New Jersey with one hundred dollars in his pocket and his skis. That was the sum total of his net worth. As Sunny drove north, he became more anxious. The drive through Connecticut seemed to go on forever. Sunny's VW only went fifty-five miles an hour flat out. Driving a

VW bug on a highway in winter, with skis sticking up in the back while giant tractor trailers tried to blow him off the road, gave Sunny an uneasy feeling in his stomach. As Sunny drove into Vermont, the temperature got lower and the snow got higher. The closer Sunny got to Stowe, the more excited he got. He had stopped a few times for gas and coffee, but he was overwhelmed with emotion when he came off the highway and headed into the town of Stowe. As he drove into town, Sunny couldn't wait to see everyone. He wondered if they wanted to see him, and after all, this was a ski town and each year was another year that waited for no one. If a skier was injured or left, it was like war; they just buried the dead and kept going. The drive up the mountain road seemed to be long and exciting. The snow seemed to be half way up the VW door. He arrived in The Horn parking lot around four in the afternoon and it was jammed. All he could see was everyone scrambling to get the food and beer out. No one noticed him.

Sunny had his car, his skis, and fifty dollars in his pocket. This was a one shot deal. Sunny walked in the door and worked his way through a sea of bodies to the bar. Richard was standing at the end of the bar pouring beer.

Richard looked over and saw Sunny standing there and blurted,

"Shit! Look who it is, it's Sunny."

Before Sunny knew it, all the bartenders, cooks and waitresses ran up to give him one of the biggest welcomes ever, almost bringing him to tears.

Richard broke up the reunion with, "Enough of this shit. Get back to work. Oh and Sunny, go change the Bud keg, line two."

Without hesitation Sunny simply said, "Yes, boss."

Sunny took off with a smile from ear to ear.

After Sunny worked that night, without saying a word to Richard, Richard turned and said,

"Get your stuff upstairs and we'll all grab a bite at the Shed, Stowe's oldest hamburger spot. You can tell me what happened to college then."

Sunny's job was to mop the floor and be the bar's ski pro. The guys at The Horn really were like a family to him. It was a great season and Sunny was home.

Rookie Year

THIS IS WHERE THE STORY really begins. You may believe in fate, but somehow between his own desire to race and a sequence of events, Sunny knew this was where he belonged. Sunny also knew that his family had higher expectations of him than mopping the floor at The Matterhorn Bar, but everyone could see that he was happy, and if nothing else, this clearly showed through in his skiing.

It was a good season and Sunny was on the mountain every day, going from Stowe's biggest moguls to the open trails of Big Spruce.

Sunny was not the best around, but he was certainly the most dynamic. He skied the mountains with a vengeance and bliss. Joubert, a famous ski coach, used to say skiing was softness in violence (violence in softness, perhaps?) and Sunny agreed with him.

With less distraction than Sunny had while attending high school across the street, his skiing came of age. Sunny skied with Richard and the gang and also with Cam and Eric, who were the hottest ski bums around.

Sunny trained with the Pro racers Arnie and Brock and did well in the local ski bum races. It was like all of a sudden, Sunny was cut loose. There was still something missing, *Carl.* Since their pro race at Waterville Valley, New Hampshire, Carl and Sunny had used the same song to get a rhythm before a run. The song was: "Here Comes the Sun" by Richie Havens, a great rendition.

They would stand at the top of the hill or the course, to get their rhythm and block everything out but the skiing to come. They would sing, or in

Sunny's case hear the beat of the guitar in his favorite song. The rhythm was perfect and motivating.

Then taking a deep breath, defogging and adjusting the goggles, he would attack the hill, pushing for more in every turn. Skiing is a commitment. Every skier knows you never beat the mountain; you just challenge yourself on it. Try to beat the mountain and the mountain will win every time. As intrinsically motivating as the song was, sharing the moment was important too. And Sunny thought of Carl in the New Jersey meat market every time he started a run and heard that song.

Carl had chosen his place as Sunny had his. Sunny had The Horn, the mountain, and his friends, not to mention the women.

Not being out of school for very long, Sunny did not have much experience or confidence in his social introductions to The Horn and the base lodge. No self-respecting ski bum would permit skiing with a woman to deter his skiing potential. Women had to wait until after skiing or ski with a "Twinkie."

A "Twinkie" is one of those impeccably dressed skiers who are there for lodge presentation and their egos. Oh, they can't ski either, but since they spend more time in the lodge than on the hill, they don't know it yet. Twinkies have their function, and that is to amuse young women until the real skiers are done.

The season went on and Sunny got better. His apprenticeship that year was perfect, and Sunny was clearly "rookie of the year." The transition to a ski bum was complete but his career had just begun. Sunny had found an area and a community that accepted him for who he was. It didn't offer much career growth, but most of the people in Stowe started as ski bums and found a way to flourish. They found a way to live the lifestyle they loved. When the Mountain closed, there was a sadness in not being able to ski so people left. The only thing to do then was get through the off season.

Surviving the Off-Season

IT IS FUNNY HOW A common denominator brings people together, and how an ideal environment can overcome so many differences and allow people to get to know each other.

Sunny was a desperately poor student in what little education he had, but was very fortunate that his parents could afford private education. All other education consisted of a fine upbringing by his father and picking up street smarts while growing up in New Jersey—and later by working in New York City.

During the early fall season, all bars and restaurants closed down in preparation for the upcoming ski season. Needless to say, work was at a premium.

John, the owner of The Baggy Knees, had acquired a motel which was partially in ruin from a fire. John had made plans for a mini-mall. So the existing building had to come down, or most of it. They needed laborers, no skills required; it sounded like a job for Super Bum. Besides, being in John's employment at this time ensured a spot in The Baggy Knees for the winter on weekends.

John had already hired another guy to work for him. Winter comes without warning in New England, and building was scheduled in a few weeks. Sunny showed up early in the morning at the job site and met a stocky, long-haired blond guy with round wire-rimmed glasses.

The job was to load rubble into a truck, drive it to the dump, and unload and to repeat this process until all the rubble was gone. Like everything else Sunny took part in, he jumped in with both feet and started ripping and tearing things apart and loading it onto the truck at an impressive pace. Sunny wasn't sure why he worked like that, except working at a steady pace was boring for him (or maybe it was the attention deficit thing). On the way to the dump, his blond-haired partner jumped in.

This short, stocky, brainy-looking guy jumped in the truck, declaring himself *Ace*. "Hi, I'll give you a hand. Besides, I want to grab something to eat on the way to the dump."

Sunny didn't mind the help. "Sure, come on, I'm a kind of hungry too."

Driving down the road to the dump, Ace looked at Sunny and said, "You've been working hard as shit; that's great, I'm impressed." Sunny smiled. Ace asked, "Do you always work this hard?"

Sunny smiled again, "Yeah, but not 'cause I like it. That work sucks! I just like to get it over with."

Ace agreed, "Yeah, but at that pace, we'll be done in a few days and we'll also be out of work afterwards." Sunny smiled again.

"You're right; we'll fuck off for a little while."

Ace turned to Sunny and surprised him.

"John says you're a hot skier."

Not sure what to say, Sunny asked, "And you?" Ace was quick to answer.

"I can hold my own. I've been coming up here all my life." It was good to know. Sunny looked at Ace, smiled and said,

"You look more like a hockey player." Ace just looked at Sunny as if he was clairvoyant.

"I am and have been playing hockey all my life. How did you know?" Sunny laughed. Ace was shorter and stocky. He looked strong, with powerful legs, and it wasn't a stretch.

"Just a good guess," Sunny said.

"My parents have a condo across from The Edelweiss, that small store halfway up the mountain road." Sunny laughed.

"You're a rich kid!"

Ace smiled. "If I were a rich kid, would I be doing this shit work?"

Sunny looked at Ace and continued,

"Yeah, but I don't know why. You probably just graduated from some preppie college like Yale and you don't want to go to work in your dad's business, so they sent you to Stowe to learn how the other half lives."

Ace huffed. "No, my parents are pissed off that I'm up here. They think I'm a fuck-off. They believe all I want to do is live in the mountains and ski."

Sunny looked at Ace and asked,

"Well, are they right?" Ace paused for a moment, thought for a few seconds and answered back,

"Partially, I do want to ski every day, but I want to get laid too."

Sunny absolutely understood, he only had one question.

"Where's home?

"Philly."

Sunny knew Ace was in the right place. He looked at him and said,

"Welcome to Stowe, you're here for the right reasons. Stick with me. Since we can't ski, we'll start by getting laid."

Ace smiled. "Great. Do you have any money for lunch?"

Sunny looked with some surprise,

"Who me?"

They got to the store on the way to the dump; and they noticed Sue who was working the Deli as they walked in. Sunny looked at the very attractive girl behind the counter.

"Hi, beautiful."

"What do you want?" Sue asked. "Don't tell me you're broke and hungry again." Sunny smiled. She was right, but it was time for charm as he had little else.

"Sue, this is Ace, he's one of us."

"You mean one of you and not another one of the pack?" Sue answered.

"Come on, you know I love you, Ace is working with me. I'll cover him," Sunny pleaded.

"Oh yeah, who will cover you?" Sue answered with a smile.

"John on Friday, then I'll cover you at The Knees. So, can I get a roast beef and tomato sandwich, no onions? Ace, what do you want?"

Ace answered with amazement, "Ham and cheese, with a large milk."

They got their sandwiches and started to the truck. While Ace was eating he turned to Sunny and said,

"She's beautiful. I've been watching her for weeks. Are you dating her?"

"Boy, are you green!" Sunny replied, "Dating? Nobody dates anybody, that's against the rules; besides, that takes money. And no, I'm not dating her. I thought of trying to give her a jump, but I'm afraid if I fucked it up, I'd starve..."

Ace huffed.

Sunny went on, "Besides I think she's smarter than that."

They drove out to the dump, put the tailgate down and sat to eat their lunch. "Thanks for the sandwich; I hadn't eaten in two days," Ace said.

Sunny smiled. "Stick with me and at least you won't starve."

After lunch, Sunny jumped up into the truck and started unloading half of the burned roof shingles.

They talked easily and Sunny asked,

"Hey, if you're new to ski bumming, what were you doing last year?"

Ace answered with pride, "College."

"No shit, I was only kidding before, which college?" Sunny replied.

"Yale," Ace replied.

Sunny couldn't believe Ace's response; he actually thought he was kidding.

"No way!" Sunny said with surprise.

Ace simply smiled.

Sunny couldn't believe his predictions were so close to reality and he had to ask,

"And the rest?" Ace responded,

"Just like you said, except I haven't told my parents. They want me out of the condo."

With some surprise, Sunny asked,

"Why?"

Ace just shrugged his shoulders and said,

"I don't know, I think they want to teach me a lesson."

"Where do you live?" Sunny paused and looked at Ace thinking he might not believe him. "The Matterhorn."

As expected, with a surprised look Ace said,

"The bar?" Sunny just smiled and explained.

"I needed a place to stay and Richard let me live upstairs, but I'm moving to a house in the back of town."

Sunny couldn't believe his evaluation of Ace was so accurate. He hadn't gone to college, but Ace was okay and he seemed to be impressed by him. Sunny guessed that was because Ace wanted to be a ski bum and Sunny was one. It was funny that Sunny wanted to go to college. They spent the rest of the day pitching shingles, laughing, fucking off and saving their jobs. After work, Ace turned and said,

"Hey, you want to go into the Jacuzzi?" Sunny had no idea what a Jacuzzi was.

"A what?"

Ace repeated, "A Jacuzzi."

He had never seen or heard about a Jacuzzi before. He needed more of an explanation.

"What the fuck is a zazuzzi?"

Ace said,

"Close enough; it's a hot bath that seats about ten people."

Looking a little surprised, Sunny just looked at Ace with a smile and said,

"Now this I have got to see!"

Ace seemed to know what he was doing, so he led the way and mentioned that he would get the key.

They went into the office to get the key and Ace introduced Sunny to this straight-looking enormous guy.

"Sunny this is Roger."

Roger was a really big guy with a big smile and seemed to be good friends with Ace, so any friend of Ace would be a good addition. Sunny just looked as Roger said,

"How ya doing?"

Ace quickly stepped in, asking Roger for the key.

"Hey Roger, throw me the key to the Jacuzzi."

On the way out, Sunny turned to Ace and couldn't help but notice how big and strong Roger was. Skiers weren't known for their size. Sunny turned to Ace on the way to the Jacuzzi and said,

"Ace, Jesus, did you see the size of that guy?"

"Who Roger? Yeah, he's pretty big, I grew up with him. He went to Princeton and was captain of the hockey team."

Sunny couldn't believe he had bumped into two Ivy League people in the same day. They were the first two Ivy League people he had ever known. He couldn't hide his discovery. He looked at Ace and said,

"Shit, are there anymore of you guys? He's huge. I want him on my side."

Ace laughed and said,

"Yeah, he's here for the season. Got a job managing these condos in order for the attendees to have a place to stay and be able to ski."

Roger turned out to be an okay guy. They spent the evening in the Jacuzzi and talking up at the condo while cooking dinner. Roger had his own place that his parents bought for him.

He seemed set, with a job and a condo. This was no way to ski bum—far too much responsibility. It's one thing to look respectable, another one to actually be respectable. No, Roger didn't have his priorities right. Skiing did not come first with him. But he was big and had the keys to the Jacuzzi; that made him okay, he was in.

Stony

AFTER MEETING ACE AND ROGER, Sunny had a pretty good group building. One day Ace and Sunny were working, cleaning up in the Center. (That was the name of John's shopping mall that they were tearing down earlier.) By this time, construction had been well under way. Ace and Sunny were the odd job men. John had already rented spaces so people were beginning to move in.

Sunny was cleaning one of the bathrooms, getting it ready for painting and watching some of the tenants move in when Ace came running into the bathroom yelling.

"Sunny, come here quick! You won't believe it!" He thought there was some beautiful girl, or an emergency or something. Sunny went outside and stood on the stairs with Ace. Sunny just stood there for a second, not knowing what to look for or what they were looking at really. He turned to Ace for some clarification. Ace just looked at him as if Sunny should know without an explanation. Ace looked at Sunny and said,

"Sunny, look." Ace pointed to this huge Nordic-looking guy sweeping.

Actually, this huge six-foot man with a Prince Valiant haircut and a chin line beard stood with this enormous chest, gripping a broom like it was a toothpick, and was sweeping the hall. He looked like the last of the Vikings, or a blond knight from the Round Table, and was fixing the Nordic Ski Center for business. The man looked up. Sunny just looked at him for a moment, now understanding what Ace brought them over to look at, this big Nordic looking guy.

"Hey, how are you doing? I'm Sunny." He looked back and simply said,

"Hi, I'm Stony."

John had at least one of the shops downstairs as a ski shop.

"Are you going to run the ski shop?"

Stony replied, with a big smile, "Yup, you guys know how to cross country ski?" Sunny did cross country ski and was happy to see somebody else who did some cross country skiing.

"Yeah, I did a little racing in high school."

Stony was eager to show what the shop had to offer. He said,

"Hey, come on in and take a look at these new racing shoes." They spent the next few minutes talking about Nordic skiing with Stony and invited him to Ace's condo for one of Sunny's famous home cooked ski bum meals. Stony met them after work.

While cooking, Stony disclosed his ambitions. He had come to Stowe to work and ski, both Alpine and Nordic styles. He had just finished his graduate research and was in the process of typing his master's thesis in Alpine vegetation. During cooking, Ace caught Sunny in the kitchen alone.

Ace came up to Sunny and asked, "Need help?" Sunny looked at Ace and laughed a little and said,

"Look Ace, you might be a college grad, but your cooking,…it's not good. So I'll try it solo, okay?"

Now it was Ace's turn to notice the size of Stony.

"Did you see the size of Stony?"

Without looking up Sunny reply, "Yeah, is he just one person?" Ace wasn't used to Sunny's New Jersey humor.

Ace remarked, "Be serious. Between Roger, Stony, you and myself, the mean weight per mass distribution is awesome."

Sunny didn't have a clue of what Ace said, but he wanted Stony to be on his side as well. He seemed to be a nice guy, sounded like a pretty good skier.

Just then, Stony walked into the kitchen. Sunny wasn't one known for his tact and a name like Stony was an unusual one. If Sunny was gonna build his team, he had to know the background on people. So he just came out and asked,

"Hey Stony, what is Stony short for? No mother looks at her son and names him Stony."

Stony just looked at Sunny and huffed, "Alton."

Sunny wasn't quite sure what to say so he just asked, "What?"

Stony clarified, "Alton Day Stone...that's my name. What kind of name is Sunny? That sounds like some flower child."

As usual, Sunny couldn't come up with just an answer or explanation. He had to be facetious. So without hesitation he decided to say,

"Well...I was born in Woodstock... No, I was at a race camp in Oregon and some girl was making fun of my speech impediment. Since I sounded so funny saying Sunny, she started calling me that and it stuck."

Sunny looked around the room, seeing Roger had come too, as he wasn't going to pass up a home cooked meal. He knew they were the crew of 1973 in Stowe and that they would set the pace; that year would belong to them. Sunny had no idea how you know you've met someone you'll want to be in your life for a long time, but after the next few days, he knew he had met some new friends who would play a large part in this for years to come.

Being the King of the ski bums was Sunny's dream, and he realized then that it wasn't one person, it would be the group. Besides, not having anyone to share his skiing with that year would leave him empty. Sunny spent the next few days at The Matterhorn helping Richard get it open for the season.

Stowe, The Season

IT WAS THE FALL OF 1973 and Sunny had just finished his official apprenticeship year as a ski bum. The attic of The Matterhorn Bar had served as perfect housing for his rookie year. It had all the essentials; it was warm and close to the slopes. It provided women, drinks and all the burgers he could eat. It was far enough from town so that after Sunny was done cleaning up for the night (even though the bar closed at 10 p.m.), he was too tired to go partying. This was fine with him, as skiing was, after all, the reason he was there. He felt like he had it all; but on the other hand, it still wasn't enough.

After a hard skiing season in which Sunny had done extremely well in the ski bum races, he had made his mark on the mountain as a real contender for the place of "THE" Ski Bum. Mind you, there really wasn't any trophy, award ceremony, or real title; it was just people within a very small group within the town.

Sunny found himself around other ski bums who were tall and athletic and charming. He was so focused on strengthening his skiing skills and advancing his abilities as a professional skier, he had failed to notice that he had turned into a six foot tall, athletic, dark wavy-haired, attractive young man with a pretty good mustache. Sunny was always that boy from high school who mothers didn't want their daughters dating, so he generally assumed rejection. That never stopped him from trying, and it generally didn't stop girls from wanting to go out with somebody their mothers didn't want them anywhere near.

Sunny felt he needed to flex some of his social muscles in the bars. After all, a ski bum's motto was "decadence, a way of life." Sunny decided it was time to leave the nest and live on his own. He believed that living with other ski bums was too obvious, so when the opportunity came to live with some people who were there for reasons other than ski bumming decadence, he jumped at the chance. Sunny had graduated late due to all the difficulties he had in high school, and his choice to drop out of college to be a professional skier turned out to be a disappointment at the time. Sunny was now in his twenties, and decided he wanted to live more respectably. He had greatly appreciated the help Richard had given to him in getting back on his feet, but Sunny was afraid that if he had continued to live upstairs in a bar, people would not take him seriously.

After all, the women Sunny had hoped to lure into his house were unsuspecting college girls, coming to town on a sabbatical from work or whatever came next after college.

The house Sunny came to rent a room in was a beautiful New England style family home, done in Early American, with three bedrooms. Being the last one in and the first one not to have enough money, Sunny got the smallest room, a room designed for children. Sunny didn't mind as it was private and had a great view and was, in short, "respectable."

Judy

It was an unexpectedly beautiful fall day in New England and Sunny was the only employee around, as no bars and restaurants were open during the off-season. At 11 am Sunny was just wiping down the bar in final preparation for its opening.

Then in she came, this terrific strawberry blond woman in an Oxford button-down blouse and a pair of faded jeans. Both the blouse and jeans were exquisitely shaped. Sunny was somewhat preoccupied by his new living arrangements, and he had just come from his first night of respectability.

Nevertheless, he was not blind. She sat down at a table with the best sunlight, having the local newspaper and a pencil with her. This was an extremely common scene in this ski town. Unlike previous years when employers would provide housing, later the employees sought their own living arrangements. This wasn't exactly the case with her. He walked over and with a smile said,

"Good morning, I'm Sunny…coffee?"

With the most beautiful of smiles she looked up and said,

"Yes please, I'm Judy."

Sunny could see at closer inspection that she was a beautiful young lady of poise, and shapelier even than she first appeared. What a great chance at the start of the season. Sunny was eager to talk with her. Finding a place to live in this town this close to the season is almost impossible, he thought.

"Do you have a job yet?" Sunny was somewhat surprised with Judy's openness.

"Yes, I'm a waitress up at the Trap Family Lodge. I'm staying at the employee dorms and they are so overcrowded, that I wanted to get out."

The Trap Family Lodge was a beautiful tourist trap, where wealthy people went for breakfast or dinner, expecting to see an actress bouncing through the halls singing the songs from the play.

All their employees were these healthy, beautiful people running around in Lederhosen and dirndl dresses designed for Swiss milk maidens. The whole idea was repulsive to Sunny; no self-respecting ski bum would be caught dead in that kind of a get-up.

Nevertheless, Judy was just beautiful, new to the area and had good prospects. As a point of enthusiasm, Sunny couldn't resist describing his new abode. After all, if it appealed to someone this respectable he knew he would be on the right track. After casual introductions, he went on to talk about his new living arrangements.

"I looked for a long time before I found this place. It's just up on Sugar House Hill, in back of town, walking distance."

Sunny continued to explain in great detail his new living quarters. Judy and Sunny talked for some time about what listings were good and where to go. She was a genuinely nice person.

After a while, more people came into the restaurant and Sunny had to get back to work. Needless to say, Sunny tried hard to make a date. Hoping she would spend the night, Sunny remarked,

"Well, good luck. I'll call you and you can tell me what you've found. You could always stay with me too."

Judy grabbed her newspaper circled with possibilities and looked at him. Sunny just looked at her and smiled.

"No, don't worry about it, coffee is on me."

Sunny figured that she was way out of his league and really didn't think much of it, but it was worth a shot. Judy looked at Sunny with that wonderful smile of hers, her beautifully shaped body with her poise and grace. She stated,

"Thanks, but don't call. I'll let you know, it's a promise."

Sunny closed the bar early. He was anxious to get home and put the final touches on his room. As Sunny approached the driveway, a green VW Bug was parked there, and it wasn't one of the other guy's cars. Since they were all single, Sunny didn't think too much of it. As he walked through the living room and started for the stairs, it dawned on him that there were no other cars in the driveway, and if one of the guys had company, his car would be there too. Talking to himself, he said, "*No, they just took off in one car.*"

Still feeling uncertain, Sunny hurried to his room, opened the door. His room looked different. It had a pink bedspread and there was "stuff," things that were not his, all around the room.

Sunny was in shock and took a deep breath, realizing what had probably happened. The guys had rented his room out to some girl, and moved his belongings to one of the other rooms. The other guys, not being ski bums, may not have understood the validity of having a house with only male residents.

Sunny quickly turned around to look for his things. It was Friday night and he was going to bartend at The Baggy Knees, and he didn't have much time to shower and change. As Sunny turned, there she was, Judy, standing before him in that full-figured blouse. The shock hit him, and Sunny could only look at her. He tried to speak but only parts of the sentence came out,

"Aha... Hi... It's you..."

Then it really hit him. Sunny looked around the room. Yes, his things where in there too! With panic in his voice along with some bewilderment, he said,

"No, you can't, I can't...I could...? No way, you can't, you don't understand..."

Now understand, even though Sunny was throwing out this beautiful strawberry blond, she stood to threaten the entire season. After all, even ski bums have some sort of twisted principle which goes: *no obstruction to decadence.* Sunny had never had any real success at a relationship, and this was really no time to chance it. He looked at her and began,

"No way, you can't live here..."

Judy was now in tears, something Sunny had no stomach for.

Judy pleaded by saying, "Please, we don't have to be together, I just need a place to sleep." Even in this emotional state, the irony had not escaped Sunny.

"Oh great, we don't have to be together...?" Judy tried to explain,

"I'm dating the manager at work and he wants me to move in with him."

Sunny was now in shock as things were going from bad to worse. He just stared at Judy.

"Oh, I see. Instead of living with your boyfriend, you move in with a perfect stranger." Judy tried a little harder.

"Look, if I live with him then I have to... well, you know."

Sunny realized at that point that Judy was a very special woman, but she really didn't know all the shortcomings of him.

"Aha, yeah...and here you don't.....Look Judy, there's a lot about me you don't know."

Sunny suddenly realized he had to be at The Baggy Knees. So he began to take his shirt off and walked down the hall toward the bathroom with Judy following him, clearly not wanting to give up.

"I know I don't know you, but you're nice."

Sunny tried to explain further, "I'm not nice, that's what I'm trying to tell you."

Judy must have seen something in Sunny.

She bluntly stated, "I trust you."

Sunny stopped dead in his tracks. By this time they were standing in the bathroom. Sunny was down to his boxers and the moment struck him.

"I don't even trust me, how can you? I'm not trustworthy."

Judy looked at Sunny with a simple smile that Sunny couldn't resist.

"It doesn't matter; I work early morning until after lunch. You work early evening until around midnight. I'll be asleep when you get home and I'm gone by dawn. You won't even know I'm here. We won't be together long enough to start anything."

Sunny was now motioning for her to turn around; after all there was no sense in starting anything that he wasn't going to finish. With Judy having her eye on his room as a residence, he jumped into the shower. Sunny yelled from the shower.

"Who's your boss?"

"Tom."

You could hear the panic in Sunny's voice as he answered.

"Tom, the Frenchman?" Judy was caught by surprise.

"Oh shit, you know him?"

"Yeah, he used to work at The Matterhorn. He taught me how to bar-tend. Forget it, Tom would rip my arms out if he knew you were here; he'd never believe the arrangement we're trying to make."

Judy pleaded with Sunny.

"Please, I don't want to move in with Tom. If he knows I don't have a place, I won't have an excuse."

Sunny knew he was caught between a rock and a hard place. He had known Tom for a long time and didn't want to be caught between Tom and his girlfriend.

"Look, I'm not allowed to live here with a girl and I don't want a relationship. Do you have any idea what this could do to me if people found out about it, not to mention what people would think about you?"

Judy pleaded further, "I promise no one will know."

By that time, Sunny was standing just about to shave, with a towel around him. Judy was sitting on the toilet next to him as Sunny was mumbling to himself, *'I'm sure the other guys won't allow it.'*

"But if I tell them you're just here for a visit, I guess…One week, and no questions about anything I do or don't."

Judy jumped up and hugged him; suddenly caught off guard, he couldn't believe what he was saying. Judy just smiled and said okay. Sunny finished dressing for work and left feeling really unsure about Judy and how he felt about her, but thinking she was special.

The Baggy Knees

SUNNY HAD LEFT JUDY AT his room and gone straight to the Baggy Knees. There were two bars in town which hosted bands, The Baggy Knees and The Rusty Nail. Both were converted barns, appropriate with their quaint New England appearance. Both were also open only on the weekends that early in the season.

Opening those bars on the weekends served many purposes. Even though the skiers hadn't hit town, all the lodge and restaurant employees, along with some native Vermonters, were looking to both those bars for a sneak preview of the season's talent. It was important to distinguish between local ski bums and everyone else, because ski town employees are the heart and pulse of any ski town. Being aware of this, neither bar imposed a cover charge on people with valid employment for the season.

Normally a season pass would be sufficient identification, and in fact it was a good backup, but anyone with money could afford one—and not all passes were in-town employees. Everyone who had attended or read the result sheet from the ski bum races knew who Sunny was. Knowing the doorman was also important if you were going to live on little or nothing and hoped to get into either of the bars. To a seasoned ski bum, it was a point of pride.

So knowing Sunny knew almost everyone in town, John asked Sunny to do the door and graciously offered to compensate him from the tips he would have earned bartending. In short, John knew how important it was to not piss off the locals.

Sunny met Ace downstairs in The Knees early to get something to eat, and right behind them Roger and Stony appeared. Sunny thought, "Okay, sure, what the hell?" After all, Sunny was also the bouncer and having the boys with him certainly wouldn't hurt to deter any trouble. Besides, Sunny couldn't handle all the girls who came in and there were plenty to go around. During dinner, Sunny must have looked a little pale, as he was asked if he felt all right and why he only had eaten half of his sandwich.

There was a code of food ethics; a true ski bum never turned down food. A true ski bum doesn't know where his next meal is coming from!

Sunny told them that he had a weird thing happen to him, and proceeded to tell them about Judy. Sunny didn't tell them everything; he just told them that he was housing some poor girl for a couple of days until she could find a place of her own. Needless to say, they didn't believe him; but that didn't bother Sunny.

Sunny had spent his entire life preparing for this season and what he had hoped for—a season of kind, caring, meaningless sex and good clean fun. What had just happened was meeting a nice girl and, at the same time, feeling really emotional, which was unfair!

However, the call to arms soon sounded to open the bar for entertainment, and in minutes a row of people formed with beautiful, unsuspecting coeds lined up for his convenience.

All the people from the previous seasons and residences came in, saying 'Hi Sunny' and proceeded to the bar. All the newcomers said 'Hi, I'm supposed to see Sunny, I work at such and such' and they proceeded into the bar NC (no cover charge).

The people visiting Stowe who didn't know him said, 'Hi, I'm a ski bum,' which meant they paid unless they were single, beautiful girls.

These weekends were important to a ski bum; it was like pre-season training or a pre-season game. The idea was the same as in sports, to get out there and get a look at the competition, scout the talent, and give them an indication of what you could do without showing them all your tricks.

It was easy to understand Sunny's concerns about Judy, showing emotions and establishing residency with a woman could constitute a real pre-season injury, which could keep him out of the game.

There was only one thing to do: go out and hit them hard. As the girls and others passed Sunny, he was in rare form, checking IDs and collecting smiles, sometimes money, but most importantly, phone numbers.

Unexpectedly, Judy and Tom suddenly approached Sunny. Sunny turned and asked Ace if he would get him a beer. Ace looked at Sunny; he could easily recognize the early signs of panic on his face, and just stood there smiling at him. Sunny quickly turned to Stony hoping Stony would get them that beer.

"Stony?"

Stony quickly replied, "No dice."

The boys were on to him. Tom was standing directly in front of Sunny. Unsuspectingly Tom said, "Good evening, Sunny. I'd like to introduce Judy. Judy, this is Sunny."

By this time, Sunny was in a cold sweat. Sunny calmly looked with a meager smile not to give anything away and as pleasant as he could be.

"Hello Judy, nice to meet you. Ah, Tom, go ahead and enjoy yourselves. I'll be back in a few minutes to say hi."

As they walked in, Ace, Stony and Roger were quick to put two and two together—as well as noticing that Judy was not just your typical poor homeless girl looking for a place to crash a few days. Ace was first to speak up, not using any sort of a filter.

"You're fucked, Warner."

Stony quickly followed with, "Don't look to me for help."

Roger was next to pile on, "Don't worry too much, the Jacuzzi is great for healing bruises, but I'm not sure about broken bones."

Now just to frame things out correctly, the most beautiful girl just came through the door with one of the toughest guys in town, and Sunny had told them that she was going to be staying with him. To make things worse, Sunny quickly opened his mouth and said,

"Wow, hold it. Nothing has happened."

And that didn't help; Ace looked at Sunny in disbelief.

"Okay, we believe you, you're gay, eh."

Now Sunny was in real trouble, but being the King meant coming up with an alternate plan. Just then, this young girl living in one of lodges walked in; he had been working on her for a while. She was really nice, a little naive and was beautifully endowed. What great timing. Sunny quickly turned his attention to her.

"Jesse, how ya doing?"

Jesse, seeing it was Sunny, walked quickly over to give him a hello kiss. Sunny grabbed her and planted one on her, a good 30-second shot. When Sunny finished, he turned to the crew and said,

"I'd like you to meet Jesse. Jesse, meet Ace, Stony and Roger. Ace, watch the door a second, I'll be right back."

Sunny walked Jesse in and apologized for the scene. Jesse who always had a big smile as wonderful as she was, quickly replied,

"No need, I liked it."

This was a chance for Sunny to get back on his feet.

"Great, how about dinner tomorrow?" Jesse was delighted, and to be honest so was Sunny.

"Okay," Jesse replied.

"I'll call you at the Inn. I have to get back to the door; those guys don't know who's who," Sunny said as he walked back.

Sunny returned to the door having saved grace; but to tell the truth, he was really new at it with the bar circuit and almost lost his first battle. Thankfully, he had squeezed right out of it.

So far, Sunny got his place to liveand let some girl move in to keep her ass from the fire; it cost him a dinner he couldn't afford, with someone he didn't want to be with. Good job so far. After the club, the gang all wound up at the condo for cornflakes after work. Roger and Ace dragged some honeys home. It was late, so Sunny stayed at the condo.

The next morning at seven, a thunderous crash of music at an earsplitting volume woke Sunny as well as everyone else up at the mountain. 'Sympathy for the Devil' by the Rolling Stones was playing at what Ace called a "motivating volume." Ace was a kind of genius with sound and electronics; this was before all the high technology, and people still had record players.

Sunny had gotten up to go to the bathroom, took one look at the girl he was with, and decided it was a good time to sound the alarm. Ace couldn't blame him; he wouldn't have gotten back into bed either. Besides having the shit scared out of everyone, nobody had wanted to get up so early, but somehow by the time everyone got to the living room, they were dancing and rocking out.

They told Ace, "good choice of music," while they were finishing off the cornflakes. The next song was "Listen to the Music" by the Doobie Brothers, while Stony, Roger, and Sunny were all working the bathroom. Sunny yelled to Ace,

"You ready for work?!" Ace yelled back from the living room,

"It's Saturday, dummy!"

Sunny said in his New Jersey humor, "I knew that...what am I doing up?" He still was a little shell-shocked from the night before. Stony yelled from the hall,

"We're going up the mountain!"

Roger decided to add his idea to the itinerary,

"I'm going back to bed."

The girl who was with Roger decided she should add to the conversation.

"No, I have to get to work, I'll come with you."

Sunny decided this would be an opportune moment to gain some needed supplies.

"Here Roger, here's a couple of bucks, grab some milk and cornflakes."

Stony added, "Granola." Then Sunny again,

"Why am I not surprised? Okay, granola". The truth was the group got along great and nobody minded helping each other out. They truly enjoyed being together, just deciding on something was the challenge.

The Mountain

AFTER ROGER GOT BACK FROM the store, they finished breakfast and Stony led the way up the mountain. The sun was shining; the sky was clear and blue. Sunny knew it was their season. He only wished Carl could have been there.

Stony kept them entertained with lectures on foliage chemistry and descriptions of Alpine vegetation. Ace and Sunny evaluated last night's game and planned strategy for that night's scrimmage. Roger wondered why he was not in bed.

Sunny had told Richard he would stop in at The Horn early that afternoon. Even though there wasn't going to be any business that far up the mountain road yet, Richard wanted to get The Horn open for a few hours to get the kinks out before winter.

Sunny wanted to keep The Horn job, but he also felt it was time to move on. On the way down the mountain, Sunny gave it some real thought. He stopped about halfway down; he wasn't his usual talkative self and Ace could sense it. Ace looked at Sunny and asked,

"Sunny, you're all right?" Sunny just looked straight ahead with a somewhat serious expression and answered,

"Yeah." Roger tried to help explain Sunny's dilemma. "Ah, it's probably that honey living with him," Roger said.

Normally Roger would be right, but for a moment Sunny quivered with the feeling of how fleeting his attachment to the mountain must be. Sunny meant he was standing on the mountain feeling like he owned it, when in reality, the town and people had been there long before he had and would be there long after he was gone. For that moment Sunny felt so insignificant, but that reality also bared the truth that nothing stayed the same. Last year had been great but impossible to repeat, so any expectations Sunny had or whatever he hoped to accomplish would only come to be by moving on. Sure, The Horn represented security, but change represented new possibilities as well as insecurity.

The whole feeling was really unsettling. After all, everyone hoped to have their work and somehow build some importance in town legend. Standing there was greatly humbling.

Sunny felt a great appreciation for the chance to experience the mountain and the people. He also felt an appreciation for those who came to the mountain with dreams much the same as his own. They really did only have each other.

When Sunny came to The Horn, he wasn't surprised to see Judy there. For a moment, he understood (understood what? love at first sight, maybe?) when she greeted him with a smile.

"Hello, Sunny. I was concerned about you; I thought I scared you off last night," Judy said softly.

Sunny just looked at her for a moment. "No, not really. I thought you might appreciate having the room to yourself."

Judy answered quickly, "No, I missed you."

Sunny tried not to show his surprise or any emotion. "Where's Tom, working?" Sunny said.

"Yeah," Judy replied. Sunny thought he'd better lighten things up pretty quickly.

"Hey, you want a beer? The gang and I just climbed the mountain, come on over."

Judy smiled, "Okay."

Sunny looked at Judy and she explained, "But only for a little bit because I've got to get home and get dressed for tonight."

Judy joined the group and mixed in with the guys as if she belonged there. Sunny could see that she was genuinely concerned for him. He finished up and went home to change, as he needed some fresh clothes and a shower. Judy came in just as he was getting out of the shower. And in that soft voice Judy asked,

81

"Hello, are you dressed?"

Hinting with his usual New Jersey humor, Sunny replied,

"No, but come on up."

Not unlike before, Judy came in and sat on the toilet and talked to him while he was shaving. This seemed to be becoming a pattern. Judy wanted to talk.

"I'm sorry, I should have warned you last night."

Maybe Sunny wasn't capable of having a serious conversation or he was trying to avoid a relationship. He said,

"No problem, I like seeing my life flash before my eyes. Don't worry. Does Tom know where you live?"

Judy tried to soothe Sunny's worries for the moment.

"No, I left my car at the Center, where he met me. From there I drove home."

"Quick thinking, though you can't really keep this up, can you?" Sunny asked.

Judy looked at Sunny and hit him hard by asking,

"Does this mean I have to leave?"

Sunny had to think for a moment. He knew what anyone was thinking; this was his chance to get his room back and escape possible death by Tom.

But after that day on the mountain, he knew she needed him. Besides, he believed she was very special, different. After a small pause,

"Nah, you can stay."

Judy jumped up to hug him in spite of the shaving cream she was now wearing.

"I knew you were great," Judy said.

Sunny just looked at her with a smile but with also some seriousness on his face. He said,

"Just keep me from getting killed and look for some place safe. If you stay too long, we'll get caught. Remember our original agreement." Judy smiled back, hugged him again and said,

"Okay. I'll see you tonight."

Sunny wanted to say yes, but that would expose the weakness he was feeling. He looked at her with a very stern look and said,

"And that's another thing. No questions, remember?"

Judy was now serious this time. "Okay. Have a good night at work."

Sunny got dressed and went to work. Stony, Ace and Roger were waiting for him; after all, they couldn't execute the strategy without the quarterback.

Oh, Sunny did go home that night and Judy and Sunny respected each other's side of the bed. The only violation was Judy giving Sunny a hug and holding him as they fell asleep. Sunny pretended not to reciprocate, but it did feel good.

The weeks passed quickly and snow finally came. Sunny had spent some nights at home and some nights at the condo; some nights with someone and some nights not. But as far as Judy went, not a question—and Sunny never, ever asked about her and Tom when she hadn't used her side of the bed. They had spent some time together over lunch, a few dinners and many talks while he shaved.

But the snow was there and the mountain opened. The excitement was unbelievable. After all, Ace, Stony, and Sunny had never seen each other ski, and although they hadn't said anything, they were all curious as to how the others skied.

Sunny was at home the first day it snowed; skiing was a very personal time for him. Sure Sunny was curious about the other guys, but he had longed for his private moment with the mountain. Sunny didn't tell anyone, he just grabbed his stuff and headed up. Sunny knew Ace and the guys would be up there, but Sunny hoped he could get some time on the slopes alone. Sunny reached the mountain, strapped on his skis, and on the way up closed his eyes to feel the fresh snow. Sunny couldn't help feeling this was it; this was the time he had been waiting for. Sunny jumped off the lift and headed for the National, one of the four runs under the lift. Only a portion of the mountain was open. Standing on top, Sunny took a deep breath and started the tune, "Little Darling." Oh did Sunny miss Carl, but this one was just for himself; he started his run.

The quietness was broken by the rhythm of ultimate violence and the softness of his skiing. It was like that for a few minutes. Sunny could feel the mountain with his skis, every turn and bump. Sunny skied like he had never skied before, non-stop to the finish.

As Sunny pulled up to the lift, there was the gang. Sunny looked and smiled. He didn't say a word. They just rode the lift, and Sunny knew then that this group was meant to be a part of the year and of him. A little nervous about their pretentiousness, they were soon reassured by their confidence and friendship, then kicked off down the mountain together.

First Ace, then Stony, Roger, and finally Sunny. Ace skied aggressively, but calculatedly. Stony possessed grace and style somewhat surprising for a man his size. Roger had a loose, carefree balance that he must have picked up from his hockey playing. Their compatibility was never more apparent as then, on the hill.

Skiing is a very personal time and to share it is very much like being in a relationship. You must have each other's acceptance, compatibility, and most of all, respect; as a group, they all shared these components.

Their presence on the mountain drew attention from all the others they shared the hill with, four or five of them bouncing from turn to turn with effortless grace—each in his own style attacking every turn; the ultimate freedom of expression.

Moving on, afterward they convened at The Horn. Sunny was suffering from this dissonance between working at The Horn and The Knees, so he went ahead to The Horn ahead of the others.

Sunny was excited to see Richard out back on the loading dock straightening up some beer kegs.

"Hey, Richard."

Richard as his usual gruff self turned to Sunny and said,

"Sunny, I should have known you'd be on the mountain today."

Richard could sense his ambivalence and sat on the edge of the loading platform with him.

"You know, Sunny, I used to live down on a boat taking care of it, and the guy that owned it was like a father to me. One year I decided to move into town and take another job. It was real hard, but things had to move on."

Sunny looked at Richard because the last thing he ever wanted to do was to disappoint his friend.

"Yeah I know, it is hard. I've always skied for The Horn," Sunny said.

"Skiing isn't the only world of bumming. Sailing has its share. I've gotta go to work, it's getting busy in there."

Somehow he knew right then, it wasn't The Horn that was important.

It was the friendships the Horn had brought him, and no matter where he went, the true friends would always be there. Richard just looked at Sunny and said,

"Give me a hand with these kegs, will ya?"

Sunny looked at Richard with a big smile.

"Sure thing, boss."

Richard and Sunny had a very special relationship. Richard had mentored Sunny through his senior year of high school, and Sunny had been there through the terrible days when the Horn had burned down. Richard believed in Sunny, even though he knew that Sunny really struggled with his academics. But Richard, being an All-American athlete, also recognized Sunny's athleticism and respected that. Richard really did want the best for Sunny and recognized the drive Sunny had.

Sunny went inside after helping Richard, feeling much better. Ace, Stony, Roger and some of the other guys were already trading stories about that day's skiing.

The better racers, in fact were Arnie, Brock, and Eric. They were all faster, better skiers than Sunny. Sunny didn't see them as competition, but as colleagues, and he hoped they saw him as a colleague. Sunny loved watching them ski and studied every move they made. What Sunny noticed the most was their humility and focus. None of them had skiing as their primary goal in life. They all had other interests; skiing was what they loved to do, but not what they counted on for an income. He realized that this must have taken the pressure off when they were racing, because they didn't *have* to race. They just wanted to ski. They knew they were better than most of the other skiers on the mountain. Nobody really talked about the great skiers but everybody knew who they were. You only had to look up and see Ronny Biedermann, and see his time skiing, to know that he was in a league of his own. It was people like Ronnie that made Sunny understand where his abilities truly lay. It didn't discourage him; it just gave him the perspective to keep him grounded. Another balancing point was that Ronnie was also a tall, good-looking man, and girls would hand Sunny their beer to go over and talk to skiers like Ronnie.

Then there were Cam and Kenny; good skiers, but better with women.

They were all there. It was like opening day reunion; time for laughter, playing pool and eyeing this year's ski talent.

People seldom came up to The Horn in the afternoon. The real skiers came down after skiing for all the girls who were there simply for the skiers. It didn't really matter how well the girls skied, they rarely ever skied with them. Sunny looked over, and Judy was there in ski clothes. Somehow Sunny had never thought to ask her if she skied. Judy was wrapped up talking with some of the people from her work, so Sunny went on about his business. Sunny decided to leave her alone, as going over to talk with Judy would be mixing her world with his world—and he had agreed to keep their worlds separate. Sunny looked over to Judy, looking natural and stunning in that ski outfit with her beautiful strawberry blond hair and wonderful natural smile. Sunny wished for a moment that he could be a part of it but turned quickly away, realizing he might not fit in. Judy was a beautiful woman with poise and grace and intelligence. Sunny frankly really didn't understand what she saw in him. As Sunny stood there talking with his friends, the "group of tall good-looking ski bums and great skiers," he wondered if he was maybe a challenge? Were the tables being turned? Sunny knew he really didn't have much to offer, compared to someone like Tom who was an educated, good-looking guy—even if he was a little older. Tom was smart, funny, and a great guy to hang with on the slopes.

Stowe was a great place to come to get out of a relationship, to be single, and to avoid confronting the emotions of a relationship. Sunny was driven by his love of skiing and to succeed. The ski industry and the environment of its decadence had allowed Sunny to be very good at not being in a relationship. As Sunny looked at Judy, he realized he had never felt so many real emotions toward someone. Maybe that's why he had avoided being with her, even though they had slept next to each other. Sunny turned around, put down his beer and decided he had to get down the road. He needed to keep focused on what he was doing. This was no time for distractions.

Love Scene

IN EARLY DECEMBER, SUNNY HAD made the announcement he was going to race for The Baggy Knees. The weeks went by fast, and the weekends were cause for celebration. The bar teams were being assembled. Stony, Ace, and Roger had decided to form their own independent team. The season was underway, filling the air with excitement and anticipation.

By this time, Sunny had gotten used to Judy being in the house; it was too late now to get her into a place of her own, and they had become good friends. The guys were used to covering for her; Sunny always had the condo for extra-curricular activity.

Sunny got pretty drunk after the party when The Baggy Knees announced its official team. Sunny got Ace to cover the door for him and went home early. When he got there around 11:30 that night, his bed was empty. This was great. As a twenty year old, Sunny had gotten used to sleeping in the nude. But with Judy there, Sunny was obliged to sleep in his underwear or sometimes even in pj's. Sunny assumed Tom had finally scored and he got the night and the bed to himself.

Sunny fleetingly thought that maybe Judy would move in with Tom now, but was really too tired and drunk to give it more thought. Sunny quickly undressed, dropping his clothes where they stood on the floor and climbed into bed. It felt good to have the bed to himself again.

At about two in the morning, Sunny was awakened by this body getting into bed. Hmm, *Judy*, Sunny thought, *no big deal*...then he woke up quickly. Sunny, somewhat wide-eyed, looked over.

"Judy?"

"Hi, who did you expect?" Judy said with a little giggle.

"Judy, I didn't expect you, I mean, I thought... ah shit, it doesn't matter. Listen, I'm not... I mean, I don't have anything on."

He waited for the disapproval, the violation of their agreement. It wasn't that Judy hadn't excited him or that he wouldn't have liked being with her. She was just special, and he couldn't address her as he did the other women.

Sunny laid back on the pillow a little hung over, only to hear Judy laugh,

"It's alright…me either..." Judy rolled over and gave Sunny a kiss, and without saying another word he pulled her closer. He felt her warmth and the amazing curves of her body. The passion of their kisses grew stronger as they began to give themselves to each other in selfless lovemaking throughout the night.

Judy's kisses and touch were delicate and meaningful, her body just perfectly proportioned and athletic. Unlike the other physical experiences, Sunny could feel the exchange of pleasure, true emotions with every kiss.

When Sunny awoke, Judy had gone to work. Sunny sat all morning looking out of the window at the town below, reflecting on the evening before. Judy met up with him in town after she got off work and they giggled about the night before.

Judy knew Sunny loved her; she also knew she had all Sunny was able to give. So they agreed to continue the way things were before, or at least they would try.

Carl's Coming?

THINGS WORKED OUT WELL AND a few weeks passed. Skiing was great. The Knees, The Rusty Nail, and The Horn were in full rock 'n roll mode. One night at work, Sunny got this phone call. The boss, John, yelled over to Sunny to pick up the phone. Sunny picked up the call, which was long distance.

"It's your dime, don't waste mine..." Sunny heard that familiar voice...

"Carl...? Is that you...? Massaro?"

"You got it. How ya doin', ass bucket?" Carl said.

"Great! Great!" said Sunny.

"You know what happened today? I was sitting on my porch, playing my git-fiddle and watching it snow," Carl said.

"Great, you guys haven't gotten much?" Sunny asked as Carl continued.

"Yeah, and we still don't. It turned into rain. You have any room up there?"

Sunny didn't have an answer.

"When are you coming?"

As usual Carl never asked permission.

"Two hours ago!"

Vermont was in the middle of blizzard conditions and Sunny should have been surprised, but somehow since it was Carl, he wasn't.

"Carl, there's a blizzard going on and Christmas is this week."

Carl had made up his mind.

"The family went to Florida and I'm in my military power wagon."

Sunny was just stating the obvious,

"You're fuckin' nuts, that thing doesn't go over 40 miles an hour."

Carl continued, "And there's no heat. I'm driving in my sleeping bag."

Sunny repeated, "You're nuts, you're fuckin' nuts!"

Carl laughed, "You're not the first to notice."

Sunny was truly excited. The Sundance Kid and Butch were back together.

"I can't wait, how much longer?" Sunny asked.

"No telling. I'll have to call you when I get into town," Carl said.

"If I'm not here, I'll be at home," Sunny said quickly.

Sunny hung up the phone, smiling from ear to ear. He turned and yelled, *"Hot shit, he's coming!"*

Carl Comes to Stowe

HAVING CARL COME TO STOWE was the completion to the year. Carl was Sunny's best friend, but it was more, he was also from New Jersey. No matter where Sunny went or what he did, there would always be a little New Jersey in him, as it was New Jersey that made Sunny the tenacious person he was.

Carl didn't have some of the advantages Sunny had; Sunny had gone to a New England private school, while Carl went to a local public high school with four thousand or so kids. Sunny had gotten formal ski instruction and coaching, while Carl taught himself.

Carl was the most naturally talented person, besides being a good athlete and a great singer. Carl was a very good artist as seen in some of his paintings. Best of all, Carl possessed creativity and insight. Sunny, on the other hand, never found anything that came easy to him; it was perseverance and fortitude which allowed him to accomplish anything.

Sunny was excited about Carl coming up. Being aware of his differences with Ace, Stony, Roger, and especially Judy, Sunny knew he would be a tremendous asset to the group and slept through the night anticipating his call the next day.

Judy was home with Sunny, and not too anxious to have someone else come up who would cut down on Sunny's time with her; she was used to having Sunny around. Although Judy would never say anything, she felt Sunny spent far too much time with the boys in the bar and on the mountain. Early the next morning, the phone rang. Sunny answered the phone and it was Carl, without his usual pleasantries.

"Where the fuck are you?"

Sunny with his usual New Jersey humor: "Standing here, talking on the phone. Where are you?"

Carl was quick to answer,

"I am at the Exxon station in town."

Sunny realized that was just down the street. "Don't move!"

Sunny hung up the phone, jumped in his car and in about 30 seconds Sunny was standing next to Carl. Now you have to understand, Carl and Sunny were pretty open-minded with each other. As soon as Carl saw Sunny, he ran up to him and jumped into his arms. Carl with his New Jersey humor quipped,

"Is this necessary?"

Sunny smiled. "You were expecting a kiss?"

"Well..." Sunny just looked at him, really happy to see him.

"No way, you didn't shave," Carl said. Carl and Sunny didn't even have to speak in complete sentences. Carl looked at Sunny: "Hungry?"

Sunny quickly remarked, "Food?"

Pointing to next door, Carl nodded; they went in and sat down to eat.

Over breakfast they discussed where Carl could get some work and could get a lift pass. Carl knew he was welcome wherever Sunny was, for as long as he wanted. That is one of the few rules of best friends. The first and most important rule is *unconditional caring*. For some reason, Carl and Sunny had never been able to live together for very long; they were just too different in their personal lives.

Sunny brought Carl up to The Horn and introduced him to the guys. Before the end of lunch, he had found room at Ace's, splitting the rent. Ace had moved out of the condo because his family was coming up to use it over Christmas, and was staying in an apartment by The Horn.

When the group met his family, they could not understand where Ace would fit in. Ace came from a socialite upper-class Philadelphia family. They all dressed like L.L. Bean mannequins. Ace's association and skiing with them was enough to make his mother cry; she found them simply dreadful. His Dad was very quiet, and Sunny thought he secretly approved.

Roger's parents had also come up. His family seemed more sociable, but they still came from the same social structure as Ace's family. Sunny never knew Stony's family. Anyway, the gang was glad to have Carl there; he was a welcome addition to the Ski Team.

The next morning they rode the lift early; again, the sun was shining on some freshly fallen snow. It was a warm winter day for New England. As Sunny looked down from the chairlift, the trail emerged as a sea of softly rolling moguls, some as big as Volkswagens. The fresh snow masked the harsh cut of the moguls that skiers had carefully sculpted.

The group had gotten to the top of the mountain early to grab some breakfast at the Octagon Lodge. It seemed every ski bum sensed this was the last chance to ski before turning the mountain and the town over to the Christmas vacationers.

It was a weekday, and still quiet on the mountain as the town below was filling up. Every serious ski bum was there. In their own way, this was their last breakfast together to celebrate the mountain and Christmas. After a bite of breakfast, all at once they filed out of the lodge, strapped on their skis, and made ready for the assault.

Carl and Sunny wore their best racing gear to provide freedom of movement. This was a special time. Carl at 5 feet 10, sandy-blond hair, Italian, stood ready in a blue well-fitted sweater and stretch pants. Sunny stood next to him in a blue race sweater, red pants and white hat. They looked like the All-American duo.

As the swarm of ski bums addressed the mountain, Carl slid to the face of the trail next to Sunny, along with Stony, Ace, Roger, Cam, and the others. Sunny looked at the descent, then at Carl. Carl started the rhythm, Sunny picked it up—and without a word, they both smiled, kicked their skis straight back, lunged forward and down the mountain with a surge of explosive power. Together in perfect synchronization, they hurled their skis into mogul after mogul, fresh snow flying.

The group catching up to them went "go for it, get it." The cheers of support heightened their pumping adrenaline. Turn after turn, they were together. Attacking every turn, throwing their skis into the air on the upside of a mogul, only to delicately touch down and attack the next. At that moment their skiing expressed their existence, their life style, and all who were watching *felt it*. Carl and Sunny were IT. As they turned and came to a stop, they heard a last yelp of enthusiasm, then silence.

"Not bad, Massaro," Sunny quietly said.

Looking straight ahead, Carl responded: "Yeah, I'm catching on."

They turned to see the others address the mountain. It was truly a sight to see that the others were skiing just as magnificently. There was no question that this was the group that would set the pace for that year. It was the year's big statement and nobody talked about it, but everybody knew it.

Christmas in Stowe

As Sunny and Carl finished their skiing, one by one their friends left the mountain for town. Some of the crew stopped by The Horn, but most had to go to work. As Christmas was only a few days away, serving the tourists was how they justified their existence. Carl and Sunny were together; both of them felt contentment and satisfaction for their skiing and the people they were lucky enough to share it with. That was the part of Carl that Sunny identified with most, the human part which allowed him to recognize others.

This was the first moment Sunny realized that days like these were few and far between—that this represented a highpoint in their lives. In short; it didn't get any better than this, just different.

Sunny and Carl talked about it as they stopped to go into The Horn's parking lot. Sunny turned to Carl and out of the blue said,

"Carl, think Idaho, just think Idaho."

Just then, Jesse (the girl from The Baggy Knees) and a friend drove up. Sunny called over.

"Hi Jesse."

Out of the corner of his eye Sunny could see Carl, overwhelmed by the sight of Jesse's smile and figure. Carl, not usually bashful, chimed in.

"Aren't you going to introduce me to your friends?"

Being the gentleman he was, Sunny quickly answered,

"But of course, how rude of me. Carl this is Jesse and Kim. Jesse, Kim, this is Carl."

Carl couldn't help but lead with his New Jersey humor.

"That's enough; we don't want them to get too much of me," Carl said.

This just fueled Sunny's response almost like a comedy team.

"You can say that again," Sunny replied. Carl was anxious to move the ladies inside where he could continue the conversation.

"Sunny, shouldn't we offer to supply some refreshments?" Jesse looked at Sunny.

"Hi, Sunny, where have you been? I've been looking for you."

Not being able to let go of his New Jersey humor, Carl said, "I bet you have. Don't hurt him."

Kim finally spoke up: "I don't know about you, Jesse, but I'll take them up on their offer." Sunny was looking for a quick way out of this conversation. He declared, "Good show!"

As Kim stepped out of the car, a closer inspection showed a young beautiful girl with blond hair, tight-fitting turtleneck, faded jeans, blue eyes and a smile that left Carl and Sunny in a feeding frenzy. Carl had just finished a great run down the mountain, and then overwhelmed by Stowe's female talent, was just starting to hit his pace.

"Kim, I'm so glad you choose to take me up on my offer," Carl said.

He hustled around Jesse's car and offered his arm to Kim.

"See you inside." Carl said. Sunny looking at Carl as if he needed a cold shower and threw a quick jab, '*Bet you can't wait*'.

"Jesse go ahead and park, I'll wait." Jesse pulled her car over and Sunny walked her to the bar.

Inside, Ace was the only one from the crew who had made it down. Ace couldn't help but notice both Carl and Sunny's entrances. However, Ace was still feeling up from the ski performances of the day. Ace and Sunny were now standing at the bar. Sunny turned to Big Paul, the bartender, and ordered "five big ones".

Paul was almost seven feet tall, with dark hair and piercing eyes, looking like Gregory Peck when he played Captain Ahab in Moby Dick. Fortunately, Sunny knew Paul to be an extremely nice guy and a good friend.

"Hi Sunny, had a good day?"

Before Sunny could answer Ace spoke up and said, "I'll say he did."

When Ace got excited he reverted back to his educational ways, something they had tried breaking him of. But nevertheless his vocabulary spurted out and he continued.

"Sunny and Carl's performances were exquisite; they actually proceeded in perfect synchronization for an entire run."

Sunny looked at Big Paul in bewilderment, turned to Carl touching his throat. "Must be something wrong with his throat."

Carl mumbled "Does he do this often?"

Taking a quick sip of his beer, Sunny just looked at Carl.

"Yeah it must be his throat, he'll be okay in a minute." Sunny said.

"Besides that, did you guys enjoy the day?" Sunny just looked at Jesse. Not knowing what to say he just smiled, kind of Sunny's way out of everything.

"Yes, I believe so, good skiing."

Kim spoke up again as she recognized Carl and Sunny.

"Yeah, I saw you guys. I didn't know that was you." Sliding her arm around Carl, she caught him by surprise.

"Oh... I liked that." Carl said. Now at about at his boiling point, Carl looked at her and said, "Shall we grab a table?"

Just then, Mike, (or Nards for short) the disc jockey at the turntable, started yelling in his New York accent,

"Do you know what time it is?"

And with that, Nards proceeded to play "Rosalita" by Bruce Springsteen. The whole bar stopped and moved toward the dance floor. Mike had been practicing "behavior modification" over the season, much like Pavlov did with his dogs; just a little classical conditioning.

When the bar heard Bruce's song, everyone stopped what they were doing and started to dance including the bartenders, managers, waitresses, everyone. If you didn't have a drink by the announcement, you went dry until the end of the song. Total mayhem struck as "Rosalita" started to play, rhythm everywhere and everybody singing along and dancing.

Nards stood there drunk and sang along with Bruce, until everyone did. It was something to see! After the song they sat for a little bit reminiscing about the day; a perfect completion to a perfect day of skiing.

Carl was helping out at The Horn for the Christmas rush and had to go to work. Sunny and Carl bid the girls goodbye, knowing they would see them in a little while: it was still early. Carl went to his place across from The Horn, while Sunny drove into town. Sunny remembered needing some supplies and stopped at the General Store.

Judy was there, too. Realizing they had to be discreet, Sunny caught her eye and smiled. Sunny couldn't help thinking that this was the true completion to the day, seeing Judy. Sunny tried to hide his enthusiasm, but really couldn't wait to say something.

"Hi Judy, did you ski today?" Sunny knew she had, but he needed small talk in public.

"Yes. It was good."

"Well, I've gotta go home, I'll see you later." Sunny said politely.

"Yes, me too, lots to do. See ya," Judy said with that wonderful little smile.

Sunny met Judy at home with a big hug and kiss. As usual, Sunny had to get ready for work and they discussed how their lives were going over a shower and a shave. This particular day Sunny was standing in the shower when he remembered he had left the toothpaste on the sink. Sunny always brushed his teeth in the shower, a trick he had learned in private school. Calling from the shower,

"Judy would you hand me the toothpaste?"

Judy replied, "Sure."

Standing in the shower waiting, letting the water run on his face, he suddenly realized he wasn't alone. Sunny heard a voice closer than he expected.

"Here's your toothpaste. I just thought I'd wash my hair while you brush your teeth." Judy said standing right in front him, more beautiful than any model Sunny had ever seen.

Needless to say, Sunny was delightfully surprised. Purposely dropping the toothpaste, they kissed. Judy's touch somehow left Sunny breathless.

Judy took the soap and helped him lather up. They kissed again and made love. Sunny finished first and started to shave with Judy behind him. Sunny could see her in the mirror and grabbed a towel.

Judy looked to Sunny and asked him,

"You coming home tonight?" Sunny was caught by surprise.

"What happened to no questions?"

"Yeah."

Sunny was experiencing feelings like he had never had before. True he was a man, but he wasn't good at relationships and didn't really know what to do. Being in love didn't mean you know what to do about it.

Judy smiled and said,

"Good, I've got Christmas off. I'm going to Boston, and I'd like you to come."

Sunny just looked at Judy and he realized that his only income depended on the people that were up for the Christmas holiday; it was not possible for him to leave. This was where he was going to start disappointing Judy, and she would have to start seeing him for who he was.

"That's impossible, I've got to work."

Sunny wanted to ask why she wasn't bringing Tom, but he stood by the rule of no questions. Judy was surprisingly supportive. This seemed wonderful and unnerving both at the same time.

"I'll see you tonight," Judy said.

Sunny went work as usual and met Jesse, Kim, Shannon, and the gang. Standing at the bar around two in the morning, John (the owner of The Baggy Knees) turned to Sunny and said,

"It's going to be a good night tonight Sunny. Big takes at the door."

Sunny looked at John with his usual smile. "Yeah, pretty good."

Carl was there, and this was his first Christmas away from home. He was curious as to what happened on Christmas Eve in this town.

"Sunny, how about tomorrow, Christmas Eve?" Carl asked.

Sunny, being from a large family, would miss being home for Christmas as well but was really glad that he would be with Carl and the gang for Christmas.

"I'm glad you mentioned that. I thought we'd meet Stony at the Center and do some cross country skiing around ten in the morning."

Carl looked a little surprised that Sunny had given it so much thought, but just looked at Sunny and said,

"Okay. See ya in the morning."

Sunny and Carl left and each returned home. It was only a short way back home, but Sunny drove slowly through town to allow himself some time to think. Sunny thought about the mountain, Carl, and his family, but mostly about Judy.

Judy had evoked emotions Sunny wasn't ready for, emotions Sunny did not want. Sunny felt as though he should be able to control his emotions, since logically he knew how he wanted to feel. Emotions have no basis in intelligence however, so Sunny was in love without a place to go with it. For now, Sunny still liked being with Jesse, Kim, Sue, etc. In his heart Sunny knew he loved Judy. However, this was the last night they would be together for a while and he could use a break from that pressure.

One thing about Carl and Sunny was that they were generous men, money or no money. Judy, Carl, and Sunny had an agreement not to exchange Christmas presents, and this meant doing Christmas shopping in secret. Carl helped Sunny pick out a present for Judy. Carl didn't approve of Judy, maybe because he knew she dragged real emotions out of Sunny, and that might threaten Carl and Sunny's relationship. This is where you believe in a friendship and where unconditional caring comes in. Judy on the other hand, also didn't care for Carl; probably for similar reasons.

Sunny decided on a matching gold chain and bracelet for Judy. Sunny wanted something that told her he thought she was special, but not something as strongly committal as a ring. Since Judy was leaving in the morning, he thought he'd wake her up and surprise her. As Sunny walked into the room, Sunny was the one who was surprised. Judy was lying next to a neatly wrapped box in red Christmas paper with a bow. Judy looked at Sunny with that unbelievable smile of hers.

"How was your night?"

Sunny was smiling from ear to ear.

"Not bad. (An understatement if there ever was one.) I thought we had an agreement?" Sunny said.

Judy didn't have to say a thing, she paused for a moment,

"Yeah but it's something you need, besides me. Besides you keep letting me get away without paying rent," she said as she laughed a little.

"Shhh, not so loud, you'll let people think I want you here." Sunny said quickly with his devilish smile.

"Merry Christmas Sunny." Judy said as she stood up, dressed in one of his flannel shirts, dangerously unbuttoned to her waist and kissed him.

Sunny opened the gift; it was a new parka. Sunny couldn't believe his eyes, people just didn't give him gifts; not like this anyway; this was just a skier's way of showing that you cared. Almost tearing up, Sunny looked at Judy.

"It's great!"

Judy was more than pleased with Sunny's reaction.

"I got tired of watching you freeze and you'll never stop skiing, so..."

Sunny was overwhelmed that Judy would think so much to do something so nice.

"I don't know why you take such good care of me. "I don't deserve it, but I do like it, thank you," Sunny said, giving Judy a hug and a kiss that let her know he meant it.

Sunny slipped into bed and turned out the light. As they were pulling the covers over them, Sunny reached down to the foot of the bed where he had put his pants and grabbed Judy's present. By this time they were used to holding each other as they fell asleep, so when Sunny reached around her, Sunny slipped the present in front of her and whispered, "Merry Christmas Judy."

"A-a-h Sunny," Judy whispered.

Flipping on the light, Judy opened the box. Sunny helped her put both the chain and bracelet on. Judy looked at both for a moment, looked up at Sunny she said,

"They're beautiful."

She leaned forward to kiss him saying, "I love you, Sunny."

He could only smile and hold her tight.

Sunny was overwhelmed with emotion. He knew he loved Judy and he had never loved any other girl before and he didn't know what to do about it. He may have looked like a big strong talented man but inside he wasn't ready. What he was afraid of most was disappointing her.

"What time do you go to Boston?"

For some reason Judy knew how Sunny felt. She just looked with her approving smile. Judy was the only woman who had ever accepted Sunny for who he was.

Judy simply said, "Early."

They fell asleep in each other's arms. When Sunny awoke, Judy was standing over him fully dressed.

"See you in a couple of days. Have a great Christmas."

Sunny really wanted to tell her he loved her, but the only thing that came out was,

"Drive carefully, Merry Christmas."

Sunny gave her a kiss, she knew he loved her. Sunny watched her drive off and went back to sleep for an hour.

After getting up, Sunny met Carl and Stony at the cross country shop. Stony was busy selling some skis to a customer. Carl and Sunny took the opportunity to browse through the shop. Carl found some gaiters he was looking for. Stony finished his sale and fixed Carl and Sunny up with skis, poles and boots. Stony looked at Sunny; remembering that he had done some racing in high school he asked,

Sunny, would you prefer these racing skis?"

As a group they had never done anything half throttle. Sunny looked over at the big Viking.

"Yeah, that's all I know how to ski on."

Carl looked at how thin and fragile the skis were.

"You better give me something more durable." He said.

Stony had a wonderful deep boisterous laugh and looked over to Carl who was the definition of a bull in a china shop and with his laugh said,

"Okay, here you go."

Stony turned to his boss Joe Pete.

"Going out for that run now, okay?"

Joe Pete was a great guy and he understood that the benefit of having Stony work at the Nordic Center was that he loved Nordic skiing.

"Go ahead, enjoy," said Joe Pete.

They went outside to put their skis on. As they were about ready, Carl was looking at one of the trails, amazed.

"Sunny, look at that!"

Sunny looked back around and saw some woman walking out of a cafe.

"No stupid, over there!" Carl said quickly.

He pointed to this incredible skier running with a full stride, moving across the field with all the grace and speed of a Pro. Whoever it was, she was hot, and beautiful to watch. You could see it was a woman by her braids and tight-fitting cross country suit. As she skied up Sunny recognized her.

He looked at her with a big smile; it was the beautiful counter girl from the Edelweiss Deli.

"Hello, Sue," Sunny said. Stony all of a sudden stood a little taller, his shoulders went back as he looked at Sue and said,

"Hi Sue, how many today?"

Sue looked at them with a big smile,

"Hi guys, 15K. I know I'm not going to run tomorrow, so I wanted to get a good one in today." Sue reached down to undo her skis. "Have a good run guys," Sue said.

She left to go inside. Sunny looked at Stony with a bit of amazement.

"She does this every day?"

Without even looking up from his skis Stony just said, "Yeah, she's great."

"Stony, you little devil, all this time and you never said a word?" Carl asked.

Stony just laughed, "Come on guys."

Stony lead the way as the group took off across the field toward the foothills on that side of town. The view was spectacular. Stony didn't ski particularly fast, but he did ski with exceptional grace for a man his size. With his Viking haircut and beard, watching him ski with his power and that size was something out of a magazine. Next there was Carl, and then Sunny followed the broad shouldered Italian.

Stretching to emulate Stony's lead left Sunny inspired. He felt great. He had his racing suit on, which felt like he wasn't wearing anything. The feeling of gliding along behind them and taking in the view brought Sunny back to Vermont. At one time, Sunny had been a pretty good cross country skier and it felt good to get out, stretch and work up a sweat. Sunny liked the quiet anonymity of skiing.

Stony wasn't a fast skier, either. He was like a train; he kept chugging along at the same speed, flats or uphill didn't seem to faze him. It was as if he had a huge engine running in only the low gears. Now Carl would never allow himself to fall off pace, although on some of the hills Sunny was sure he was ready to hook himself up to Stony and let Stony pull them both. Sunny was used to more of a sprint technique; a little out of practice, Sunny was still able to execute his kick so he could save some energy on the flats and hang on the hills. As they got further from town all their cares seemed to slip away; some things just didn't appear to be all that important.

This seemed a most appropriate way to spend Christmas Eve day, gliding through the woods, passing old farms in Vermont and being with good friends. They skied out and up to the hills overlooking the town. It took them a little over an hour. They stopped at a field and sat on a stone wall. Stony had brought a backpack with some juices and granola, of course. The backpack didn't affect Stony's skiing; a house would not have fazed Stony's skiing.

As they sat munching they could see the town below. People were scurrying from shop to shop, buying food and last minute gifts. Seeing people in their fur coats and parkas on the snow covered streets full of decorated shops was just what you would expect to see on a Hallmark picture postcard. To Stony, the scene below seemed a little too commercial. Carl and Sunny agreed; they were thankful to be able to get away.

Carl broke the silence, as he was always fascinated by architecture; the church below really made the town. "It makes it look like a postcard." Stony paused looking at the church and asked, "Yeah, you guys going tonight?"

Sunny was somewhat surprised at the question. Sunny was raised a good Episcopalian and he hadn't missed a Sunday in 12 years growing up, but had replaced church with skiing on Sundays. Sunny missed going to church and was a devout Christian, surprisingly enough. Still, Sunny was a little surprised to hear of Stony's involvement in the church; pleasantly surprised though.

"To church?" Sunny asked. Nonchalantly Stony simply replied,
"Yeah."
Carl was raised Catholic, but had his own beliefs.
"Why?" asked Carl. Stony looked over at Carl with a declaration.
"I'm singing in the choir."
Sunny shouldn't have been all that surprised, he was actually an altar boy at one time.
However, he had to ask, "You? A choir boy?"
Without a blink or hesitation Stony simply stood up and declared,
"Yep, I like to sing." "Great. What time?" Carl asked.
Stony looked at him with a smile. "First mass, 7:30 to 8:30 tonight."

Carl looked at him saying, "I'm impressed. We'll be there."

It seemed surprising because of their decadent lifestyle, but each of them was carrying special talents. So it wasn't really too surprising to see Stony's. They had worked up a good sweat on the way up after spending a late night, and it had felt good to get back into some running. After all, the bar scene was relatively new at this point. Sunny couldn't help but wonder if his priorities had gotten a little twisted. They talked about how good they felt and started back to the Center. On the way back, they skied like the wind.

Stony and Sunny taught Carl how to Telemark: make long, sweeping turns. On the steep hills, they had skied a cross-style between Alpine technique and Telemarking. Still double poling, they made it home quick.

Stony hustled back to work. Carl and Sunny thanked the Stone man and headed off to Sunny's house for a shower. Carl and Sunny killed most of the day walking through town, taking in the sights and watching the tourists.

This was a time when the locals turned the town and the mountain over to the Christmas vacationers, and it was time to make your bread and butter. Still, it was nice to just watch people get such great enjoyment out of being there.

Stowe went way out to be picturesque during Christmas with a minimum of glaring lights. Everything was traditionally decorated with all kinds of Christmas scenes in the shop windows, Christmas wreaths and trees everywhere you turned.

Stowe, Vermont is the poster child for the Vermont town with the general store in the middle, the white steepled church, and town hall, while downtown was beautiful with its drugstore and the Green Mountain Inn on one end of town. The mountain was packed with people who had been anxiously waiting for this time off from their 9 to 5 jobs, to try out their new skis and boots.

Since Carl and Sunny worked at night, it was fun just to mosey around and watch during the day. Although neither of them said anything, seeing Ace and Roger with their families, as well as watching all the other families in town, made Sunny and Carl miss their own families that much more. Both Sunny and Carl were close to their families, and at Christmas time it was tough to be away from them. Stony's family lived in New Hampshire; having the day off, he planned on heading home after choir.

Carl and Sunny decided to have dinner at a Danish friend's restaurant, as Stein was by far the best chef in all of Stowe. Carl was the closest to family that Sunny could be with now and vice versa. They enjoyed being able to have each other, now that they couldn't be home with family for Christmas. After dinner Sunny and Carl drove to The Baggy Knees to get their parking space early. Even though Sunny didn't really expect a crowd, he thought the quarter mile walk to the church would be nice.

It started to snow on the way to Main Street just as they were crossing the creek. As Sunny and Carl approached the corner, they could hear the church choir singing "Silent Night". It felt like something out of a Bing Crosby movie. If you had to be away from home and family on Christmas Eve, being in Stowe, standing on Main Street watching it snow, and listening to Stony and the choir with your best friend wasn't too bad.

As Sunny and Carl walked up the stairs to the church, they could see Stony standing in his choir vestments, singing Christmas carols by a beautiful decorated altar. Sunny and Carl listened until they were finished and found Stony following mass to wish him a Merry Christmas, as they weren't going to see him the next day.

Christmas Brunch

SURPRISINGLY ENOUGH THE BARS WERE open; back at work, and again the bar was pretty busy. There were many people away from home in town. After work, Carl decided to stay at Sunny's house as his roommates had left for a few days.

The telephone woke Sunny in the morning. Unsurprisingly it was his family. Since Sunny's family had been up early with his nieces and nephews, they decided to call him early to be sure to catch him. The phone call took well over an hour. Everyone in the family personally wished Sunny a Merry Christmas and filled him in on the latest happenings in their lives. Talking to everyone made Sunny feel much better about being away.

As soon as Sunny hung up, he dialed Carl's family and called Carl to the phone without telling him who was on the line.

"Okay, Merry Christmas, hold on for a second."

"Carl, it's for you." Carl answered the phone somewhat surprised,

"Hello, who is this? Hello Dad, Merry Christmas."

Carl was surprised, as he didn't have his parent's telephone number in Florida. Sunny had gotten it because they had called him looking for Carl a few days earlier. Sunny had decided to keep their phone number secret and surprise Carl on Christmas.

Carl talked for a while, and you could see the joy and relief on his face since he thought he wasn't going to be able to contact anyone at home that Christmas. As soon as he hung up, Sunny came over from the kitchen with coffee. It was Christmas morning and Sunny just handed some coffee to Carl.

"Here's some coffee, Merry Christmas."

It was just the two of them Carl smiled.

"Merry Christmas, how'd you know?" Carl asked.

Sunny replied, "Your Dad called a couple of days ago looking for you and gave me his number in Florida. So I thought I'd surprise you."

Carl had never been one for a lot of emotional things, but the stakes here were truly heartfelt.

"Thanks. I thought they'd forgotten about me. That's the best Christmas present you could have given me."

With a smirk Sunny looked at Carl and said,

"Well, I guess this will have to be second best then, here."

Carl looked with surprise and commented, "You asshole, we agreed no gifts."

Of course Sunny and Carl never followed many rules before so why should this be any different? Sunny just looked at Carl and said,

"Yeah, I lied."

Of course Carl never cared for rules much either. He turned to reach behind the couch and said,

"Here, Merry Christmas." Sunny just smiled and looked at Carl.

"This no present thing was your idea. What's this? I just didn't want you to spend your money," Carl said.

They opened the gifts. Sunny and Carl had bought each other sweaters. Carl got Sunny a beautiful rag-knit red sweater, Sunny had bought Carl a gray turtleneck. Sunny realized that these were the moments he would remember, the Christmas when they only had each other. They didn't think alike all the time and giving each other the same gift was just a coincidence. Sunny looked at Carl and said,

"Carl, it's beautiful, thanks."

Of course he couldn't show all the emotion, it just wasn't manly. So Carl looked at Sunny and replied,

"Yea, I liked it. I bought it so I can steal it back on certain occasions."

Sunny knew he wasn't kidding as he looked at Carl and said,

"Don't you dare, I'll get yours." Carl finished the conversation with,

"Sunny, I like this one better anyway, thanks."

By this time Sunny and Carl were getting hungry and most of the restaurants were closed for Christmas, but there was only one place open. Sunny knew where it was and suggested to Carl,

"Hey let's walk through town to Bumpies restaurant, they're having a Christmas brunch."

Carl never turned down a meal. It sounded like a good idea so he replied,

"Sure, the walk will be nice. You know, it doesn't seem right without the other guys around."

Sunny agreed; somehow Butch and Sundance should have the Hole in the Wall Gang.

"Yeah, they'll be back in a couple of days and things will be back to normal." Sunny said.

They walked to town, as it was snowing pretty hard then. On the way they talked about what their phone calls had revealed. The town was unusually quiet, and all but two of the shops were closed.

Church was in mass and once again, they could hear the choir in full voice. The walk felt good. They got to the restaurant and sat down for a nice brunch. As Sunny and Carl were eating, Carl turned to the door to see Ace standing there. Surprised and delighted to see them, Ace greeted them with a big, "Merry Christmas." Carl was equally delighted to see Ace. It was surprisingly how close they had come to be in just a little while. The common denominator of skiing together and being a ski bum is a very strong one. Carl looked at Ace and asked,

"Hey, how come you're not up with your family?" Ace replied,

"They're up skiing. Roger is here too, his parents are skiing with"....Just then Roger walked through the door. Carl and Sunny laughed and said,

"It sure is nice to see you guys, sit down. Merry Christmas!"

Then from the hall outside they could hear this bellowing deep voice singing "Deck the Halls with Boughs of Holly" and there appeared Stony, beard covered in snow, smiling. Singingin a bass voice, in walked their own Viking. With a big smile, Stony said,

"Ho, ho. Merry Christmas, hello guys." Carl looked at Stony with a big smile and asked,

"Stony, what about going home?" Stony replied,

"This storm closed the highway. I'm stuck with you guys here."

Realizing the gang was back together Sunny spoke for the group saying, "Well at least you have to come on over."

They had started their own Christmas gathering and within the hour Cam, Eric, Richard from The Horn, and many others appeared at Bumpies, and Christmas for the ski bums was complete.

They ate brunch and drank. As soon as they were good and drunk (and frustrated by being off the mountain), they chose teams, grabbed a football from Roger's car, and got a game of touch football going. It was snowing hard and the ground was soft, wet and slippery, but who cared? They had a ball, score 100 to 100. Who was counting? Then, one by one they left for Christmas dinner, wishing each other once again a Merry Christmas. Carl and Sunny returned to his house for some dry clothes and to shower before work. It had been a great ski bum's Christmas.

The Ski Bum Races

A FEW DAYS AFTER CHRISTMAS, the town started returning to a slower pace. During a regular week, the town belonged to the locals and the ski town employees. During the weekend, people from the Montreal, Boston, and New York areas dominated the town and the mountain.

Every store, restaurant, and bar employee headed up the mountain to do some training before the first ski bum race.

This year, the team turnout was exceptional. Over 30 teams had signed up, which meant more than 120 competitors. This was the first year the mountain had entertained the thought of having the race over two days, rather than trying it all at once. In later years, that is exactly what happened.

Each team consisted of four people to make it fair. They had even developed a handicap system. However, there was a certain prestige to the team who produced the fastest skier.

Getting your own ringer was THE thing to do. Sunny was not the fastest skier, but he had always managed to come into the top five and score some points for his team. From time to time, Sunny would feel good and be able to pull off a win, but he knew he was not the best racer.

Like any competition, some people can take racing and keep it in perspective; others get bitter and upset at the prospect of losing. Somehow, Sunny had managed to keep his sense of what the races were all about and ski for fun.

Sunny loved ski racing and wanted to do the best he could, but from his first experience of racing, Sunny learned that there was always going to be someone better. Sunny's goal was to be the best he could be just simply to ski to his fullest potential.

Sunny knew good skiing and skiers when he saw them. Eric, Greg, Brock, and a few others were truly in another league. But through pure tenacity, Sunny was able to hang in there; he was flattered just to be recognized as one of them. Carl was always a wonder; he rode on pure natural athletic ability, without any formal instructions in skiing at all. Anyway, the pressure on the top got pretty heavy some days. Sunny really enjoyed the races. It was a chance to get all the skiing employees together and have an event that everyone could partake in. The fact that Sunny excelled was somewhat a bonus. To be honest, when Sunny saw the disappointments some had, he felt bad at times about doing well. The bottom line; winning was not everything.

Further, the way to score points in the ski bum races was to bring someone into the top ten.

Having Carl come up was exciting for Ace, Stony, and Roger as they were counting on him to be their ace in the hole. Sunny could see Carl enjoying the boost and he was excited too. Sunny always skied better when it came to racing against Carl. They really got one another pumped. Carl and Sunny were competitive against each other, but not so much that they wished bad things on the other while skiing. Sunny wanted Carl to do the best he could, Sunny just wanted to do better. If Sunny couldn't win a race, he wanted Carl to win; they always helped each other.

The ski bum races were fun to 98% of the people. There was always that 2% of racers who took competition way too seriously, blew it out of proportion, and tried to ruin it for others. In the top ten there were always some guys who had to prove something, reinforce their virility. Fortunately guys like Arnie, Eric, Carl, and Sunny knew skiing and were real racers, able to keep a healthy perspective and keep things fun. The ski bum races were about getting together, sharing something in common, having fun doing it, and getting together again later to share the results at The Horn.

The day before the race, Carl and Sunny decided they would depart from the guys and head over to Little Spruce and train with some of the racers there. As they got up to the mountain, they stopped in at the Race headquarters to turn in their entries for the race.

While they were there, Sunny introduced Carl to a friend of his, Ronny Biedermann. Sunny had known Ronny's sister, who had worked at The Knees. To describe Ronny, well.., he was this tall, blond, handsome surfer who was clearly the best racer and skier on the mountain or on most any mountain in the country. He was one of the aces on the US Ski Team. Ronnie was a really nice and okay guy. Ronny never got to spend much time in Stowe; he was too busy bouncing around in Europe with the team. Not many people in town had a chance to know Ronny.

Sunny introduced him to Carl, not mentioning his attachment to the team. They talked for a while, and then Ronny went up to ski and do some training. Sunny turned to Carl and said,

"Carl, come on with me." Not sure what Sunny was up to, Carl trusted him. Carl just said,

"Okay."

They left just behind Ronny as they got off the lift at the top, and skied down to the course with him. As Ronny gathered himself at the top of the course, Sunny turned to Carl and said,

"Carl, come here."

"I thought we were going to run gates?" Carl said.

"Come on, trust me. I want you to see something," Sunny explained.

Sunny brought Carl halfway down the course so they could see Ronny's entire run. Ronny fired onto the course like Carl had never seen. Carl and Sunny had seen some really good skiers in the time they had been up to the pacesetter finals, but Carl had never seen a skier like Ronny.

"Holy shit, did you see that? Unbelievable!" Carl said.

Ronny raced through the gates with more power and grace than anyone could possibly imagine. Sunny laughed because he knew how good Ronny was.

"He makes us look like dog shit." Carl said next.

Sunny laughed again and said,

"Compared to him, we are dog shit."

"Don't feel bad, he's one of the hottest guys on the US Ski Team."

"You're kidding, why didn't you tell me? Carl replied.

"I didn't want you to get star struck!"

They skied to the bottom. Watching Ronny gave them a real boost, it also gave them an example of how skiing was really supposed to be done.

Carl turned to Sunny and said,

"After watching Ronny, training for the Ski Bum races doesn't seem to be so important."

"No. It's important to do the best we can; we're the same as everyone else in the races, down to the last guy who's trying to do the best he can," Sunny replied thoughtfully.

Carl thought for a second and said,

"And compared to Ronny, not much better."

Smiling and nodding his head Sunny replied, "That was just the point. Yeah, Ronny's a World Class athlete, and we're just ski bums."

Sunny and Carl trained for a while, more relaxed with a better perspective of who they were and what they were trying to accomplish. By the next day, they achieved the warm-up they needed.

Sunny met Carl on the hill the next morning. Sunny skied up to him and the other guys. Most of the teams were together inspecting the course. It was nice to see everybody again. Sunny turned and said to everyone,

"Good morning."

Carl replied, "Morning." Sunny asked,

"How's the course?" Carl was always confident and never short of an opinion.

"Not bad, a little light," Carl replied.

Ace, always the competitive one, was quick to speak up. He said,

"Hey, don't give out any information!" Ace didn't understand that this wasn't hockey and it wasn't the Stanley Cup.

"Easy Ace, it's just a ski bum race, we want Sunny to do good too," Carl replied. Stony laughed.

"I'm glad to hear someone has his head on straight about this," Stony said.

Sunny asked, "Where's Roger?"

"Where else...eating." Sunny was the only one with any formal race training so he was more than happy to help out the gang.

"Come on guys, we can look at the course together. Maybe I can help too," he said.

They inspected the course and went to the start to get ready. Carl and Sunny just naturally got together and started helping each other. Some of the guys on Sunny's and other teams were a little confused by this. Especially some of the guys in the first seed, which Carl and Sunny were in. Sunny got a start number just ahead of Carl's. In the gate, the familiar countdown: 3, 2, 1, GO! Sunny exploded onto the course. Sunny skied hard and felt he had a good time: 32.4678 seconds.

Carl was next. Sunny stood cheering as he too exploded onto the course. He was skiing very well, not a fluke. As he skied across the finish line, he spotted Sunny and skied over.

Sunny looked at Carl and it was like old times and said,

"Great run, Carl." Carl was a little shocked by the remark, but said,

"Thanks, it felt good."

Then over the P.A. system they heard, "Ladies and Gentlemen, we can hardly believe this, but we have an exact tie for the first time, down to one hundred thousandths of a second. The time is 32.4678, the same as Sunny Warner from The Baggy Knees." Carl and Sunny gave each other a high five.

Carl, never short of wit looked at Sunny and said, "I guess you had a good run too."

"Yeah."

They had been beaten by three other guys, giving them the tie for 4th. They felt great; but while they skied a good race, they promised to try to improve next week. To Sunny, the tie was a reflection of the closeness between Carl and himself. Stony, Ace, and Roger also did well. As a matter of fact, their team won the race. They headed off for the last run. Skiing together that last run, they were all loose and hot on the hill. When it was over, they went down to The Horn for a celebration.

The Ski Bum Hustle

NOW IT WAS TIME FOR the other competition in town, The Ski Bum Hustle. This game was played by sitting around the bar, spotting your female targets. You would be as discreet as possible; introducing yourself, buying a few drinks, leaving the bar without getting caught, and scoring. You lost points by not being discreet, a poor introduction, or by being cheap, by being caught leaving the bar, and of course by not scoring.

The town was small; so to make things interesting, the other game was to catch one of the other guys, to give them a score reduction. This was a hard game in some ways, a game of life. If you took a good look at the ski town, especially the skiing community, it really didn't emulate life or society. You see, skiing is an expensive sport and ski towns are expensive places to live.

So if someone was old or unhealthy and they couldn't ski, or someone wanted to raise a family, unless they could afford it, a ski town was not the ideal place to be. There were some people raising families, but there were two classes of people in every real ski town. Wealthy people owned lodges, restaurants, second homes, didn't need to actually work for a living at all. Then, the people who worked for the lodges, restaurants, etc. were distinctly not wealthy. They justified their lack of financial portfolios by skiing. In case one wondered, Sunny was in the latter class.

The bottom line was, the town consisted of the "beautiful" people; young, healthy, wealthy. This alone connoted some decadence. Playing the Ski Bum Hustle was just a fitting extension of a distorted, decadent life.

Sunny had grown to love it! The only problem was rich or poor, people were playing with real emotions. Everyone was looking for happiness.

The town consisted of people who came and went with the seasons, so although sincere, the odds of finding a lasting relationship were slim to none. Newcomers and rookies came to town with the traditional dating understanding. Unfortunately, it was the despair and dismay of investing sincere feelings in a fleeting relationship was the price to pay for living with the "beautiful" people.

Any seasoned ski bum protected him or herself from this pain with the knowledge that relationships were fleeting and withholding any real emotions. To Sunny, this was too big of a price to pay and eventually it drove him out of ski bumming. Nobody can deny real emotions and live with themselves too long.

Now back to the Ski Bum Hustle. This year's ski bums who were most proficient were Cam, the tall, blond, intelligent skier; Kenny, the manager at The Rusty Nail; Peter, a photographer from the Cape; Carl, The Stone Man; Ace, Sunny, and too many others to name. Cam was clearly in the lead. He could walk into a bar and command the attention of all women in sight, a tough competitor. Sunny was the best skier of the Ski Bum Hustlers. Arnie, Eric and Brock had disqualified themselves by either a permanent monogamous relationship or by having poor hustling techniques. Sunny was up for the overall event.

With Sunny's position at the door at The Knees, he was tough competition and climbing fast. You see, the town was small and there were only so many women. Fortunately, none of the women coming into town were aware of the decadent game or the players, nor did they know to talk to any of the seasoned ski bum women.

However, it wasn't long before they caught on and started to talk to one another. So the strategy was to score as hard and fast as you could before you got your reputation. Discretion was the only hope for survival you had when your flagrancies were finally discovered. Cam was leading by having dated one of the prettiest girls on the circuit. After a brief disappointment of discovering Cam's deficiencies, she rebounded to Kenny. Sunny was hoping to catch her at the third round. They all knew what they were doing was cheap, meaningless and decadent. Great stuff though!

Where does Judy come in? Judy had Tom and Tom was a senior retired member of the Ski Bum Hustlers Association; he had placed Judy off limits. So what was she doing in Sunny's house? Sunny had no idea, maybe she didn't want all that protection or maybe she was just nuts. Maybe she knew how to play the game better with ultimate discretion. Maybe she just liked Sunny. Sunny thought '*Nah, she must be nuts, but she wasn't stupid and that could be dangerous.*'

Carl was coming in as a strong contender even though he was new to Stowe. He was good looking, a great skier, and had done his fair share of team work at home in the local home town hills.

As for Ace, Roger, and The Stone Man, they had only been exposed to normal college level decadent dating and needed a rookie year in the Ski Bum Hustle to get going.

Now the hardcore part of this game was the rules about which women were eligible. There was one simple rule, and that was, that there were no rules. Any woman, married, unmarried, under age, over age, pregnant etc. was eligible. Even the girl friend imported for a few days was okay for recognition and points. Roger and .Stony had just done that. Ace was off to a slow start, but tagged some chamber girl at one of the lodges and came in for some last minute yardage. Sunny had scored some great points with three or four girls, a nice representational cross section. He also had Judy secretly at home. Now that was decadent, not to mention dangerous and a little stupid.

The Bathroom Scene

STUPID OR NOT, SUNNY ALWAYS had loved women and loved being with them whenever he got the chance. Every once in a while the gang would end up at Ace's parent's condo, since his parents only came up there every third week for a visit.

For Sunny it was great, because if he wanted to be with someone and he couldn't go to their place, he would have been stuck. Sunny certainly couldn't go home; besides the condo had lots of beds and was centrally located.

If the Hole In the Wall Gang knew there was a good day of skiing coming up, they would all stay at the condo overnight and go up together. The condo was their time to get together and have some sort of slumber party in anticipation of skiing together.

One night, Ace, Carl, Stony, Roger, and Sunny agreed the skiing would be ideal the next day and it was time for the condo again. It was a Sunday night, so they all had the night off from work. Sunny consented to cook one of his fabulous ski bum meals. On that night's menu was baked chicken breast in a mushroom sour cream sauce over rice with freshly steamed vegetables, wine, and last but certainly not least, women.

They all dug into their resources and acquired a dinner guest and hopefully also slumber partner. Attire was extremely casual, dinner was family style sit down and turned out to be delicious. After dinner, they actually did the dishes for a change, and then proceeded to laugh and drink until the moment was right for more. Couple after couple, they headed for the appropriate places to continue before going to sleep.

In the morning as usual and on time the stereo awakened everyone with thunderous volume with "Listen to the Music" by the Doobie Brothers. Although everyone was still hung over, no one got mad as this was the signal for getting ready to ski.

Ace started the coffee while Carl jumped up with his slumber partner and headed for the shower. Roger was just finished brushing his teeth as Carl entered the bathroom and even though this was a group of ski bums, there were still manners and etiquette. Carl turned to Roger,

"Morning Roger," without even looking over, Roger offered his toothbrush to Carl, "You want this?" He handed his toothbrush over to Carl.

"Sure," Carl replied. Alice, Carl's date had made it to the bathroom just looked at Carl and turned to leave Carl turned to Alice, and said,

"Hey, you don't have to go. Roger is just headed for the shower," and Carl proceeded to brush his teeth. Alice, a little disgusted, still joined them in the bathroom as Ace entered the bathroom almost directly behind Carl and proceeded to take a leak while fumbling for his glasses. Alice looked at Ace with disgust barked,

"What the hell is he doing?" Carl looked at Alice as if puzzled she needed an explanation and said,

"Urinating?" Just then, Sunny appeared, a little hung over still, but anxious to go skiing. "Hi guys." Alice was a little overwhelmed with the crowd in the bathroom. She looked at Sunny with disapproval and asked,

"What's he doing here?"

Carl turned and handed Sunny the toothbrush. Sunny decided to shortcut both Ace and Carl, who was now waiting for the head to squirt, and proceeded to the shower to brush his teeth. Climbing in the shower, Roger's date Sally screamed for Sunny to get out of there. Sunny just looked at Sally with a half hung over smile and said,

"Good morning Roger, Sally." As Roger was finishing his final rinse, he replied,

"Morning, Sunny."

Sally jumped out of the shower, and he guessed that the sight of so many men in the shower was just too much for her. Alice was now standing in amazement, watching Roger and Sally emerge from the shower. While wearing only his glasses, Ace joined Sunny in the shower, Carl urinating.

Alice was still overwhelmed, not understanding that getting through the morning showers was just a formality says,

"What are you guys, gay?" Sunny ignored her, realizing she really didn't understand what was going on. He looked at Ace.

"Ace, you forgot your glasses again!" Sunny stated. Ace looked up through his fogged up glasses. "Hhmmm. I thought I'd been playing with myself and was going blind." Sunny laughed and said,

"Sorry Ace, they're just fogged. You want the toothbrush?"

"Sure, here's the soap," Ace replied.

Just then, Sunny's date Jesse comes running into the bathroom stark-naked yelling,

"Oh no, you guys don't you're not going to do this to me again, I'm going with you." Jesse now jumped into the shower. With a simple politeness, Ace looked at Jesse somewhat astonished, but managed to say,

"Good morning, Jesse." Jesse looked back and said,

"Good morning, Ace. Your glasses..."

Jesse and Sunny kiss just as Ace removes his glasses. Ace felt he probably should've kept his glasses on so he couldn't see so well.

"You guys aren't going to start, are you?" Sunny was anxious to get ready to go skiing, he knew that Jesse was too, but with his New Jersey humor he said,

"No, you can have her."

Sunny got out of the bathroom and headed toward the door as Stony waltzed in and said, "Morning." Ace called from the shower,

"Stony is that you?"

"Yeah"

"Stony here, hold my glasses?" Ace asked. Stony laughed.

"Oh no, not again. Pass me the toothbrush." Carl climbed into the shower as Sunny left.

Alice decided this was too much and too weird for her and just left the bathroom while Roger yelled,

"Which car today?"

Yelling from Sunny's room, "Ace's, let's leave yours and Stony's here."

Roger and Sunny were sitting with their cornflakes and coffee as Carl, Ace, Jesse, and Stony, finished with their showers to join them; there was not much conversation. Roger finished up and headed outside to start Ace's car, while Sunny walked away saying,

"I've got the skis covered." He followed Roger outside to the car to start loading the skis.

Alice turned to Jesse and asked with some surprise,

"Where's he going?" Jesse just looked at her not really knowing what to say as if she didn't understand what the whole group was about. Jesse simply replied,

"Skiing!" Alice turned to Carl asked again,

"Carl, where are you going?" Carl even more amazed didn't give it a second thought as he replied, "Skiing." To make things worse Alice asked, "Now?"

Carl knew the answer, but some lessons had to be learned the hard way, "Yup, you coming?" Carl asked. Alice snapped,

"No."

Ace was ready and opened the door to his date's room. He threw her some keys and said,

"Here, it's to the brown Caprice."

From Ace's room, you heard a pleasant voice respond,

"Thanks honey." Now this must've been just the final straw for Alice as she didn't understand the hard-core skiing community and the preference for skiing. By this time, Alice was screaming,

"What do you mean, thanks honey? You guys are going to leave us?"

Sunny with his charming smile looked at Alice and asked,

"Can you ski?" The light bulb went on with Alice now. She looked at Sunny and simply replied,

"No." Carl with some astonishment looked at Alice as if not being able to ski was some sort of exotic disorder and said,

"Really? I didn't know that." Sunny just looked at Alice, smiled and said, "Yup, we're going to leave you."

Jesse passed them in the hall all dressed to ski with a big smile saying,

"Wait for me, I'm coming."

Stony opened the door to his date's room and tossed a set of keys. "Gray Volvo, don't give it too much gas, and easy on third gear." The voice from the room says, "You asshole, I can't drive a stick." Carl couldn't resist the set up on that line. He had to chime in and say,

"That's not what I heard."

Stony, always a gentleman, quickly replied,

"Oh yeah that's right. Alice will take you, she can't ski. Alice you don't mind, do you?"

Sally understood and was happy to help as she said,

"No, I'll take her."

Turning to Alice,

"It's okay, I'll explain later over breakfast." As Stony closed the door behind him he said,

"Girls be sure to lock up, thanks."

Jesse

As everyone headed up to the mountain, Sunny could not help noticing Jesse. Having a woman along was something new and quite unusual. Sitting in the car and looking at her, he couldn't help thinking about her transition.

When Sunny first met Jesse at the door of The Baggy Knees she was a modest, sincere, naive girl; and yet since she had come over the day before with her equipment anticipating skiing, she stayed the night, made love, took a shower with the guys, and now tried to keep up on the mountain.

She may not have known it, but she had just passed her initiation to the greatly honored Ski Bum Association. The self-appointed president and chairperson Sunny made her a member. She was actually more than becoming one of the guys; Jesse was a good sport. Sunny also felt sorry for her; he knew that the naive, sincere part of her which was so attractive to him was the price she had to pay for her membership. In exchange, skiing and decadence will now emerge in its place. Sunny wasn't really proud of himself; yet he knew she would thank him later.

As they drove into the parking lot, they saw that the lift lines were far more than any respectable ski bum was willing to endure. The group decided to head over to Big Spruce, which was to the right of Little Spruce and was relatively hidden. It was the older part of Stowe's ski area. One of the original founders of the mountain built Big Spruce to provide open intermediate skiing, emulating skiing in Europe.

The chairlift was the original two single chairs welded together. From time to time in high school, Sunny would sneak away to Big Spruce to do some fast, open skiing and to be alone. Now it was a forgotten area for visitors.

Stowe had a great reputation for being the most challenging area in the east, so the majority of the skiers who came to Stowe came to challenge the mountain. Most weren't ready for the mountain and its moguls. You never challenge the mountain; it never changes, a skier will only challenge himself on the mountain. For many of those weekend warriors, the challenge was to see how they could desecrate their body and endure the punishment. Sunny was glad it would always be his retreat.

Even to the good skier, there was a physical price to pay, pounding the bumps day after day. On Big Spruce they cut all the trees for open skiing and the long ride up in the chair was a cold one. A blanket with a hood to keep the skiers warm was provided when they got on. Sunny days were a rare commodity in Stowe in the winter; nonetheless, today was one of them so they didn't mind the cold.

There was a lodge at the top which had some coffee and sandwiches, and an old guy named Joe who had been the lodge's attendant for years. In many ways Sunny preferred this lodge to the other mountain lodges, simply for the chance to get away from the crowds and the hustle. During high school, Sunny would ski Big Spruce, stopping in at the lodge to listen to Joe tell his stories about the town and skiing some twenty years ago, while sipping hot chocolate.

Sunny had been thinking for some time, this year so far had lived up to all his expectations and it would be hard if not impossible to duplicate. This scared him somewhat.

Sunny had heard many of the old ski bums tell of their great year as they sat down in the bar slamming down their beers. Sunny was afraid of becoming one of those guys, hanging around waiting for a repeat year instead of moving on to make something of himself.

In many ways being a ski bum can ruin someone. Being a ski bum is basically unproductive to everything in life except improving your skiing. All too many men and women who love skiing get caught up in ski bumming and somehow lose perspective and productivity. Sunny didn't plan to be one of those people; he was determined to do something with his skiing and himself. On the way up Sunny turned to Carl and said,

"Hey Carl, what's next?"

Carl just looked at Sunny as if the question came out of nowhere and answered,

"Well, we get off the chair and start skiing."

Sunny knew Carl was avoiding the question.

"Come on Carl, I'm serious."

Carl did not want to think about it at that moment, yet replied,

"What do you mean, what's next?"

"We'll never be able to have a better year than this one in Stowe, there's got to be more." Sunny said. Carl looked at Sunny and said,

"I don't know; this is okay." Sunny looked at Carl paused and said,

"Idaho!"

Carl looked at Sunny who now was a little annoyed.

"You keep saying that, would you please stop?"

"No, I mean it, I read somewhere that Idaho has great skiing and big mountains, powder skiing" Sunny continued. Carl looked at Sunny, still a little annoyed.

"First New Jersey, then Vermont, now Idaho."

Sunny just smiled. He may have taken the line from Butch Cassidy and the Sundance kid, but it seemed to be working.

"Just think about it. If we can ski this mountain, Idaho is just there for the picking."

The type of skiing they did on the mountain was fun, and Sunny was pretty good at it. But the fast, open skiing where you worked your ski from top to tail and really felt the ski move was the type of skiing Sunny liked best. Sunny enjoyed skiing fast, with big turns, smooth and dynamic; the type of skiing which brought a grin to his face the whole time.

He had an advantage in knowing the terrain and when they skied this fast, they loved to know what was coming up. The most fun was to swoop across the flats, set up and pop off a leap onto the steep while finishing a turn. On this one part of the hill, Carl and Ace had stopped to inspect the terrain before a steep section. Coming from behind, Sunny blasted by them catching about thirty yards of air. As Sunny went by Carl, he yelled "Idaho!" and faded down the hill.

Jesse actually kept up. The unwritten rule was, let no man slow down before his time. If you couldn't keep up, it was like war; just bury the dead and keep going. After some hard skiing, Sunny brought the group up to the top and introduced them to Joe. They honored Jesse, for her perseverance as well as her change from naiveté to the ski bum world.

Good Times

IT WASN'T EASY TO GET time alone with Judy, so when Sunny got home, he offered to take her to dinner. Judy and Sunny had grown to be good friends as well as lovers. Sunny realized how this must have looked with him romping all over town with other women, and Judy dating Tom. Judy was a good girl; she and Tom had established a strong relationship before Judy met Sunny. Since Sunny was committed to being anything but monogamous, there was no reason for Judy to disrupt what she and Tom had.

On the other hand, it was unfortunately evident that she and Sunny were falling in love. Judy was the only woman who accepted Sunny for exactly what he was. If Judy fell in love with Sunny and felt she had to leave Tom, she would undoubtedly cause pressure on their relationship.

Instead, she would find great humor in catching Sunny with other women and play little jokes on him. Judy had a great sense of humor. To isolate one instance, Sunny was at the bar in The Baggy Knees doing his utmost to impress this young coed from Massachusetts, when Judy spotted him. As soon as Tom was elsewhere, Judy strolled by and smiled.

"Hello, Sunny."

Sunny looked up knowing he was caught with a red face.

"Hello, Judy."

"Judy, this is Kim. Kim, Judy." Judy just grinned,

"Nice to meet you, Kim." Unsuspectingly Kim replies,

"Thank you." Now Judy just closed the deal with,

"Sunny, I was curious as to whether you're coming home tonight. Remember, you promised to bring me skiing."

Sunny knew he wasn't going to be with Kim that night; he just looked up and smiled.

"I haven't forgotten, Judy." She turned to Kim.

"Sunny is one of, if not the best skier on the mountain. Okay, there's Tom, I've got to run, see you later at home. Bye Sunny, Kim," Judy said. Without even looking Sunny said,

"Goodbye, Judy."

And Judy was off. Kim looked at Sunny and asked,

"Who's that?"

"Oh, no one," Sunny replied.

It took Sunny the better part of the hour to talk his way out of that one. When Sunny would get mad and confront Judy, she would only laugh and say, *'It's only because I want you to myself.'* Sunny would always make the same remark, *'I can't, not now, that's not part of the deal.'* Knowing that Judy would say, *'You wouldn't be you if you changed, but I don't have to make it easy; besides, it's fun seeing you panic.'*

At first, her little jokes would piss Sunny off, but as time passed, he realized she did it because she loved him and most of the time, it was funny. Besides having a good sense of humor, Judy was kind and always there to listen to Sunny or nurse him through one of his hangovers.

That week, Sunny took a couple of days to just go up to Big Spruce to be alone for once with Judy. Judy was a pretty fair skier herself, and the whole time Judy and Sunny were growing closer and closer.

In the fifth week, Sunny's team for The Baggy Knees won that week's ski bum race. Sunny was skiing well and consistently. His regular performances in the top five qualified him for the Stowe-Sugarbush challenge.

This was a series of two races, started when the ski bums of Stowe challenged the ski bums of the town of Waitsfield to a race. Each town selected their top 15 teams and had a duel in the giant slalom. The race format was dual head to head racing, which was exciting. Also, it was great way to meet ski bums from another town. Neither town took the races too seriously; after all, decadence implies not taking anything too seriously. It did however, give a great excuse to celebrate and scope out new talent.

Sunny had done well in the race and Stowe won by a considerable margin. However, during one of the races, one of the competitors from Sugarbush fell and broke her leg.

Later in The Horn, Sunny discovered she had no insurance and wouldn't be able to work. Feeling enormous empathy, Sunny quickly called a summit with Gar, the leading town promoter who organized the race and Richard of The Horn and his new guardian, John. Within seconds, Gar stood up and announced the bad news and the dilemma, and asked for donations. Richard offered free beer for two hours to generate some funds, and John pledged to match the pot. Within 20 minutes, the girl had enough to pay for her broken leg and have a few dollars to live on for a while. Some of the bar and restaurant owners from Sugarbush returned with their own pledges and several job offers she could do until she recovered. Overall, it was a happy ending.

If the real world could only get together in human interest the way a bar filled with ski bums did, the world would truly be a better place. Thanks to Gar, Richard, John and all who donated, it gave Sunny a glimmer of goodness and hope.

After several more weeks of ski bum races, it was our turn to go to Sugarbush, for them to host the race. Sunny was again selected. The group had continued to ski hard, they even took time to join one of Gar's promotions where they cross country skied from his house over and up the back hills to town.

These constant good times were starting to get to Sunny. Sunny was skiing well, and his performances in ski bum races and Ski Bum Hustle, were right up there. Sunny was shooting for the overall award.

A couple of days before the Sugarbush challenge, Sunny actually took time out not to drink or to eat, but catch up on some much needed sleep.

The Race

STOWE'S SKI BUM POPULATION WAS well represented. Some car-pooling efforts were actually made to enable some the liberty to drink in excess and return home safely. With that little rest, Sunny felt pretty good. As it had been in Stowe, it was a head to head competition. After the Stowe challenge, all the ski bums were pretty familiar with one another, so the race was fun. The town of Sugarbush turned out in force to cheer for their team. Sunny wasn't used to skiing before such a large crowd; it was like being at one of the pro races.

Carl and Sunny both skied well, and both had established a fair lead over the competition after the first run. Carl always helped Sunny to relax and concentrate and that particular day, it paid off. Carl took third place overall, and Sunny took first place overall on the times. Needless to say, Sunny was Stowe's pride and joy. Sunny felt good because he had beaten Eric and Arnie, who had made good runs as well.

After the race, Carl and Sunny decided to postpone their celebrating and disappear on the mountain for a few hours. Sunny personally wanted to ski to place things in perspective and to spend some quality time on another mountain with Carl. Besides skiing well with Carl, they laughed a lot. Carl had a great sense of humor.

Cindy

As soon as Carl and Sunny were done, they went to the Sugarbush rendition of The Horn for the awards. Stowe had won again by a considerable margin. Still Sugarbush was a gracious host, so the festivities began. Though Sunny felt really good about skiing so well, he was a kind of apprehensive about ruining how good he felt physically by getting drunk. Carl and Sunny were standing at the bar after the awards.

Sunny turned to Carl.

"Hey Carl, we should be thinking about getting something to eat and what we want to do tonight."

"Yeah, I'm getting hungry, but you're not taking me out just like that. I want some advance warning if you want a date; besides, you didn't shave."

Sunny grinned and laughed,

"Guess I can't win them all."

Now standing with John, his boss from the Baggy Knees, Roger and Stony came over. It felt comfortably familiar standing with the group again. Looking around the room, Sunny saw Ace pushing his way through the crowd to get to them. Ace was always the instigator and looked at Sunny.

"Hey Sunny, look over there," he said, pointing in some general direction.

Sunny looked at Ace like he was nuts, because he was. The bar they were in was an old, dark barn packed wall to wall with people and Ace told Sunny to look over where?

It was noisy, and Sunny could hardly hear Ace, so Ace yelled above the noise. Sunny looked at Ace and said,

"Calm down Ace, gather yourself." Stony with his Viking humor, turned from the bar to Ace and said,

"Ace you've been drinking a lot lately, relax, here have a beer."

Ace persisted.

"No, you guys look over there," he said.

Carl was obviously not looking in the right direction.

"You mean that fat chick playing pool."

Ace took another sip of beer and by this time, he was delirious. He grabbed Sunny by the arm and pulled him over to look out to the back porch. Carl, John, Stony and the others follow.

Stony stood there like a giant Viking statue with his beer and proclaimed,

"Jesus, look at that."

Standing out on the porch was the one of, if not the most beautiful woman Sunny had ever seen. She was tall with blonde braided hair, wearing a blue turtle neck and well-fitting stretch pants. Sunny recognized the outfit immediately; it was the Sugarbush Ski School uniform. She had beautiful eyes, a great smile, and laugh. John with his great smile looked at Ace as if he just found a ruby and declared,

"Good find, Ace."

Roger somewhat nonchalantly added, "Pretty girl."

Sunny looked at them all and replied,

"Roger, you have a talent for understatement!" Ace turned to John.

"What are you thinking?" he asked.

The challenge was on. At that point having done so well in the race it was up to Sunny to establish his true title if he were to be King. Ace declared,

"Sunny could get her." That was it!!! Sunny was faced with the ultimate challenge and it wasn't on a mountain.

John just looked and made it worse by saying,

"Maybe; if there wasn't that sea of men around her, she probably has some rich guy, anyway."

Ace, one of the new Knights of the Round Table, stood up to the challenge replying,

"No way, if she had one guy, all those guys wouldn't be out there."

Ace was pretty smart. .At that moment Sunny felt he had to do something. Sunny knew what was going to happen, but this had to play out.

"Good point," Sunny said.

"You stay out of this."

"John, what do you want to bet?"

This was not going in the right direction. This whole environment was a feeding frenzy. Ace knew he was in charge and the bidding had started. John smiled; this was true sport.

"Ah… Okay, fifty dollars," John said.

Carl chimed in; "I'll take a piece of that action, even if he didn't shave." Now the friends were going at it with each other.

Stony said, "I'll take Sunny, for twenty."

Even Roger wanted the piece of this one as he said, "Stone man, for twenty."

Sunny couldn't believe his ears as he tried to stop it, but it was like stopping a freight train.

"Wow," Sunny said, "Hold it. Even if I could, or would be willing to try, I got no place to take her and no money to take her with, and…I'm supposed to work tonight. Sorry, guys. One of you will have to face the ultimate rejection."

Carl was happy to sacrifice himself. "I'll try," he said.

Ever the sportsman, John spoke up.

"No, wait. Look, Sunny, I'll give you dinner for two and the night off if you can get her to The Knees."

Ace was happy to up the ante, as he said,

"I'll throw in the condo if you get her to *her* knees!"

Sunny was feeling pretty good. He had just won the race. Sunny was sober and a little hungry. So before Sunny could talk himself out of it, he looked at the porch again. God, she was beautiful, the ultimate girl. Sunny had been scoping women all year and this face stopped him dead. Looking at John Sunny said,

"Wine with dinner, the night off with pay…"

John smiled and said, "You got it."

Sunny stood up straight, took a deep breath, walked out on to the deck, pushed through all the guys, looked this stunningly beautiful girl straight in the eye, grabbed her hand and said, "Hi, I'm Sunny."

The girl looked back with a smile and said, "I know!"

Sunny raised one eye in surprise and smiled in delight. The girl looked at Sunny.

"I was in the race today. You won it. I'm Cindy."

Sunny looked at her a little stunned and quickly said,

"Well Cindy, I'm also hungry, would you care to join me for some dinner?"

There was a good 10 seconds pause. Sunny looked straight into her eyes and smiled, while his heart was going Mach 10.

Cindy just smiled and said, "Sure."

Sunny felt relieved. Sunny didn't show a sign of anything but confidence. To be honest he was scared to death. Sunny just looked at Cindy and said,

"Come on, I've got an idea."

He gently squeezed her hand and led her across the bar to the door. Sunny knew that the guys were all staring at them, he could even hear them talk, but the bar was too noisy to understand what they were saying. They emerged from the crowd into the fresh air. Sunny looked at Cindy; she was more beautiful than Sunny could believe.

Cindy asked, "Where are we going?"

"Well, how'd you like to go to dinner in Stowe? Thanks to you we just won dinner for two with wine at The Baggy Knees!"

Cindy looked at Sunny and smiled, she knew what Sunny was talking about.

"It will be a really nice dinner."

Cindy looked at Sunny and said,

"It is nice to meet someone being honest. I'd love to go, let me go home and change."

Her car was blocked in so they left it there and went to her house in Sunny's car so she could change. She shared the house with some other ski instructors and as he drove they talked.

Cindy looked at Sunny and said,

"You were great today. You beat some really good guys from here." Sunny looked at her trying to be modest and said,

"Thanks, I got lucky."

"What was the bet, anyways?" Sunny knew what she meant but didn't want to answer and instead replied,

"Stowe was favored 3 to 1." Cindy persisted.

"No, the dinner bet." Sunny, a little embarrassed, realized that the only way out of this was to be honest.

"Nothing bad really. They bet you wouldn't go to dinner with me," Sunny said. Cindy looked a little surprised and asked,

"Why?"

That question was verging on being naive, or she was fishing for how Sunny felt. So Sunny decided to tell her straight out and said,

"Because you're beautiful."

Cindy laughed.

"Come on, tell me."

"Really, I think you're beautiful, so do the guys I came down with." Cindy smiled and said,

"You guys are crazy." Sunny just looked ahead with a grin and said,

"You're not the first to notice. Dinner, wine and the night off with pay as well."

Cindy looked at Sunny with a smirk and asked poignantly,

"What if I had said no?" Sunny just shrugged his shoulders and said quickly,

"No problem... would have quietly left the bar and cut my throat."

Cindy smiled and replied,

"Well, to keep from seeing your throat cut, I'll save you if you'll teach me to ski like you did today. Here's where I live."

With his heart in his throat Sunny leaned over to kiss her as they stopped. The kiss seemed to last for hours, actually may have only been a minute, but Sunny was devastated. As they went into her house he felt uneasy; elated, but uneasy. Sunny was so infatuated, he could hardly breathe; but what bothered him most was that he didn't feel in control. Usually Sunny was able to talk fast and sweep girls off their feet. At the moment, Sunny could hardly talk and he was swept of his feet. Actually Sunny was just scared.

Sunny turned to make small talk, only to see her stand in front of him and take off her stretch pants, then her turtleneck. Sunny froze at first, but he could see that she didn't mean anything by it; she just quickly changed to a white turtleneck and faded jeans. Sunny couldn't help but flash back at the bathroom scene at Ace's, where they had learned to throw modesty to the wind.

Sunny knew then she was a seasoned ski bum. Within an hour Sunny, had seen her in three ways, ski clothes, undressed, and in faded jeans. It would be hard to pick his favorite, but undressed certainly exposed possibilities.

On the way to Stowe, they talked about the usual stuff; where they came from, how many brothers and sisters, etc. Cindy was from Massachusetts, just outside of Boston. She had a brother and a sister, and her dad was a banker. Backgrounds certainly could tell you a lot about someone. Sunny wasn't surprised to hear Cindy's background, she fitted it perfectly, and she was the perfect looking Wasp, (white Anglo-Saxon Protestant). Sunny had to change clothes as well. Fortunately, he'd had the forethought to throw some jeans and a clean shirt in his car. When they got to The Knees, Sunny changed there. Why Sunny had not thought of changing at Cindy's he didn't know, but none of his thinking was really going too well.

Cindy was impressed with The Knees. Sunny was pretty hungry and ate a big steak; so did Cindy. As they talked, Sunny noticed something that had given him that uneasy feeling. It was simply that Sunny was nervous, infatuated, and wearing his heart on his sleeve. Cindy on the other hand was obviously at ease, not nervous or seemingly infatuated. She was just having a good time, seeing Stowe and eating a nice dinner. Sunny wasn't used to this; when he took a woman out, he expected *her* to be infatuated and apprehensive. That was another thing, Cindy had no apprehension about traveling somewhere with someone she knew nothing about. Whatever she did, Sunny would be in trouble; he knew for the first time that he wanted more from her.

After dinner they went upstairs and danced. Cindy was a good dancer, and Sunny introduced her to the guys. She was the talk of The Knees and Stowe, as everyone saw Sunny walk her out of the bar in Sugarbush. Sunny got the credit for bringing her up to Stowe. He couldn't help but feel that he didn't bring her, she brought him.

However, Sunny also had won the race which gave him a victory and something to celebrate about that he felt he deserved. They danced and drank for a few hours. Standing at the bar, Cindy whispered in Sunny's ear to come down to Sugarbush with her and to go skiing with her the next morning. Sunny turned to look at her. As he turned, she kissed him long and hard. From any other girl Sunny wouldn't have been surprised. Coming from her, Sunny was actually more delighted (God, did he want to go!) than surprised and only had one reply.

"Sure, why not? I'll be right back," he said.

He went over to Carl, Ace, and the gang, standing together. Carl looked at Sunny.

"Hey Sunny, how does it feel to be King?"

At this point, Sunny didn't want to be the King of anything. He knew he was in over his head, but there was no way out. He just looked at Carl, still hoping to get out of this.

"What do you mean?" Sunny asked the boys of the Roundtable who were proud of Prince Valiant at the moment. Ace chimed in,

"Look at Cam and Kenny standing over there, drooling over your date. When she kissed you, I thought Kenny was going to cry. It's great," Carl said.

"Yeah, and today you smoked everybody, good skiing," Stony added.

"Thanks Stony. Look guys, I just got lucky. Ace, call Judy and make some excuse and tell her I'm not dead."

Carl looked at Sunny and asked, "Why, where are you going?"

"Idaho," Sunny quickly replied. "No. I'm only kidding, Waitsfield. I'm going to ski Sugarbush tomorrow."

Roger, as the giant that he was, raised his beer glass and said,

"I underestimated you. Long live The King."

Sunny didn't want to hear this. You'd think he'd be okay with the praise, but he looked at the guys with a smirk and said,

"Enough of that shit, I'll see you tomorrow night; if not, Ace, cover me, okay?"

Ace nodded and said, "Sure Sunny. Go for it."

Now you'd think Sunny would've been ecstatic to claim the title at last, but he wasn't. He was scared. All the guys could see that Sunny had done the ultimate skiing and the ultimate grab. Sunny looked over at Carl; he couldn't even smile. He turned and left with Cindy. Sunny didn't say much on the ride to Sugarbush; while driving he turned to see Cindy asleep.

Sunny wanted this to be the happy ending to the ski burn story. He wanted to be the King of the ski bums, to run off with the prettiest girl and live happily ever after.

When they got to Cindy's house, Sunny expected to proclaim her to be a nice girl and offered to graciously sleep on the couch. Instead, as soon as they closed the door Cindy grabbed his hand and pulled him straight to the bedroom. This actually upset Sunny somewhat, because this is what he had done with every previous girl. Sunny wanted this to be special. Cindy stood in front of him, quickly undressed and jumped under the covers. Sunny leaned over and kissed her while telling her he would be right back.

He went into the bathroom and took a deep breath, washed his face, brushed his teeth, and took a piss. Sunny really didn't want to turn and go do to Cindy what he had done to so many other girls; Sunny wanted this to be different. What hurt was that it hadn't been special throughout the evening. Sunny hadn't gotten any indication from her if she liked him for anything but his looks, friends, and skiing. She wanted to have fun with the King of the ski bums and she didn't care who he was. When Sunny walked out of the bathroom she was dead asleep.

Normally Sunny would have awakened her and finished the evening. Instead, he looked at her for a while, slipped quietly into bed so as not to wake her. Sunny was pretty tired; it had been a long eventful day, and his mind was running at a hundred miles an hour.

Suddenly Sunny woke up unsure of where he was, looked around and saw it was almost dawn. He looked over at Cindy; God she was beautiful. How could he to get her to fall in love with him, he thought. Sunny stepped out of bed and went over to the sliding glass door to watch the sun rise. It had a beautiful view. The ground in front was covered in a foot of snow, the mountain and a part of the town showed in the background. Without the sun, everything turned black and white.

Watching the sun rise was like watching a picture turn from black and white into full color. More importantly everything was still and quiet. Standing there, Sunny felt alone. He couldn't help but think of the day before. Sunny wondered what Ron Biedermann would have thought of his win. What was really bothering him was when he talked to the guys at The Knees, he wanted to tell them how he felt about Cindy and more importantly, to share his fears. Sunny had a real moment of clarity when he realized that there was no king of anything, especially King of the ski bums. It was just somebody pretending to be self-important and Sunny didn't feel important to anybody, especially himself. Sunny knew that guys like Arnie and Eric were still better skiers and racers; and guys like Ron and Greg were in a class of their own. Sunny knew he wasn't fooling anybody but himself. Sunny still loved skiing and what skiing had brought him, and wondered what was going to happen next. He stood for a long time just staring at the horizon. Suddenly, he felt arms coming around him from the back and he jumped a little. It was Cindy. "Good morning. What's the matter, couldn't you sleep?" Cindy asked softly. Staring straight at sun, he said,

"Oh, you startled me."

"Yeah I guess it's the excitement from yesterday." Cindy gave Sunny a hug and kiss,

"Yeah, you were great yesterday. Go ahead and jump into the shower, I'll make us some coffee."

Sunny did just that. As he was standing there, Cindy joined him and without a word, they embraced in a passionate kiss. As they pulled apart, Cindy said,

"Good morning, and sorry that I fell asleep on you last night. It's hard to keep up and stay up."

Sunny didn't want to let on that he really wasn't disappointed; instead, he said,

"No problem, I was pretty tired myself."

They kissed again and Sunny was as aroused as he had ever been. The shower was too small to make love, but Sunny wasn't totally inhibited. He paused to look at her athletic body, hard and wet, it was breathtaking. The passion was great, but Sunny wanted the real thing, so he stopped and took a deep breath and said,

"Let's hit the hill."

Cindy realized that there would be time later and skiing couldn't wait for the real skiers. "Good idea," she said.

Sunny felt good and bad, he had Cindy but not the way he wanted her. Sunny didn't want the ski bum game anymore. They got dressed and went up to the mountain. Cindy brought Sunny to the ski school and introduced him to everyone. Sunny was recognized immediately for his accomplishments the day before. Sunny didn't want the adulations from other skiers, he wanted to spend time alone with Cindy. He felt he was Cindy's trophy, which was fair game from how he met her the night before, but now he wanted to get to know her.

As they skied, Cindy asked Sunny questions about skiing. Sunny was skiing, but his mind was somewhere else. After a couple of runs and just as they were getting off the lift at the top,

Cindy turned and asked Sunny,

"Hey Sunny, I have to go the little girls room. You want to come and grab a cup of coffee?"

Sunny needed to think so he looked at Cindy and said,

"Yeah, okay, but I'm gonna take a run first."

Sunny gave her a little kiss and skied over to the top of the trail. His muscles were so tight he could hardly stand up properly. Sunny thought a run by himself might be just the thing to make him relax and place his priorities back in perspective and return to his old self.

Sunny kicked off with explosive energy and flew. Sunny skied as hard and as fast as his body could handle, first open fast turns, smoothly and gracefully. Then short radius fast turns, quick with a violent snap of aggression. Sunny skied nonstop and so hard, he broke a sweat. Sunny skied all the way to the bottom.

Panting, out of breath and sweating, Sunny just stood there staring at the trees for a while. He did manage to get some aggression out, but the perspective he had hoped to gain wasn't there. Sunny couldn't shake his feelings for Cindy. Just then Cindy skied up, standing in front of Sunny gasping for air.

"Christ, I can't believe it. I've never seen anyone ski like that." Sunny looked at Cindy she took him by surprise he had to hold her up. Sunny was still a little confused, as he still had to refocus.

"Wow, just slow down," he said.

Cindy gasped and said, "I remembered I didn't have any money, so I thought I'd catch you before you took off. I've been trying to catch you ever since."

Sunny realized what she'd done.

"I'm so sorry, I didn't know." Cindy was still gasping for air.

"Are you kidding? That was great! I was right behind you and you took off like a jet. I've never had anyone lose me like that."

Sunny, still apologetic, looked at her and admitted,

"I don't usually ski like that, I just needed to." Cindy had caught her breath as she looked at Sunny understandingly.

"Yeah, I thought something was bothering you. Are you okay?"

Sunny paused for a moment and looked at her; she was beautiful, and now she was being very understanding.

"I'm okay; you just have to be patient with me. Come on, let's get some coffee."

Over coffee, Sunny was introduced to yet more of her friends. As Sunny sat there, he realized that he wasn't going to get to know Cindy like he had planned after having met all her boyfriends. So Sunny thought he would plan a quiet dinner. Sunny turned to Cindy and touched her hand.

"Hey, Cindy listen, let's get some dinner tonight."

"I can't, my mother and brother are coming up to have dinner with me tonight. Wait a minute, why don't you join us?" Cindy said.

This was not the answer Sunny had expected. Now remember Sunny was not the person that mothers wanted their daughters going out with, especially a tall, beautiful, statuesque blonde daughter of a banker from Boston. Sunny was from a proper upbringing, but this was not a good idea. Sunny looked at Cindy with a little bit of panic on his face.

"Nah, that's not a great idea," Sunny said. He continued, "Besides I've got to work."

Cindy was fearless and she wasn't going to take no for an answer.

"Come on, you can call in. Ace will cover. Mom will like you."

Boy did Cindy not know what she was in for. She wanted to introduce a 6 foot tall, dark-haired uneducated ski bum with learning disabilities whose greatest skills at this moment were to be bad at relationships and strengthen his abilities drinking people under the table. Cindy wanted to brag about bagging the King of the ski bums, but he doubted mom would be impressed. Not exactly the talk of the country club. If Cindy was to get the two introduced one day, this would be a good way to do it; but not *now*. Sunny looked at Cindy again and reinforced,

"I doubt it, but okay I'll see what I can do."

They skied the rest of the day and Sunny was somewhat more relaxed. Cindy kept up fine and Sunny helped her with her skiing. It was pretty cold, so they kept going in for food and coffee. After skiing, they went down to the bar where Cindy and Sunny had met. Gar was standing there. Sunny was happy to see a familiar face and asked Gar,

"What are you doing here?"

Gar was somewhat surprised to see Sunny there. He replied,

"I had planned to stay and ski Sugarbush today. I heard you went to Stowe with Cindy."

Sunny actually wasn't surprised to hear that Gar knew, it was a small town and a smaller skier community. Gar was one of those guys that was a leader in the town, and really kept himself aware of the pulse of everything. News traveled fast.

"Welcome back."

"Hey Gar, I'm kind of short, do you have any cash?" Sunny had known Gar for a long time, and he had helped him shovel out the barn to make the Rusty Nail. Gar was more than happy to help Sunny out.

Gar, with his usual astute observation stating the obvious, handed some money to Sunny and said,

"It figures that the most broke bum is with the prettiest girl. Sure."

Gar lent Sunny enough to cover dinner. Cindy picked the restaurant and fortunately it was within his budget. Sunny managed to borrow a clean shirt from one of the instructors staying with Cindy. They waited a long time for Cindy's mother and brother to show. Sunny took the opportunity to grab a few drinks. Things may have looked great on the surface, but he was still in turmoil.

Finally Cindy's mother and brother arrived. If Sunny had any doubt about Cindy being the perfect Wasp, looking at Cindy's mother and brother removed it all. Cindy's mother was a tall, beautifully gorgeous woman, who carried herself with poise and grace, conservatively dressed in slacks and a turtleneck sweater. Her brother was a tall blond of about 16 years old, who looked like a model from an L. L. Bean catalog. After the formal introductions, a little drunk and a lot nervous, Sunny joined them for dinner.

All Cindy's breeding had been evident in her mother. As they sat, Sunny politely answered questions about where he was from, what his father did and what his plans were for the future.

Sunny answered everything except what his intentions were with her daughter. It was actually pretty funny, for the first time Sunny had honorable intentions. What would have been a more appropriate question was what her daughter's intentions with Sunny were.

The biggest drawback seemed to be Sunny's lack of a college education. Sunny was sure he wasn't viewed as an appropriate match for a girl with such a promising future. Just then, he heard from the bar in the next room *'Well all right, look here, it's Sunny!'*

One of the unique things about Vermont was that there weren't very many black people. In Stowe, there were five, one resident and the four guys of the band playing at The Knees. They were not only good musicians, they were also nice guys. Coming from New Jersey, Sunny had more readily accepted them and they had become good friends. Looking over, Sunny saw the guys from the band; they had the night off, Sunny found out later, and wanted to get out of Stowe for some dinner. Bill, the lead singer, came right over and the others followed. At first Sunny thought, 'oh shit.' Then it was so good to see some friendly, familiar faces. Sunny jumped up and gave them a hug. He introduced each band member to Cindy and her family, her mother obviously was not impressed, even Cindy looked a tad nervous, her brother was impressed. Any doubt her. mother had about Sunny being the sort of man her daughter should be with just went into the next room with Bill and the band as they had dinner. All Sunny could think was 'fuck it.' Sunny wanted Cindy, but Cindy didn't want him for anything but for being the King of the ski bums. So fuck it, it didn't matter what her mom thought anyway.

After dinner, they went into the next room where there was a couple singing and playing the guitar. Again Sunny heard,

"Hey Sunny, what's happening?"

The couple had played at The Horn in the summer.

The Group

"Congratulations."

Sunny stood up for a round of applause and sat down to finish his drink. By that time, Sunny was pretty drunk and decided it was a good time to make his exit. So Sunny thanked Cindy's mom and brother for allowing him to join them, said goodnight to Cindy, and headed for the door. On the way he noticed Gar and waved. As he got to the door, Cindy cut him off. Sunny was more than a little drunk, and surprised when he heard Cindy.

"Sunny wait, where are you going?" Sunny turned andsaid,

"Stowe."

Cindy wasn't sure she understood, but she knew Sunny was a nice guy somewhere in there.

"Stay awhile," she said. Sunny just looked at her.

"That's not a good idea, I'm pretty drunk, and so far I don't think I managed to impress your mother. Besides, I'm out of money."

Sunny wasn't really proud of himself at that moment, yet Cindy didn't seem to care.

"I've got some money. Come in and have some coffee. I'll leave in a minute," Cindy said.

Cindy knew that Sunny should not be driving, and that it was really too soon to have introduced him to her mother. Sunny just looked at Cindy and said,

"I should get back to Stowe tonight, Cindy."

Cindy wasn't going to let Sunny drive in his condition and she did want to be with him.

"Why don't you let me come with you and ski Stowe with you tomorrow?"

Oh shit, now Sunny was in real trouble. Cindy wanted to come to Stowe, and he couldn't show her where he lived. Well, technically he could. Sunny looked at Cindy and said,

"What about your work?" Cindy just smiled,

"It's not a problem, the director likes me." As if the director wouldn't. Sunny now just mumbled to himself, '*Well, I'm not surprised.*'

Cindy asked, "What?"

"Nothing," he replied.

"Okay, let's try some coffee," Cindy said.

They went back inside, and Sunny had sobered up a bit by the time Cindy's mother left. Her mom actually had a good time and was throwing a few back herself. Once again they said goodnight, they headed for their hotel while Sunny and Cindy headed for Stowe. Cindy had told her mom there was a ski instructor's clinic the next day in Stowe, and she bought it.

Sunny needed a place to bring Cindy; so on the way out of the bar, he stopped and talked to Gar. Gar had the perfect house; it was huge with plenty of bedrooms and out of the way. Not to mention, it also had a gorgeous view. Gar offered Sunny his top floor. They picked up Cindy's car and she followed him closely, as he was still plenty drunk.

On the ride up, Sunny couldn't help but think that things had gotten out of control. Somehow he had gone from not wanting any relationships to now being caught between two women and not being able to have either. That really bothered him; even though he was going to spend the night with Cindy, he knew he couldn't really have her.

When they got to Gar's house it was his turn to fall asleep. Sunny was out like a light. He probably could have stayed awake a few moments more, but he was avoiding meaningless sex; this from the kid who defined meaningless sex as a sport. Sunny still wanted Cindy to be special so he could project their relationship in the future. However, this is what he meant by not being able to have her. Sunny knew that although Cindy was sincere with her feelings, this relationship's longevity was maybe to the end of the season, which was fast approaching.

In the morning, Sunny woke up to Cindy sleeping on top of him. As Sunny looked at her, he still couldn't believe how beautiful she was with her blond hair and long sleek body. Just then, Gar decided to bless them with some morning music, the song "I Can See Clearly Now" by Johnny Nash. As Cindy woke up she smiled and looked at Sunny.

"Good morning, how do you feel?" Cindy asked.

Sunny looked up. As bad as he felt, looking at her made everything feel a lot better.

"Good morning, hung over!" Cindy looked at him with some concern, "I can't believe how much you drank." Sunny just held his head knowing he wasn't really proud of himself.

"Yeah, in my case stupidity comes in large volumes. God, I can't imagine what your mother thinks of me."

Cindy laughed. After a shower with Cindy and a cup of coffee with Gar, Cindy and Sunny headed to The Baggy Knees.Sunny knew John would be there setting up. Sunny brought Cindy in because if John was mad, the sight of Cindy might put him in a better mood. Standing in John's office, Sunny said,

"Good morning, John." It worked. John looked up and saw Cindy, and smiled.

"Hey Sunny, I thought you and Cindy ran off?"

Feeling relieved Sunny looked at John and said,

"Not exactly. Sorry about being gone, you mad?"

John with his big smile looked at Sunny,

"Shit no, that's what's it all about, love."

Sunny just said, "Yeah."

"Hey John, do I have any money coming?" John chuckled a little bit.

"Yup, here.

"Good, I have to pay rent and get breakfast. John, you care to join us?"

"Sure," John said.

"Great, but first I have to go to the ladies room." Cindy said.

"Around the corner to your left," replied John.

"Thanks."

Cindy left the office. John looked to Sunny with some concern. Sunny thought he was in trouble but then John said,

"You look like hell. You've got to slow down, or these young women will kill you." Sunny looked at John and asked,

"Have you seen Judy?"

"Yeah, she came in looking for you." John said.

Sunny looked at John and turned a little paler than he already was.

"Oh fuck." he replied.

John could see that Sunny was really on the edge. He said,

"Don't sweat it, we all got together and we told her that your brother is sick and you had to go south for a while. Besides, she was with Tom."

"Thanks John. I owe you one," Sunny said as some color came back to his face. Then he continued, "Come on, I could use some breakfast."

John went on, "Yeah you got to pull yourself together. There are only two weeks left of the ski bum races. If you do well, we could be the season's winners."

Cindy returned and they went for breakfast. Afterwards, they went up the mountain over to Big Spruce for a few warm up runs. On the way up, Ace spotted them. He and the guys had the same idea of warming up. After the run, they joined up and Sunny let Ace jump on the lift with Cindy so Sunny could get a chance to talk to Carl. They got on the chairlift with the blankets. Carl looked over while pulling the blanket aside and said,

"You look like you were rode hard and been put up wet."

Sunny felt that way, but wasn't thrilled everybody noticed it. He just looked at Carl with a pale face,

"Great, Carl."

Carl was serious if anybody could tell Sunny the truth it was Carl.

"No really, you look like death warmed over."

Sunny knew he was right.

"It's nice to see you too! Yeah I got pretty drunk last night."

Sunny told Carl about the night before and what had happened with the band, the couple singing, and described Cindy's mother. Carl looked in amazement.

"Holy shit, you've been through the wringer."

Sunny knew he was out of control.

"Yeah, I have."

If there was anybody Sunny could talk to it was Carl, and he knew that wasn't the end of the story.

"There's something else isn't there?" Carl asked.

"Why?" Sunny asked.

"When I looked at you at The Knees the other night, I thought there was something wrong. Now I know what it is," said Carl.

There was something wrong, but they didn't have time, they had to get off.

"Don't worry, I'll live." Said Sunny as they got off the chair. Carl pushed away saying,

"Well if you don't, can I have your skis?" Sunny was right behind him, and taking a few skiing steps to keep up replied,

"Yeah, but not the bindings, you asshole."

They laughed and he felt better; Carl always knew how to make him laugh.

As they skied the guys were impressed with Cindy, by how well she could ski. Between all of them, Sunny didn't get much chance to ride the lift or even to ski with her, but that was okay with him. Sunny didn't feel like putting in his best effort, he just skied with Carl and relaxed. Sunny didn't push the subject and he didn't want to talk about it yet, just being around Carl and the guys helped. Carl was right; they always knew when there was something wrong with one of the others. But they also knew when to give each other a little space. After skiing, they got together again at The Horn.

Alice had been waiting for Carl. Cindy was having fun, she had just been introduced to a whole new world of ski burns where she had the pleasure of being crowned Queen by being one, so beautiful and two, being with Sunny. She grabbed a beer and within moments Cindy was surrounded by a sea of men.

Sunny wasn't surprised. After all, this was where he came in. Sunny needed a moment for himself and went to his favorite place to think, the loading dock out back. Sunny was sitting on the loading dock when Richard showed up, sat down next to him and said,

"Saw you come out here. This was always the place you went when something was bothering you, even in school. You okay?"

Sunny just sat there; he knew Richard was right. He was staring off the loading dock.

"I guess so. I was just thinking how things have changed since I started coming over here to teach you guys how to ski."

Richard knew, if anybody, the changes Sunny had made.

"Yeah, you're in the fast lane now and you look it. It's tough to keep up, that girl inside isn't going to help any."

Richard could see that Sunny was in trouble. Sunny looked at Richard.

"She's beautiful, I'm in trouble."

Richard never minced words. "Don't tell me you're in love."

Sunny looked over in a bit of a panic. "It's not quite that bad."

Richard wasn't going to cut Sunny any slack.

"Well, it's nice to know there's some real feeling in you anyway. You'll be all right; it's all part of growing up."

Sunny just laughed a little. "I think I liked things better before."

Richard looked at him seriously for a moment.

"Yeah, but you can't go back, you got to keep looking to what's next. You'll be okay. I believe in you."

Sunny needed to hear that. He didn't believe in himself right then.

"Thanks, Richard."

That was about as much conversation as you ever got out of Richard.

"I've got to get back inside, it's getting busy in there. Sunny, try to get some sleep. You look like hell."

Just then Carl walked out, sitting beside Sunny.

"Hey Sunny, I've been looking for you. How you doing?"

"I don't know Carl, things got all screwed up." Carl looked at him as if he should know.

"She's beautiful," he said.

Sunny agreed, "Yeah, I just want this one to be different. Instead of me out to have a good time, the tables are turned."

Carl just looked at him and with a smirk he said, "Long Live the King."

That really hit Sunny where it hurt.

"Yeah, and that's another thing. I want to go back to just being Sunny."

Carl looked at him and he was serious this time.

"You can't go back."

Sunny looked at Carl. "That's what Richard said."

Carl continued, "But you're still Sunny to me."

Sunny said, "There's something else. Carl couldn't imagine there was anything more."

"You don't have a dose of the clap, do you?"

"No, it's not that. We've been together for two nights and we haven't..."

Carl just looked at Sunny. "No?"

Sunny explained, "No! I want this one to be different."

Carl was really baffled by this.

"It's that you can't keep this one. There isn't anything wrong with you physically, is there?"

Sunny replied quickly, "No."

"Well, I know you're not gay, so you'll work it out. Come on in, Cindy's looking for you. It's tough to see through all those guys," Carl said.

"Yeah, but she knows a good time when she sees it," Sunny said.

They went in, and as Sunny walked by the bar toward Cindy the group

150

of men parted to pay respect to Sunny's accomplishments. Cindy and Sunny talked for a bit.

Cindy looked at Sunny somewhat pensively, "I've got to meet my mom for dinner again, do you want to come?" Sunny just looked at Cindy; he knew she knew the answer, but he did the polite thing and simply said,

"No thank you, I think your mother could use a break from me."

Cindy asked, "When am I going to see you again?" This kind of took Sunny by surprise. He thought that Cindy might've had enough of him by now.

"Cindy, I've got to ask you something. There are a dozen fun guys here who would

give their right ski to be with you, so why me?"

Cindy surprised Sunny with her answer.

"Because you're the best Sunny, that's all I've heard. You're the leader; they all look to up you."

That wasn't the answer Sunny was looking for, but it was flattering.

"I'm just one of them."

Cindy looked at Sunny and said, "Well, I like you."

Sunny looked back at Cindy and was still not really sure why she wanted to be with him,

"I'll call you in a day or two. We'll get together. Cindy, I do like being with you."

Cindy gave him a convincing kiss, one he was not soon to forget.

Cindy looked at Sunny and said, "Please do call, Sunny."

Cindy left and Sunny headed home. All Sunny could think to do was to take a shower and a nap, and to finally put on some clean clothes. In the front of his mind was Judy, too. Sunny kind of hoped he would get some time alone, but he did look forward to seeing Judy. Sunny went home and Judy wasn't there.

After a shower, Sunny lay on the bed looking around the room at Judy and his things together. He couldn't help but feel a little confused about Judy and Tom and himself. Sunny felt like he had everything, but really had nothing. After a nap, Sunny dressed and went to work. It felt good to be back at the door. Things weren't the same though; when a pretty girl came in Sunny thought about his dilemma, feeling a little guilty. Nevertheless, he went right back to the Ski Bum Hustle. He loved women. Sunny wasn't sure it was the women .though, he just wanted to go back to when it was fun.

Just as things seemed to be returning to normal inside, Judy walked in with Tom directly behind her. Sunny knew there were a lot of questions Judy would have for him. As yet Tom still didn't have a clue, so they had to keep their distance.

Immediately, Sunny caught Judy's eye and broke out in a huge smile. He was really glad to see her.

Judy looked at Sunny and asked politely, "Sunny, how was your trip? I hope things are okay?"

Sunny hated to lie. He had an agreement of no questions with Judy, but lying was not part of the agreement.

"Yeah, I think I'll be just fine Judy. Nice to see you, how have you been?"

"Okay while you've been gone," Judy said.

Sunny wanted to talk, but he couldn't. All he could say was,

"Yeah, but now I'm back. Well, you guys have a good time now."

Judy and Tom left to walk into the bar. Just then, some guy with his date walked up to him, looked him straight in the eye and said,

"Hi, I'm a ski bum, I know Sunny."

Sunny just looked at him a little stunned and said,

"Oh?!"

Ace as quick as he could looked at the guy and asked,

"What does he look like?"

The guy looked at Ace and tried to bluff them. "Come on, everyone knows what Sunny looks like," he said.

"Yeah, I guess they get the ski bum special. You pay five dollars and your girlfriend goes free," Sunny said. The guy looked at Sunny angrily.

"Hey, that's not fair." Ace smiled.

"Yeah, but that's the game, right Sunny?" Sunny just looked at Ace and said,

"Yep."

The guy left, but his girlfriend stayed and Sunny was on her like a dog on a bone.

It was good to see Sunny back to his old self.

The Day After

SUNNY NOTICED TOM HEADING FOR the bathroom and decided to corner Judy at the bar.

Sunny caught Judy somewhat by surprise, and he had to hurry as he didn't have much time. Sunny really didn't like the sneaking around. He didn't dislike Tom; he really admired Tom, but his feelings for Judy were much stronger.

"Hello, Judy," he said.

Hearing Sunny's voice, she turned quickly.

"Hello, Sunny," she said.

Sunny wanted her to give him a hug and a big kiss, but they both knew they couldn't do that.

"Where have you been? I've been worried about you. Are you okay?" asked Judy.

Sunny knew he couldn't explain what he actually would've liked to. That was out of the question.

"Yeah, I'm fine," Sunny replied.

Judy looked at him for a minute, concerned, and said, "You look drained."

"That's it, I'm not getting a good night sleep," Sunny replied sharply.

That was the last straw, as everybody had noticed.

"You're the fifth person who's said I look bad."

Judy had a somewhat stern look on her face, as she spat,

"Serves you right." Then, she laughed and said, "Does that mean you'll be home tonight? I like the place all to myself."

This actually hit him a little hard, especially that Judy actually liked it when he wasn't home. Sunny tried to make light of it.

"Oh yeah, don't get used to it. Will *you* be home?" Sunny asked.

Judy just smiled, "Maybe."

Sunny had to finish up this conversation quickly.

"Well, maybe I'll see you then," he said. "Here comes Tom. I got to go."

When Sunny got home, Judy was there waiting for him. As Sunny walked through the door to his room, all he saw was her fist coming at his nose. Fortunately, Sunny had taken the night off from drinking. Sunny ducked quickly and caught her fist with his hand. Being part German and part Irish, Sunny had a bad temper when it came to people trying to punch him. Sunny was tired, confused, and didn't need this. Holding Judy's fist, he squeezed so she could feel it and see the fury in his eyes. Sunny looked at her for a moment, and as mad as he was, he was happy to see her as well; it's a good thing he didn't believe in hitting women. He could also see that Judy was not only mad but hurt as well.

"You asshole, do you know how worried I've been?" She said angrily. "You take off for one day to race and you come back a week later!"

Sunny tried to defend himself. "Two days later. I've only been gone two days."

Judy looked at him and snapped, "Two nights and three days!"

Sunny conceded the point. "Okay, who's counting?"

"Me, you asshole. Then to top it all off, the guys get together and feed me some bullshit story about you being at your brother's."

Sunny had to put a stop to this quick. "Hold it, hold it."

Sunny grabbed her and kissed her. They fell onto the bed and made love as they did that first time.

"I'm sorry. I couldn't help it. I get scared when you leave. I'm afraid you won't come back," Judy said with a very concerned look that Sunny hadn't seen before.

Sunny paused for a moment. This was the first time they actually really talked about a real relationship, and it just all came out at once.

"Wait, I've missed you too, but what about no questions? Judy, you've been dating Tom every day, he's in love with you. It's bad enough with you're being here. Even if I could stop being—well, you know—you would have to dump Tom. Even if I wanted you to, you'll never leave him."

Sunny wasn't sure he really wanted to hear her answer.

"How would you know, you've never asked me?" Judy said, and she was right.

The truth was Sunny never really believed that Judy would choose him over Tom, and Sunny really didn't have anything to offer Judy. Sunny didn't have a home, didn't have any money or an education, and he was a ski bum. There really wasn't much of a contest.

Sunny had to confront Judy with what he knew. "I heard Tom asked you to marry him."

"How did you know? Okay, that was a stupid question." Judy said.

Sunny had to ask, "Did you say no?"

Judy didn't want to answer the question. "No, and I didn't say yes either," she said softly.

Sunny just looked at her and knew this was going to change everything. "I see," he said.

Judy looked at Sunny and asked what Sunny was most afraid of: "What are you offering?"

Sunny had to tell her what she didn't want to hear.

"You already have all I can give you right now," Sunny said.

Judy looked at him, "I know, that's what scares me."

Sunny looked at her very seriously; he wanted to tell Judy he loved her, and not to marry Tom. But Sunny realized that he didn't have anything to offer and he couldn't support himself, much less Judy. Most of all, he knew he wasn't done pursuing his dream to be a professional skier and that wasn't what Judy wanted. Meeting Cindy had confused Sunny, but it hadn't confused him about his feelings towards Judy.

"I love you Sunny. I'm not expecting to hear that from you yet. Just don't scare me like that," Judy said.

Sunny looked at her and wanted desperately to tell her how he felt. But he knew that would change everything and it wasn't fair to Judy. "Okay, but no questions."

Sunny held Judy close to him all night and when he awoke, she was gone. This time it was Sunny who was afraid *she* wasn't coming back.

Sunny got up and knew what he needed. There were only a couple of races left that season, and he wanted to be in shape. Sunny called Carl; he needed a good run. They called The Stone Man, and the trainers were waiting. Sunny met Carl at the Center and he was already a ball of nerves, yet what he wanted was to run hard and sweat. Normally they took turns taking the lead in the run. The others would sort of draft off him while he kept the rhythm and broke track from any windblown or fresh snow.

But today, Sunny took off hard and fast, leaving Carl and Stony. Sunny ran about 5K out and up the hill where they had gone the day before Christmas. Sunny sat on the rock wall, sweating and out of breath and proceeded to cry. It was like someone opened the flood gates. Sunny wasn't even sure what he was crying about. He guessed it was just a release from all the frustrations he had built up inside of him. Sunny suddenly felt bad about all the times he had stolen emotions from women under the name of ski bumming. Sunny could see Carl and Stony coming up the trail, so he grabbed a handful of snow and washed his face. Stony got up the hill first. Carl was a minute behind. Carl was standing gasping for air.

"*Fuck* Sunny, are you trying to kill yourself?" Carl asked.

Actually Sunny thought he'd given it a try for a moment; maybe the run was his way of finding something cathartic.

"You're trying to kill us. I didn't know you could even run like that. How long have you been here?" asked Stony.

Sunny, staring off down toward town answered, "A few minutes."

Carl could see Sunny had been crying, and it didn't take Stony too long to recognize it either. Carl never really showed a sensitive side, but at this moment he just looked and said,

"Things are kind of twisted around, eh?"

Stony with some unusual insight said,

"Jesus Sunny, I'm glad to see you're human. Between Judy, Cindy and god knows how many other women, I would have cracked a long time ago. I thought for a while *you may not have* any feelings."

Sunny looked at both of them realizing that he had two really good friends.

"Thanks guys, I'm human, let me assure you. I realize I have been over my head and I fucked up. But I do feel better."

Carl looked to Sunny; he knew he was right. Carl paused for a little self-reflection.

"Yeah, things have been getting to me, too."

"Sunny, you don't realize how people look to us to initiate things. I think we've got to get back to doing things for us, like before," Stony said, being a pretty smart guy.

Sunny sat for a second. He looked at the new Stony, knowing he was exactly right. Sunny wanted nothing more. "We can try, but we can't go back," Sunny said.

"Maybe we can get back to the Center and eat," said Sunny. "I'm starved and I'm starting to chill."

They skied back together, shooting the hills and striding with double poles on the flat terrain. After eating, Sunny felt a 100% better. The conversation on that hill between Sunny, Carl, and Stony had shown him many things. Sunny couldn't help thinking of the pain and the consequences of his actions—and that all the others that came before him had done the same. What was most important was what Sunny would decide to do next. Carl and Sunny took a walk through town to grab some Vermont cider and an apple for dessert.

"Hey Sunny, what you need is some condo time," Carl said.

"Nah, I think I'm going to get home and catch up on some sleep," Sunny said.

Sunny had realized that doing the same old thing would have been the wrong thing to do.

"Yeah, a good night's sleep wouldn't hurt either." Carl was right on board with that decision.

They walked around town going from restaurant to coffee shop discussing the problems of the world over coffee. Sitting in one of the coffee shops, Sunny had made a decision. It was just a matter of implementing a plan at this time. Sunny said,

"You know Carl, we don't get much powder skiing. They say Idaho has good powder skiing."

Carl tried to dismiss the conversation:

"I don't know, I can't imagine skiing getting more challenging than the Star (Stowe's steepest trail) in January."

Sunny looked at Carl with a little smile that worried Carl a little bit.

"*Idaho* Carl, think Idaho."

Sunny knew he had to pull it together and call Cindy. Sunny couldn't explain how much he wanted to be with her. Yet before Sunny met Cindy his life was decadent, but not this crazy.

Sunny called her the next morning. Cindy was at home and glad to hear from him. This was something Sunny just could not understand, when Cindy obviously had her pick of any boy on the mountain. Sunny's claim to fame was being a good ski bum; he always considered himself boring compared to Ronny Biedermann, or even some successful businessmen. Sunny almost started to question Cindy's taste. Nevertheless, it was good to hear her voice and enthusiasm over the phone.

"Hey kid, what's up? How's skiing?" Sunny asked.

"Pretty bad. There are only a few good runs left open," Cindy explained.

"I guess we're lucky here. Most of the mountain here is still good," Sunny said.

Sunny didn't think that Sugarbush was all that bad. He knew what was coming next and it probably wasn't a good idea, but he also knew he probably wasn't going to be able to say no.

"Can I come over and ski with you guys?" Cindy asked.

Sunny's heart was racing. Just the thought that she wanted to be with him left him breathless, even if he knew it was just for skiing.

"Sure, you can stay at the condo...with me," Sunny said.

Sunny went home that night after work; he hadn't seen Judy at work either. When Sunny got to his room, Judy was awake. Sunny was somewhere between really needing to see and talk to Judy, and ready to admit himself for a nervous breakdown.

"Hi Sunny," Judy said softly.

"I didn't mean to wake you," Sunny said.

"That's okay," Judy replied.

"Sunny, I'm going to visit a friend in Boston for a few days."

Sunny looked at Judy for a moment. "Judy, is there something wrong? Something with you and Tom?"

"No, no, nothing. I just want to get out of town."

Sunny just looked at her, really concerned that there must been something going on; but it was clear that she didn't want to talk about it.

"If you need me for anything, I'll be around," Sunny said.

In the morning after Sunny and Judy got up, they had breakfast together. Sunny told her to drive carefully and watched her drive off. Sunny usually would have questioned her leaving for Boston just like that, though he remembered their agreement; no questions. And so he left it at that. Sunny met Carl and the whole gang at the Center for a tour as a group. Cindy and several other girls were there as well. It was a nice day of skiing, eating Vermont cheese, and drinking a little wine.

It was Sunday, so the party moved to the condo for one of Sunny's gourmet specials. That night Sunny made filet of sole, sautéed in wine and lemon butter, fresh vegetables, and served wine. Sunny had managed to stay away from drinking. Soon Cindy and Sunny went for the master bedroom. Cindy went in first, and Sunny closed the door after him. Sunny started to say,

"Cindy, I..." Before he could get another word out, Cindy looked at him and said,

"Shhh...,Don't say a word." She kissed Sunny, and before he knew it, she slid her hand up his legs and undid his jeans. They proceeded to make love for hours; it was like an addiction for him. Sunny just couldn't get enough. The passion was as thick as honey.

They made passionate love until they collapsed in steaming sweat, then lay there and talked for a few moments and started again. Sunny just could not seem to get enough of her. From moment to moment, Sunny wanted to tell her he loved her, but the best he could tell her was he loved being with her—and that was not the same. Cindy didn't tell him she loved him and Sunny did want to hear *her* say it. More so, Sunny wanted her to *mean it*. Finally before dawn, they both fell asleep. In the morning, the Ski Bum Alarm woke them up. Cindy jumped up to say,

"Holy shit, what the hell is that?"

Sunny had his non-reacting face on and looked at Cindy.

"Oh that? That's Ace's rendition of an alarm clock."

Cindy laughed a little and said, "What happened to the radio alarm clock you can turn off?"

Sunny just jumped up and looked at her and said, "I'll explain later. Listen, we better use the master bathroom. I don't think you're ready for the other one yet."

They took a shower and made love, and even though he hadn't gotten much sleep he felt great. As Cindy went for coffee and cornflakes, there was some poor girl in shock over Ace in the shower with Stony.

Over breakfast, Cindy looked at Ace and asked,

"What's that all about?"

Sunny laughed and said yet again, "I'll explain later."

As they all got in the car, Cindy asked,

"Are you just going to leave those girls?"

Carl in his usual tactless way, commented,

"Let me think... yes."

Ace tried to soften the explanation some by saying,

"They'll be okay; Alice will take care of them."

Cindy made an observation they weren't particularly proud of.

"You guys are a little hard on girls," Cindy said.

Nobody said a word, and then Carl broke the silence with his straightforward thinking by saying,

"There's a price to pay."

Sunny knew exactly what Carl was referring to. Skiing was good, all of them knew the season was coming to an end. So they had to savor every ski moment together as they could.

That night Sunny had to work so Cindy was on her own. Sunny wasn't jealous, but he didn't like seeing a horde of guys constantly around her. Sunny and Cindy grabbed the master bedroom for an abridged version of the night before.

Cindy and Sunny, having been seen in public together, were now starting to pose some problems. Besides having Judy find out, also remember one of the golden rules of being a ski bum was: *Thou shalt not have a steady girlfriend.* Right then, Sunny wasn't real sure he still wanted to be a member of that Royal Order. But people had developed this portrait of how Sunny should be, and he was *now* subject to their opinions and ideas of what he was doing. The people's opinion, which made Sunny King of the Ski Bums, didn't matter anymore; so where did he fit in? Sunny didn't think he could say *no* to Cindy. The more Sunny got, the more he wanted.

The Last Ski Bum Race

It. was the day of the Last Ski Bum race. Carl and Sunny made a point of being prepped. Everyone showed up for this race; it was a clear, warm day. Carl and Sunny both drew early starting numbers. As usual, they all inspected the course together.

Cindy was the cheerleader. Sunny had to go before Carl. Carl gave Sunny a quick rub down and Sunny climbed into the start; 3, 2, 1, Go! Sunny blasted off in a fury. When Sunny got to the second gate, he hit a. hole that threw him back on his skis. Sunny didn't fall, he just lunged his body forward and moved down to the next gate.

Sunny skied the rest of the course like a wild man with nothing to lose. As he crossed the finish line, he heard the announcement: "Ladies and gentleman, skiing for The Baggy Knees, in spite of his near fall the fastest time of the day, Sunny Warner."

Sunny hustled over to the finish shack, grabbed the headset to the start and got them to put Carl on.

"Carl, watch for the pothole in the second gate. Keep a high line and go over it. The rest is cake," Sunny said.

It was important to Sunny to end the season as it started—with Sunny and Carl together, working as a team.

"Good run, Sunny. Way to kick ass," Carl said. Sunny just ignored him.

"Get the rhythm, Carl. You can do it," Sunny replied.

The announcer suddenly said, "Skiing for Mountain Road Enterprises is Carl Massaro; 3, 2, 1, Go!"

Then Carl skied as Sunny held his breath. He took the second gate just right and finished with a great run; no flaws. Carl skied over and they waited for the time to be announced.

"Time: 36.432–for the fastest time of the day, inching out Sunny Warner by two one-thousandths--Carl Massaro."

Sunny jumped straight up and down and hugged Carl. Afterwards, Cindy pulled him aside.

"Sunny, you didn't win?" Cindy asked. Sunny looked at her with a big smile.

"I don't always, and besides, *this is almost as good*, as Carl won."

Cindy looked a little confused, "But you could have, if you hadn't helped him," she said.

Sunny smiled as Cindy was about to learn a valuable lesson and something important about him. Sunny loved to ski race; and if you get to ski race *you ski to win*. Sunny always skied competitively and wanted to make everybody else didn't beat him. But, if he couldn't win, then he wanted his friend Carl to be the guy who won the race.

"Cindy, winning is great. But helping out a friend so he can ski the best he can , is just as important." Sunny explained, "If I can't win, I want Carl to win."

Cindy got it. "You guys are great," she said.

You can take the kid out of Jersey, but you can't take Jersey out of the kid. Sunny smiled said, "No, just good friends, but thanks."

That day had been special. Not only did Carl and Sunny ski well, but Stony, Ace, and Roger all turned in their best finishes. The next stop was The Horn. Since it was the last race, everybody was up for a farewell party. It took time to publish the results, so everyone convened at The Horn to wait and say goodbye to the season and to friends who were not going to return the next year.

The Horn was the perfect place to be, and everyone could dance and drink in ski boots or anything they wanted. Mike provided the music with just one or two turntables and four well-placed large speakers.

Mike and his disc jockeys had been doing this for a couple of years, and The Nards would have to rotate disc jockeys—because most afternoons, each disc jockey would start partying with the crowd and end up drunk, stand on the furniture, and sing along with his or her favorite song. The Nards had purposely come back up for the party.

Bruce Springsteen had released the song "Rosalita" that year in 1973 as a part of the 'Wild, the Innocent and The Street Shuffle' album. This quickly became the anthem of the Matterhorn. Nards had programmed the crowd to stop everything and dance when "Rosalita" began. To dance with anyone or everyone near you, it didn't matter; just start to move your feet.

Most of the regulars knew all the words, so when Nards' anthem sounded, it was total boogie. It didn't take long for everyone to get into partying, drinking a pitcher of beer, and dancing up a full sweat while trying to pick up some girl; it was the perfect way to end the season's ski bum races. Ninety percent of the teams had persisted in showing up and racing in rain, snow, freezing cold or occasional sunshine for the chance to take the season's overall championship.

Later that night, there would be a ski bum banquet, where the awardees would be honored. However, everyone was waiting for the day's result sheets, which would disclose not only the day's finishes, but the overall team winner as well as the day's team winner. The results came in perfect timing, by immediately following "Rosalita." Gar stood up by the microphone to announce the top ten finishes for the day.

They all knew Carl won and Sunny was second, but they yelled louder than ever when Gar announced Carl's name and Sunny's.

"And todays number one team, and by the way, *overall season's champions...*"

Sunny was standing in anticipation with his team, as well as Cindy, John and the gang.

Gar announced, "The Baggy Knees."

John and Sunny jumped up and hugged each other and John yelled in Sunny's ear, "We did it, you son of a bitch!"

They jumped and screamed and fell on the floor and poured pitchers of beer on each other's head. John turned to Sunny to say,

"Sunny, I knew it when I talked you into skiing for me. Thanks."

Sunny didn't say a word; he just gave him a big hug.

Gar spoke up and continued the announcement.

"Ladies and ski bums, everyone who has partaken in the ski bum races this season, please sign your name to the list up here by Nards for the Cow Shit Cotillion. And remember, it is black tie and by invitation only. Please get on the list so we can get you your invitation."

Sunny had already explained the Cow Shit Cotillion to the guys, but it was completely new to Cindy. Cindy just looked at Sunny. From her social status, she may have known what a cotillion was, but he doubted they were referred to as Cow Shit.

"Hey Sunny, what is the Cow Shit Cotillion?" Cindy asked.

"This may be a little difficult to explain; it's just what Gar said, a formal," explained Sunny.

Cindy laughed. "No way, you guys."

Sunny didn't quite know what to make of this. He didn't know whether she thought this was beneath her, or she thought it was going to be cool. So Sunny looked at her and said,

"Okay, if you don't believe me, don't get a gown."

Cindy looked like a deer in the headlights and said,

"Wait, are you asking me?" Sunny hadn't realized what he had done, but he was stuck then as he replied,

"Since you can't ask me... Yes Cindy, I'd be greatly honored if you would join me as my date and the honored guest for this year's Cow Shit Cotillion."

Cindy had a big smile on her face and said most politely, "I'd be delighted. When do we attend such an auspicious occasion?"

"In one week's time, my lady," Sunny explained.

Cindy broke the formality with,

"Holy shit, you expect me to come up with a formal gown in less than a week?"

Sunny laughed and said, "I would have asked you sooner, but I didn't know you."

Cindy turned to Ace for a reality check.

"Is this for real? Ace, don't bullshit me."

Ace with his usual logic replied,

"Let me rephrase that. It is as real as a night at the condo."

Stony overheard the conversation, laughed, and looked at Ace and said,

"That's two strikes."

Alice, who was standing next to Stony, looked at Cindy to bail her out some:

"Cindy, it's for real, they have it every year."

Cindy, looking at the group replied,

"You realize I have to go home to get something to wear. I can't wait to see my mother's face when I tell her you're bringing me to a cotillion."

Sunny just looked at Cindy, not really realizing what he had done but he said,

"Good idea, we'll leave it at that."

Then Cindy put the image of everybody being together, dressed up in formal wear, having dates and confronted everybody with this thought:

"Wait a minute, that means you and the guys are going to get dressed up in tuxedos and bring dates."

Carl with his eloquent summation:

"Yup, equipped with table manners and flowers, if you're lucky."

Sunny with his follow up: "Well, don't press your luck."

"I won't recognize you. I've never seen you guys in anything but ski pants and jeans," said Roger.

Sunny laughed. "I think that's the point of this whole thing, Roger."

"Wait, you've seen us in the shower too!" Roger said.

"Oh, this is great. Thank you, Sunny," said Cindy after taking a sip of beer.

Sunny knew it was going to be great; he also knew it was going to be the final hurrah, which was kind of sad. They partied and stayed just sober enough to attend the awards ceremony. Sunny got a chance to sneak out to go home to take a shower and get some clean clothes; he knew Judy would be there. Sunny also knew Tom had asked Judy to the cotillion and she had accepted. As Sunny got in, Judy met him at the door.

"You did it. I'm so proud of you. I knew you could do it," said Judy

"It's been a good day. I'm a little drunk, but you should see Carl and the guys," Sunny said

Judy continued, "I was at the race. Carl did great."

"I do wish we could be seen in public," replied Sunny. Judy had seen Sunny and Cindy together.

"It didn't look like it," Judy said.

"If we could, I would," said Sunny.

"You're going to the awards banquet?" Judy asked.

"Yeah, you're going?"

"Yeah, with Tom."

Sunny knew the answer to these questions, but it was time that they both talked about them and got it out the open.

"And the cotillion?" asked Sunny.

"You know," Judy replied.

Sunny just looked at her and said,

"Yeah, I hoped we could go public by then, but I guess it's not in the cards."

Judy looked at Sunny and came over to give him a hug and said,

"Sunny, listen. I don't know what's in the cards. I just know I can't celebrate with all of you tonight, so I want you to know I'm proud of you."

Sunny went to the shower and Judy joined him.

He was somewhat surprised and asked,

"What are you doing in here?"

Judy with her beautiful smile said,

"I thought we'd have a little party before THE party." They made love until the hot water ran out. Then the cold water sobered Sunny up and they had to go to meet their dates. As they were leaving, Sunny stopped.

"Judy, you'll look beautiful in a formal. Save me the last dance, will ya?" Sunny asked.

Judy knew she probably wouldn't, but she smiled and said, "You bet."

And they left for the awards banquet. They went to The Rusty Nail where the Ski Bum Awards banquet was to be held. It was actually pretty boring. Gar was a great promoter, but somehow a traditional awards banquet didn't fit the ski bum races. After all, this was about ski bumming, not the racing. As Sunny sat there, he had the feeling he was at the end of the year's swim team banquet he went to when he was just a kid. In spite of all of this, Gar flattered Sunny and his merry band of bums.

"This year's overall winner and King of the Ski Bum Races: Sunny," announced Gar as Sunny arrived at the head of the table to accept the award in the midst of applause and whistles.

Gar continued, "This has been my pleasure for several reasons. In past years, we all left our jobs; took time off to go to the mountain and race two runs. It seems each year we became bigger and busier, and work dominated our time. We think of Sunny as one of our own, because he has been here with us for so long. But Sunny is from New Jersey and along with Carl, also from New Jersey, and Ace as he is better known, Roger, Stony to us, from New Hampshire." They all looked up as their names were mentioned. "Sunny along with his friends have shown us what we came to this town for—skiing. On any given day this past season, you could go up to the mountain, and if you could keep up, you could ski your legs into the ground with these guys. So Sunny, for winning, I say *congratulations for being here* to provide us with an example of what Stowe and the mountain represents. I say thank you, thank you to all of you."

Sunny had been standing next to Gar feeling embarrassed and was then expected to speak.

Sunny started: "God Gar, thank YOU. I just did what I thought everyone on the mountain did. When I stood up there on the mountain and looked out, I felt all the troubles and problems were down below somewhere. When I felt the freedom and challenge of the mountain, all I could think of was, *this is life*, the best of it. The only time it got better was when I looked over at my friends and could share these feelings. And you know, this is what life should be—and anything else is just waiting. Without my crew of friends, this whole experience wouldn't be… as for the *decadence*, it was just our way of saying that things aren't so important. Only people are. And that's YOU. So, thank you for letting me share this with you."

The banquet crowd exploded with cheers and hollers. Sunny chugged part of a beer and poured the rest over his head. Standing on a chair, he said: "Hold it, one more thing. As long as there's skiing, there will be dreams. Here's to the dreams and people to ski and share them with."

There was a moment of silence as Sunny chugged another beer and placed the mug on the table upside down. Everyone did the same.

They partied into the night; they drank and danced, hugged and kissed. The band at The Knees was the same one that played when Cindy and Sunny were at dinner.

At one point, Cindy turned to Sunny and said, "I'm really glad I could share this with you and the guys."

Sunny was a little drunk then. He looked at Cindy and said,

"Thank you, too."

"Really! I didn't know how much you wanted me."

Sunny looked at Cindy and took a deep breath and said,

"To be honest, this whole experience wouldn't be the same without you. If I'm the King, you're the Queen. And I do want you, I just know I can't have you."

This really took Cindy by surprise. He didn't think anybody ever had told Cindy they didn't want her.

"You have me now," she said.

Sunny smiled as he looked at the Queen.

"Yeah, for now. I won't always be king and things won't always be like this. You'll always be the queen, even if it's not of the ski bums. It will be of the women's auxiliary or some other thing, and I will always be just Sunny." Cindy just looked at him, a little surprised at his perspective. She knew his insight was a little more on target than she would like to admit.

"But I like this Sunny," Cindy said.

"Let's hope so, we'll see. Come on, let's go upstairs," Sunny replied, taking her by the hand.

As Sunny got to the stop of the stairs, he saw Maureen, his old friend from the Matterhorn.

It was great to see Maureen, and he didn't forget that none of this would have happened if it wasn't for her.

"Hello Maureen!" Sunny said.

"Congratulations, Sunny." Maureen said with a very poised smile.

"For what? If it weren't for you," Sunny reminded her, "none of this would be. I wanted to tell them, but who would believe us?" Maureen smiled as she remembered.

"It's not important, what's important is you," Maureen said.

Sunny gave her a hug.

"I knew someday you would be the one to lead the town," declared Maureen.

"No, I'm just following where you and Richard and all the others were before me. Thanks," Sunny answered.

Maureen looked at Sunny. She was in a little bit of a hurry and said,

"I've got to go. I've a date waiting. I love you Sunny, keep well."

"Love you too Maureen, see ya."

Maureen walked out, and all Sunny could think of was how she and Richard had believed in him and what that meant to him. Sunny didn't know it then, but that was the last he ever saw of Maureen, as she stood in front of him with her short black hair and even shorter dress, without underwear. Sunny would never forget her.

Cindy and Sunny wound up at the condo, and in the morning, Cindy took off for shopping in Boston. Sunny and the gang headed for the mountain. Things were quiet on the ride up the gondola, just the five of them sitting there.

Sunny knew that the guys were hung over, but that never kept them from a blow by blow description of the evening's events before.

"What's up?" Sunny asked.

Ace spoke up first, "Well we didn't want to say anything before, but Roger got an acceptance letter to medical school."

"You're kidding! Roger, I didn't know. That's great," said Sunny.

"We'll still have you on weekends, won't we?" asked Carl.

Roger laughed. "I'm afraid not, I'll be pretty busy."

Sunny realized that this was when the Hole in the Wall Gang was going separate ways, one by one. It was happening.

Stony with his usual wisdom said,

"There's only one thing left to do.....party. How's tomorrow night, the condo?"

"Great!"

Ace may have been partied out at the condo by this time, He said, "How about if we keep it small?"

Everybody agreed.

Skiing was good. They all stuck close together and wound up over at Big Spruce, as that was where the best snow was left. On the chairlift up, Carl turned to Sunny.

"Hey Sunny, you wouldn't go off to school without me?"

Sunny looked at Carl with a surprised look, "I wouldn't go off to school, period!"

Carl just laughed with relief as they got off the lift. "Come on," directed Carl.

"And you?" Sunny questioned.

"I'm not going anywhere. I like Stowe."

"Yeah, Stowe's great. Aren't you afraid things will change? No matter where we are, someday, we will have jobs and bills will have to come first. And then what, marriage?"

Carl looked at Sunny as if he was crazy, "What about it?"

"Someday you'll get married and she'll come first," Sunny said.

"Why can't things stay the same?" Carl probed further.

Sunny just looked out across the mountain and replied,

"They never do. Come on, let's run Stony into the woods."

They unloaded and proceeded to do just what they had set out to do—a game of tag, or a sort of roller derby on skis. Everyone knew in the back of his mind that this might be their last run.

Sunny went directly home after skiing and Judy was there. She looked serious.

"Sunny, I want to talk."

"Shoot," declared Sunny.

"What's going to happen with us?" asked Judy.

Sunny looked at Judy, took a deep breath and said,

"Jesus, what a tough day this has been. First Roger gets accepted to med school, Carl is afraid I'll run off and *now you*."

"Well, are you going to run off?"

This was the pivotal question as to whether Judy would want to be with a ski bum, somebody without an education, who wanted to be a professional skier; or somebody who had a house, a car, and a job. Judy and Sunny both knew that this question was unavoidable:

"Do you want me to stay?" asked Sunny.

"I don't know," Judy said.

You could see that Judy was really wrestling with this decision. Feelings and love weren't enough; Judy deserved stability. Sunny was a man and he wished he could be more, but he wasn't. He just didn't see himself as more at the time. Maybe it was all those years of growing up and seeing himself, *and of being told*, that he was less. But the reality was that he was who he was.

"Okay, what's going on?" Sunny continued to push for an answer.

"Tom asked me to marry him." Sunny wasn't surprised by this, and he knew he didn't want to lose her.

"And you said...?" asked Sunny

"*Let me think about it,*" Judy said.

She wanted Sunny to come out and say, "Will you marry me?" He knew he couldn't, and that it wasn't fair. Sunny knew he couldn't be there for her—not only as the lover, but as her friend which was important, if not *more important.*

"That's going to be tough; he'll have to get his own bed."

The tension was broken and Judy laughed.

"You asshole."

Sunny looked at her, held her hand, and quietly explained, "This has been a strange year for us. We never wanted this, but yet... we're into it up to our eyeballs."

"Speak for yourself," Judy said. "I got what I wanted, but now I can't have it. Sunny listen, I love you, but I can't have you. You're not going to change. Tom wants me."

Without any emotion, Sunny looked at her and, stated clearly,

"I want you."

Judy called his bluff. "And go public? It's time to put this on the table."

"That's not the issue. You want security; you've flung your fling. I want you, but I still want to see how far I can go as a professional skier."

Judy looked at Sunny and thought for a second.

"If I stopped you... you would resent me. You'll get your dreams too, Sunny.

Unfortunately, I'm not one of them," Judy said with a quiet, sad voice.

Sunny paused and looked at Judy for a moment. He didn't like giving up or giving in.

"I wouldn't be so sure; it's just too soon to tell. Do you love Tom?"

Sunny didn't really want to know the answer to this, but he needed to know when the new Judy would be honest. Judy answered,

"Well, kinda."

"Kinda!" Sunny replied.

"He's good to me, he's there, and he's in love with me," Judy went on to explain.

"But do you love him?" Sunny asked again.

"Well…" Judy replied.

Sunny looked at Judy with a very serious look,

"I can't tell you what to do, but I do want you. You are the only one who loves me for who I am. You believe in me. Let me see where my dreams lead me to," said Sunny.

"And *my* dreams?" This time it was Judy's turn to talk about her dreams.

Sunny looked at Judy, brushed her hair back, and gave her a kiss.

"Hang in there and don't ever give up your dreams."

Judy and Sunny stayed in the whole night making love and talking about her dreams. She showed Sunny the dress she was going to wear to the cotillion and modeled for him. She was beautiful. It was a deep red gown with ivory lace that accentuated her red hair. It was modestly low cut, showing a pearl necklace and earrings.

"Wow, you're beautiful," observed Sunny.

"Don't act so surprised," sneered Judy.

"I'm not surprised, just envious!" Sunny quickly countered.

"Of what?" Judy questioned.

"Tom. He'll have the prettiest girl in town."

What Judy came out with surprised Sunny and hit him hard. "No, you have the prettiest girl in town," Judy commented angrily. Caught by surprise Sunny wasn't sure he agreed.

"I do?"

"Yeah, if you want her." Sunny smiled with a sigh of relief.

They made love again and fell asleep in each other's arms. In the morning, they went out for breakfast.

"I'm going to Boston for a few days," Judy informed him.

"With Tom?" Sunny felt compelled to ask. This was the first time he broke the rule and asked a question.

Judy knew she didn't have to answer, but replied reassuringly,

"Yeah, but don't worry, you're still number one. Besides, we're staying on a friend's couch."

"Sure, be careful and remember your dreams," said Sunny.

Judy left, and Sunny went into town to get some things done and meet Carl as well.

"Hey Carl, do you ever think of getting married?" Sunny asked him. Sunny really took Carl by surprise with this question.

"You didn't just say that," Carl replied a little stunned.

Sunny answered quickly, "No, come on..."

"Yeah, I think about it. I even think Alice would be a nice girl to marry. But there is one thing," Carl continued. "She's not Italian," Carl said frankly.

"No, she is a Wasp, and so am I," Sunny said with disdain.

"Yeah, but I'm not marrying you. I've always wanted to marry a nice Italian girl," Carl stated.

"Good, Carl. I'm sure Alice will be thrilled to hear she's not acceptable because she isn't Italian."

Carl looked at Sunny and remarked, "Yeah, she wasn't thrilled."

Sunny was stunned, "What...?!"

Carl looked at Sunny and said, "Yeah, I told her last night."

"What happened?"

"She hit me! She was kind of taken aback."

"Really! I'm surprised...surprised she didn't run you over with her car!" Sunny laughed.

"Almost...she grabbed her things and went back to her place. When I went out to talk to her, she almost ran me over on the way," Carl finished.

Sunny just shook his head and said, "Good job. Well, Judy took off for Boston with Tom."

Carl returned the compliment, "Good job, Sunny."

Sunny looked up and grinned,

"At least she didn't hit me or try to run me down. Come on, let's get some food for tonight."

While they walked through town, they continued their discussion.

"Sunny, do you think we'll ever get married?" asked Carl.

"I don't know, you haven't asked me, besides I'm not Italian!" Sunny came back.

They went to the butcher shop and spent their last dollars on some steaks. They arrived at the condo around five in the afternoon.

"Hey, anybody home?" Sunny called when he walked through the door.

There was no one home, but they went in anyway. They went to the kitchen and sitting on the counter was a letter from Stanford addressed to A. Carlyle Frank, and Carl read it.

Sunny had to ask, "Carl what's it say?"

"It says that Ace is accepted for an M.B.A program at Stanford, starting this coming September."

"Jesus, Ace must be smarter than we thought. That's a great school."

Sunny said, "What's an MBA?"

"A master's in business administration, a business degree. We're losing the gang," Carl said.

"Yeah."

Ace walked in.

"Hey guys, you should try the Jacuzzi."

Ace looked at them and saw Carl holding the letter.

"Oh. You found the letter," Ace said.

Carl was now feeling a little guilty that he had read Ace's mail, which wasn't exactly hidden.

"Well, I wanted to tell you before, but I didn't want to take anything away from Roger's acceptance letter," Ace replied.

"I think it's great. You're going to do it?" Sunny asked.

"My parents are psyched. Probably," Ace replied.

"We're going to miss you," Carl said quickly.

Ace looked at Carl and Sunny and said,

"Don't start getting soft on me, Massaro. Let's cook those steaks. Stony is right behind me, and you know how mean he is when he hasn't eaten."

Sunny asked, "How about Roger? Is he coming?"

Ace replied, "Probably. He's at home saying goodbye to his little honey."

"No, he meant, is he going to join us for dinner?" Carl clarified.

"Yeah, that too," said Ace.

Just then Stony came lumbering through the door, singing one of his English drinking songs in his deep voice. And in this deep voice, he said,

"Food, I smell food."

Carl spoke up, "Quick, throw him some granola or something before he eats one of his wool socks."

It was great to just have the guys together like it was in the beginning of the season. It was a time to just reflect and get back to basics, maybe for the last time.

"No little lady tonight?" Sunny asked.

"Later. I knew you were buying dinner and I didn't want to give anybody my share."

Sunny walked over to Stony, put his arm around him and said,

"Ah, a true romantic."

Just then, Roger popped through the door.

"What smells so great? Did I miss dinner? I'm starved," Roger declared.

"No, it's still cooking," Carl replied.

Sunny looked over and said,

"In that case, you better let me into the kitchen, Carl. If you fuck up dinner you'll be lynched. Those guys mean business."

"That was quick, Roger!" Ace stated.

"I'll see her for the Cow Shit Cotillion. Besides, I didn't want to miss dinner."

Sunny looked at Roger and said, "I hope you're not going to be an obstetrician!"

Stony observed, "You guys, do you realize we all got the night off?"

They stood around and drank some wine while Sunny finished cooking dinner. Sunny was in the kitchen flipping the steaks when Ace walked in.

"Sorry I didn't tell you guys about the grad school before. The truth is, I didn't know whether I was going or not."

Sunny just smiled to let him know that whatever he decided was okay.

"Hey Ace, no problem, let's eat."

They sat down for dinner. As always, they ate family style. That night's menu was all American with New York Top, mashed potatoes and gravy, broccoli, and Brussels sprouts. For dessert, they warmed up apple pie a la mode. No one talked much; they were all pretty hungry. Roger proposed a toast.

"Here's to skiing and our accomplishments..." They all drank.

"Here's to women, may there be plenty of them..." They all drank some more.

It was Ace's turn; he raised a glass and said,

"Here's to the King..."

Again, they all drank.

Then, Carl raised his glass and said,

"Here's to Stowe, it'll always be better skiing than New Jersey..." They all drank once again.

Sunny thought for a second. He appreciated everybody's sentiments, but with his lack of eloquence, he said,

"No, shit, give me a break. I'm no king; I'm just me, Sunny. I'm just the same as when we met. The real thing is the mountain and that is what counts. You all made the season. To all of you, thanks." Sunny continued, "Oh, and here's to Ace's acceptance to Stanford's grad school."

Everyone spoke at once, congratulating Ace.

Sunny put a motion on the table. "Why don't we all retire to coffee and pie on the couch?"

They sat around asking Roger about what to expect. Carl was particularly curious as to Ace's MBA program.

Roger asked, "Hey Stony, shouldn't you be almost through with your Master's by now?"

Stony replied, "I think I'll be ready in about three weeks. I just have to get to UVM for about a week and I'll be ready."

"That leaves Sunny and Carl. What are you guys going to be doing after the season?"

Carl thought for a second and said,

"I think I'm going to stay, I like Stowe. I think I can do some building and be real happy."

Stony asked Carl, "What about Alice?"

Carl said, "Well, I don't know. I told her I wouldn't marry a girl who wasn't Italian. I just hope she cools down in time for the cotillion."

Ace asked Stony, "Stony, I've seen you hanging around with Sue. You've been doing come cross country skiing with her lately?"

Stony laughed.

"No, but she is going to come to Burlington while I'm finishing up my thesis."

Ace, always the observant one, asked, "Sunny, you're awfully quiet, are you okay?"

177

Sunny looked at everyone and said,

"Not much to tell."

The truth was that Sunny didn't know what he was going to do. He realized that he was with a group of really smart guys, and they had some really good plans for the future and Sunny did not. All he knew was he had finished one hell of a season, he was skiing really well, and if he was going to fulfill his dreams of being a professional skier, it would have to be then. There wasn't really a college for that.

Ace looked at Sunny and said, "Come on, you still have Judy at home and Cindy on the way up. Which one gets the pick?"

Sunny wasn't thinking about picking women. His priorities were still the same; it was all about the mountain that was all about skiing. Skiing was what allowed Sunny to move forward and build a dream and he didn't want to stop then.

Sunny looked at Ace and said, "You got me on that one. Judy's with Tom in Boston and Cindy... well?"

Carl spoke up and asked a difficult question,

"Do you guys think this was the Last Supper?"

"I hope not, I'll starve," said Roger. Always thought-provoking Stony spoke up,

"It could be."

Carl showed some unusual sentiment.

"What about seeing you guys again?"

Sunny looked at the group, took a drink of his beer and said,

"I don't think we'll ever fade. Don't worry, Carl."

They reminisced about the season all night and got really drunk! Nobody said goodbye, but they knew that was the last condo gathering. To avoid the pain of goodbyes, they all vowed to meet the next year for Christmas and ski together. They even sang along to "Listen to the Music", "Sympathy for the Devil", and yes, "Rosalita." Most of them were drunk and fell asleep into the early morning hours. Sunny couldn't get much sleep. He just kept on thinking about the things they had all done and how close they had all become in such a short time. As Sunny stood by the glass door, he could see the mountain in the full moon with the large, dark spots where the snow had melted. Sunny thought of Judy and what fun they had. Judy was the only girl who accepted him unconditionally for himself. He knew he loved her for that, but he just was not ready to commit to anyone.

There was still Cindy, who was so beautiful and independent; she made Sunny catch his breath every time they kissed. On the other hand, the entire gang saw Sunny when he was up and when he was down, even when Judy was there. Sunny couldn't imagine not having her be there. There were also all the other women and his ski racing. Some Pro racers were in town, and the next year Sunny could do okay at it if he stayed and trained hard.

Sunny didn't have any answers. All he knew was that all season he had gotten more than he could ever have hoped for. And then, just like the snow melting, he felt it was all slipping away. There was nothing he could do about it. Sunny had to pick a direction and make some fast choices, or he could be left with nothing. Sunny looked around the room as everyone slept on the floor and the couches. Sunny looked at each one and he uttered softly: "Thanks Roger, Stony, Ace, for a great season. Good luck, guys. I know you'll all be great—and for you, Carl, you always got me." Sunny went into the master bedroom and finally fell asleep.

Feeling Uneasy

SUNNY WOKE UP SUDDENLY THE next morning and looked at the alarm clock. A bad feeling came over him. For the first time, the sound of the Ski Bum Alarm had not awoken him. Sunny jumped up and sat on the side of the bed. He knew what that feeling was. The season's skiing was over, at least for them as a group. Sunny went to the kitchen where Roger was making coffee.

"Mornin' Sunny. We thought we'd let you sleep in," said Roger.

Sunny was still half asleep and a little stunned by the realization that the season had ended.

"Thanks, I didn't get to bed right away."

Roger could see that Sunny was struggling with some stuff and said, "Oh?"

"I was just thinking. Where's Ace, Stony, Carl?"

"They went for a run," Roger replied.

"Hung over? Wait a minute, we don't run. Or we haven't in a while."

"We do now; we all thought we'd get in shape," Roger explained.

Sunny looked at Roger.

"I guess we'll always be on the same track forward. Yeah, if I'm going to race I'll need to be in better shape."

Once the guys arrived back home, they all rode together into Burlington to get their tuxedos for the Cow Shit Cotillion.

They spent the day looking through stores and the university. Stony, being familiar with the university, was their guide. It was great to spend the day outside of Stowe with everyone. That was the first time they had gone anywhere together besides Sugarbush. Walking around the streets of Burlington was really different. It was the real world opposed to Stowe, which was New England's version of a decadent Disneyland. Things seemed more real in this town.

As Sunny and the group walked and talked, the prospect of research, careers, and buying real estate, things like that, seemed more exciting and tangible than anything Stowe had to offer. Watching Ace, Stony, and Roger made Sunny envious of their education. They seemed far more equipped to deal with the real world. Fortunately, Sunny wasn't looking for anything tangible or even meaningful; or was he?

As they drove back to Stowe, Sunny couldn't help but feel a little uneasy. Sunny knew that for all purposes, the season was over and that was hard enough to adjust to. To add to Sunny's unrest, it was evident that they were driving back to say goodbye. He knew that his relationship with each member of the group was much more than just a winter season of good times; they had all become very close in many ways. First Ace: Ace and Sunny had come from opposite ends of personality to thoroughly accepting and understanding each other for what they were, no pretenses. They trusted and cared for each other, and thus were able to learn about each other's world. From the beginning, Sunny thought he was coaching Ace through his rookie year. He could now clearly see he was the one to learn from Ace far more than he could have ever given him.

Roger was a lot like Ace. However, he was always the constant reminder that ski bumming was a transition. Even though it was their life style at the moment, they all knew it wouldn't always be the case. Roger's looseness and decadence came from his knowledge that there was a time and a place for everything, and this was their time for Stowe.

Stony represented intelligence integrated with powerful solidity and an appreciation for nature. Seeing Stony's snowy beard and his huge strength, gracefully gliding across the Vermont scenery was a constant reminder of a healthy involvement with the basics of nature. The Stone Man gladly drew Sunny from the decadence into his world of health, aesthetic appreciation, and genuine caring.

Carl and Sunny had grown even closer throughout the year. For many, the integration of new friends could cause problems in a close relationship.

Carl and Sunny only drew closer with the security and knowledge that their relationship of being best friends would endure. That didn't mean that Sunny liked or approved of everything Carl did, but for whatever reason Sunny would always be there as his friend and vice versa. Carl and Sunny sat and dreamt about the future. They dreamt about building houses, having a family, or skiing other areas. Not once did either of them not include the other.

Sunny was overwhelmed by the feeling of how fortunate he was to have had the time to develop the closeness with the others as they drove into town. The other thing that was bothering Sunny was this; as much as the real world was harsh and ever changing, Stowe was the fast lane, fleeting to the tenth power. As Sunny and the group would return soon, their accessibility to one another would fade and that year would become nothing but a memory.

All Sunny had left were John and Richard, who provided him with food, shelter and many moments of sincere, fatherly advice. However, both John and Richard would see ski bums come and go as all time goes on. Sunny knew they would never forget him, and that he would not soon forget them.

Now what about Judy and Cindy? Sunny loved them both, but in greatly different ways. Judy was the only woman in his life who truly knew him and accepted him for exactly who he was. She was beautiful, kind, and always there somehow. She always seemed secure and sure of what she wanted. The truth was Sunny wasn't sure he was in the driver's seat with her. Sunny didn't feel he could handle committing himself to a full-time, monogamous relationship. He also couldn't see being without her, and he didn't want to lose her.

Cindy was just the opposite. The only things Cindy was sure of were that she was beautiful, wealthy, and she wanted all of life's fruits. Her long hair and carefree smile could lure the most sedentary person to thrust himself into any adventure, just to be near her. Sunny did want her, but he knew he could not keep up.

As the group got back, Sunny hopped out and walked through town up to his house which he had to himself for the night. Sunny spent a long time sitting on the bed, staring out of the window. As Sunny sat, he knew he had to make some big decisions. Actually all Sunny could think of was, if life could be this exciting in Stowe, how adventurous and exciting could it be in other towns? Sunny had been able to conquer Stowe, but what about Aspen, Vail, Sun Valley? Sunny knew he was not done. He just didn't know what would come next. One thing Sunny was sure of; he wanted to race.

Figuring Out What's Next

THE NEXT DAY SUNNY WOKE up early. The first thing he did was to look out of the window at the mountain. The snow was fading fast. The next night was the Cow Shit Cotillion, and most everyone was taking the day off to prepare. If Sunny wanted to get some last time skiing in with anyone, today was the day. Sunny threw on his ski clothes and headed for the condo. Driving into the condo parking lot, he met Carl.

"Morning, Carl. What are you doing, out here in the parking lot?" Sunny asked with a puzzled look on his face.

"I just came to get my skis. I ripped one of the bindings out last time up and want to get it fixed," Carl explained.

"Shit, I'm headed to the mountain and was hoping you could come." Sunny said with a worried look on his face.

"Let me see how long this will take. I'll meet you up there if I can." Carl said.

Sunny went into the condo and there was Ace.

"Hey Ace, where is everyone?" asked Sunny.

"Carl just left to get his skis fixed." explained Ace.

"Yeah I know, I just saw him." said Sunny.

"Stony went out on a cross country run, and who knows where Roger is, and why are we standing here looking at each other?" Ace questioned quickly.

"I'm headed for the hill, you coming?" Sunny asked.

"Sorry Sunny, I can't. I've got to get some transcript stuff done today. I'll be in town most of the day," Ace explained.

Sunny had a cup of coffee with Ace and headed up the mountain. Sunny didn't mind skiing by himself; he liked skiing alone sometimes. He just wondered if the group would all ski together again.

Going up the road by The Horn, Sunny thought he would stop by and say hello to Richard. When he walked in, Richard was sitting on a barstool talking to Big Paul who was stocking some beer, getting ready to open. Chandler, one of his old schoolmates from across the street, had now taken his place as floor mopper and bar ski bum.

"What's up guys?" asked Sunny.

Chandler was a great guy, always with a smile.

"Hey Sunny, what's happening? I haven't seen you in about a week or so," he said.

"Hi Chandler, how's ski bumming treating you?" asked Sunny.

Richard, always straight to the point said, "A little hard, he was late today."

"What? From upstairs?" replied Sunny.

"No way, there's only one Sunny," Richard said.

"Thanks, Richard," said Sunny.

Richard in his usual gruff way looked at Sunny and said, "No compliment intended."

"Speaking of ski bums, I haven't seen you up at the mountain lately," said Sunny.

"It's tough for me Sunny. I have a real responsibility here," Richard explained.

"Yeah, you look busy to me, why don't you get off your dead ass and let's head to the mountain? It's a beautiful day; come on, it will be like old times," Sunny prompted.

"Go ahead Richard, the air and exercise will do you good," said Big Paul.

"Yeah go ahead, I'll stay here with Paul," Chandler said, supporting Paul.

"Ha, and your honey eh Chandler! Well, what the hell, let's do it," Richard said finally giving in.

They drove up the mountain and talked how they missed the old days, when Sunny would run over from the school and wake up the guys at The Horn to go skiing. The mountain's bumps looked pretty shabby, so they went over to Big Spruce. They skied for a couple of hours, just like in the old days. Skiing with Richard was great. It reminded Sunny of when the only thing that mattered was getting to the slopes to ski. As they skied to the bottom, Richard was a little out of breath. He stopped Sunny.

"Hold it Sunny, you've skied me into the ground. I've got to head back; I got some things to do."

"I'll go back with you. The snow's getting too soft to be much fun anyway," Sunny said.

They loaded their skis onto the car and headed down the mountain.

"Jesus Sunny, you've gotten good."

"Thanks, Richard. I can't return the compliment, though. I think you've gotten out of shape," Sunny said with a smile.

"No really, your skiing has gotten much better, you pulled off some moves up there that I could hardly believe." Richard said with a serious look on his face.

"Well, if you do it every day, you're bound to get better," noted Sunny, trying to explain his progress.

They talked, for a little while and arrived at The Horn.

"Are you hungry?" asked Richard.

"Starved!" exclaimed Sunny.

"Come on in, I want to talk to you," Richard said.

"Okay, but first I have to use your phone. I'll charge it to my home phone," said Sunny

Sunny went up to Richard's office and called Cindy in Boston.

"Hello Cindy," Sunny said.

"Hi Sunny! I was just thinking of how I could get a hold of you," Cindy replied.

It was good to hear her voice.

"What's up? Are you coming back?" asked Sunny.

In Cindy's usual upbeat manner she replied,

"You bet, I got a beautiful dress for tomorrow night. Have you missed me?" It seemed to be a silly question.

"I missed you today, skiing was good and yeah, I've missed you."

"You're sweet Sunny," encouraged Cindy. Sunny never to be one to take things seriously replied,

"Hey, not so loud, someone might hear you. I've a reputation to keep up, you know. Though, you are sweet."

"I can't wait for tomorrow night. I'll be up around 3 in the afternoon. Where should I meet you?" asked Cindy.

Sunny knew the only place he could meet her was the condo so Sunny replied,

"At the condo, we'll get dressed there."

"Great. Listen Sunny, I got good news. I've got to go now, but I'll tell you tomorrow. I'll see you, Okay?" Cindy said quickly on the way out.

Then Cindy hit Sunny right between the eyes when she said,

"I love you Sunny, goodbye."

Without thinking, Sunny replied,

"Me too, take care and drive carefully."

Sunny was a little taken aback by Cindy's statement. Sunny wanted to tell her he loved her too, but somehow the words didn't come out. Sunny went downstairs where Richard was waiting with their lunch.

"Who was that?" asked Richard.

If Sunny could tell anybody it would be Richard,

"Cindy."

"That's been going on for a while. That's not like you," said Richard.

"Yeah, I know. I needed to know when she was coming back. She's going to the cotillion with me, explained Sunny.

"Let's sit down here and talk," directed Richard.

They went down to a table which provided some privacy. The Horn was still empty, but in a little while it would be filled up and Nards would be on the turntables.

"What's up?" asked Sunny.

Richard got right to the point.

"What are you going to do next year?" he probed.

Sunny knew that Richard wasn't going to tolerate long answers.

"Funny you should ask; I don't have a clue. I keep thinking I should be moving on," Sunny answered.

"The way you skied today, you should get into Pro racing. They're starting up a B circuit in the east next year, you'd be perfect. I'll bet you'll kick some ass."

"That sounds great," stated Sunny.

"You could have Cindy or Judy live with you and work here," Richard said with some unusual enthusiasm.

"Very funny Richard, I'm in enough trouble," Sighed Sunny

"Look, Sunny, I was in the same position with sailing. I had gotten real good in my yacht club and it was time to either stay and be a big fish in a small pond or move on and try my luck with the big boys," Richard continued.

"I don't know whether I'm ready for the big league," Sunny explained.

"I wasn't kidding before when I said I need a manager and no one knows the Horn like you. You can work here and I'll cover for your races." Richard was pushing hard.

"Sounds great, Richard, but I'll need to train," Sunny said.

"No problem. There's a morning training session up at the mountain. I'll come in and open and you take it from 11 on, after training," Richard offered.

"You're not shitting me, are you, Richard?" Sunny blurted.

"No Sunny. The only thing that worries me is you'll have to get serious and give up a lot of your partying," Richard said with a serious look on his face.

"In this town? That's not easy," Sunny replied, also being serious.

"I know, but if you want to try racing, you'll have to get serious." Richard accentuated the point.

"Thanks Richard. Let me sleep on it a couple of days," Sunny said quietly.

They finished their lunch just as the place was filling up. Nards came in to get the people going. On the way out, Sunny thanked Richard for lunch and told him he would see him after the cotillion or at the .cotillion, whichever came first.

Sunny headed down the road and stopped at the condo. Carl was there and he had gotten his ski fixed. Ace, Stony and Roger were still out. Carl and Sunny talked and sat in the Jacuzzi while Sunny revealed what Richard had offered him.

"Great, Sunny! I think that sounds perfect for you," Carl said with enthusiasm.

"Yeah, almost too perfect," Sunny said.

Carl could see something was bothering Sunny.

"What's on your mind Sunny?" asked Carl.

"Well, now that you ask, I know things can never stay the same, but things are moving a little too fast for me," Sunny said.

"Yeah, like what?" Carl interrupted.

"A few months ago, the only thing that mattered was skiing and having fun. Now I'm looking at a commitment to a job and possibly a woman," Sunny continued to explain.

"Oh yeah...which one. Cindy or Judy?" Carl asked.

"I don't know. I don't want to lose either," Sunny said with distress in his voice.

"How will you do that? No one gets Cindy, that's just Cindy and Judy's got Tom. Don't worry Sunny, you've always got me," Carl said with his usual facetious, correct insight.

"Great, but can't I have a girl and you too?" Sunny said understanding exactly that Carl was correct.

"Maybe, I didn't tell you what deal I've got," Carl said enticingly.

"Shoot," replied Sunny

"The boss of the construction company that's building these condos just offered me a job as a foreman," Carl explained.

"Great. You're going to take it?" asked Sunny.

"I don't know, I told him I get back to him in a few days," Carl said.

"Hey Carl, can't we get back to where things weren't so important, so serious?" asked Sunny.

"I don't see how Sunny. It's time to grow up," Carl said. This time, Sunny knew he was right.

"Hey, don't ever say that, let's go somewhere else," said Sunny.

"Where? Don't tell me..." Carl replied with some intolerance.

Carl and Sunny both said together, "Idaho!"

"Come on, we have to get to work," Sunny noted.

Carl just looked at Sunny a little frustrated and annoyed, but excited at the same time then he asked,

"Where the fuck is Idaho anyway?"

Sunny looked at Carl with a little smirk and said,

"A little west of Chicago I believe. Nobody knows us there. We could start from scratch. With what we know we could take the town by storm."

"Sunny you're a dreamer. A big time ski area and two bums, come on. No, we finally have a chance to have something, let's stay," Carl pleaded.

Sunny grinned a little bit not wanting to push the issue at this time, but knew he longed for something bigger.

"You're right Carl, we'll stay," said Sunny.

They were finished with the Jacuzzi and got ready for work. They ate at The Knees and celebrated their job offers and potential futures. Both of them had to keep their job offers to themselves as there were others who would like to move into their available positions. The Knees was slow that night, just another sign that the season was coming to a close.

When Sunny went home, Judy was there asleep. As Sunny climbed in bed he kissed her gently on the cheek, waking her up.

"Hi Sunny," Judy said.

"I'm sorry Judy; I didn't mean to wake you," Sunny whispered softly.

"That's okay. I've been home for a while and in bed for hours it seems."

"Are you feeling okay?" asked Sunny.

"I'll be okay," Judy explained.

"Good," Sunny said looking somewhat concerned.

Sunny held her close all night. In the morning she got up to go to work.

"Sunny, wake up a second," Judy said. Sunny knew something important was up.Judy had never awoken him in the morning before.

"Listen, I need to talk to you. Meet me here at 3 when I get off work."

Sunny went back to sleep, not thinking Cindy was due at the condo at 5. This would be close. When Sunny woke up, he couldn't help but being a little worried.

Sunny went up to Carl's room to grab him to go to the mountain.

"This is Sunny here to see Massaro," Sunny announced.

"It's Carl to you, asshole. Come on in Sunny," Carl said.

"I'll call you asshole for short. Hello Alice, looking forward to this evening with Carl?" Sunny asked.

"If it was anything like last evening then NO!" Alice said with a sneer.

"Should be the same, just in formal attire." Sunny explained with a smile.

"Right, let's go skiing," said Carl.

Carl quickly got dressed and he and Sunny jumped in their cars to drive up to the mountain. Carl had to come down early to talk to the construction company boss. As they were loading the lift Sunny asked,

"What was all that about with you and Alice?"

"Oh, we had a fight. I told her about my job offering and asked her if she would stay with me," explained Carl.

"So what's wrong with that?" asked Sunny.

"She wants me to marry her. Besides her not being Italian, I'm not ready," Carl continued.

"Do you love her?" Sunny asked poignantly.

"Yup," Carl answered.

"Well...?" Asked Sunny

"That's the problem. I love her, Shannon, Kim, Sally, Sue...," explained Carl.

"Okay, okay, I see what you mean. Hang in there!!I've got the same disease. I was hoping maybe you had a cure, but I see there isn't one," Sunny said.

"Sometimes, I think time will cure this disease," Carl said thoughtfully.

"What if we fuck up and blow it?" Sunny asked.

"How?" asked Carl.

"What if we don't find girls as nice as the ones we've got?" Asked Sunny.

"Do you have any idea how many girls there are in the world?" Carl asked.

"Not yet. But I keep on looking," Sunny said.

Carl and Sunny made it a point to ski every trail which was open. Skiing with Carl was just what Sunny needed. As they started each run, Carl would start the rhythm of their skiing song ("Here Comes the Sun"), and they skied as fast as they could. After all, if you broke a leg that day, you had three seasons to heal.

Sunny skied with Carl, hurling himself down the mountain. That moment, the only things that mattered were their friendship and skiing. This was what Sunny was looking for, back to basics. Carl and Sunny stopped in the Octagon Lodge later for coffee. Sunny saw the best sight he could see; Stony, Ace, Roger, and about 15 of the hard core skiers were there. Sunny was excited. No one had mentioned they were going to ski, as everyone assumed the season was over and that day was a chance to rest for the night ahead.

Sunny didn't have to ask what they were doing up there. They were all up there for the same reasons. First to get in some last runs and second to say goodbye to the season, as the lifts would be closed the next day. The next few runs they took were great, everyone skied as hard as they could to try and get skiing out of their system until next year's season. Skiing with the group always got Sunny up, and today he was able to pull it together and uncork one. Sunny skied as hard and as fast as he could, dancing down the mountain. Little by little, each one of the group left the hill to prepare for the night ahead. Carl had left to talk to the construction company. Sunny didn't ask what his decision was; he knew Carl would tell him later.

Sunny rode up the almost empty lift alone. Sunny listened to the quiet, the wind, and felt the afternoon sun on his face. It was a time to feel the calm and enjoy the last ride. When he got to the top, he waited until all the others had gone for their run. Sunny stood there looking at the beautiful Vermont scenery; he reflected once more on the season and all the wonderful things it had brought him. Standing there alone at the top, listening to the quiet and feeling the cold air with every breath was one of his favorite things in life. As all the skiers below turned out of sight, Sunny was now alone. Sunny was a religious man; he couldn't believe that this moment of beauty could happen without God's help, the beauty of nature and the strength of the mountain. Sunny straightened his goggles, gloves, boots, and poles and with a smile kicked off, knowing this was the last farewell run of the season. Sunny carved, savoring every turn down the mountain, stopping from time to time to gaze back. As Sunny reached the bottom of the mountain he kicked off his skis, turned to look up at the mountain for a moment and said with a smile: *'Goodbye for now and thanks.'* It was a moment of sadness, but in consideration of what the year had given him, he couldn't help but smile. Sunny wondered if this was a goodbye for now, or for a long time to come.

It was close to three o'clock when Sunny drove straight home. Judy was waiting. Sunny's timing in meeting Cindy might be close, so since his tuxedo was here he thought of getting dressed with Judy. As Sunny walked up the stairs he could hear the shower going.

"Hello Judy, I'm here," yelled Sunny.

"Hi, Sunny," Judy called from the shower.

"Yeah, who were you expecting?" Sunny said with his usual wisecrack.

"You, about half an hour ago," Judy said.

Just then, he quickly undressed and jumped into the shower. "Well... here I am," Sunny said.

"Where have you been?" Judy asked. This time she did have a right to ask.

"The mountain, taking my last run," Sunny explained, thinking Judy would understand this was the one explanation that made sense.

"You know Sunny; I've always felt I could hold my own with any of the women in town, but I've always known the mountain came first with you. How do you compete with a mountain?" Judy asked.

"You don't, it's just a part of me," Sunny just looked at Judy and stated the truth.

They stepped out of the shower and dried off. Judy sat as Sunny shaved as she had done so many times.

"What was this you wanted to talk to me about? How was your trip to Boston?" Sunny asked.

"Okay," said Judy.

"Did Tom enjoy himself?" Sunny asked.

"Very funny, Tom didn't go. Sunny listen, I went to Boston because I had to go see a doctor. I thought I was really sick," Judy explained.

"You're kidding. Why didn't you tell me? What was it?"

Sunny stopped shaving and looked at Judy concerned, angry, and disappointed.

"I didn't know what to do, I was scared and I just wanted to go home. It turned out that I'm going to be fine," Judy explained.

Sunny looked at Judy with relief, but realized that she hadn't counted on him when it really mattered. This was a game changer. To Sunny being in love wasn't all about the good times, but more about what happened during the bad times.

"Sunny, you don't understand, you aren't ready for me, much less to deal with my problems. You're just starting to come into your *own*. Just like today, your priorities are not ready. No woman will take a back seat to a mountain. Sunny, I love you and I do want you, all this year I've wanted you. You're living in the fast lane and you're the King. If I forced myself on you, even if I could have you, you would feel trapped and frustrated. Eventually you would wind up hating me. At least now we're friends and I have as much as you're able to give," Judy said with all the warmth and seriousness Sunny had seen before in her.

Sunny was mad and disappointed, not so much at Judy, but at himself because she was right.

"God damn it Judy. Why don't you let me make those decisions?" Sunny asked.

"Sunny, you did. You haven't been here all year and I know you love me, I can feel that when we're making love and hold each other all night," Judy continued.

Sunny could feel Judy slipping away and he wanted to throw up.

"What about Tom. I assume you've been with Tom."

"No, Tom doesn't know," Judy said.

Now Sunny really didn't understand, "Why?" Sunny asked.

"Sunny, I couldn't tell Tom either, I love YOU!"

He didn't say a word; instead, he reached down and pulled Judy up to hug her.

"I love you too Judy. Why didn't you tell me?" said Sunny, then in tears.

"I couldn't Sunny. I knew from the beginning that the only way I'd be able to stay would be to let you go. Each night you came back, I knew it was because you wanted to, not because you had to. I knew if you didn't want to stay, you would have either thrown me out or moved out yourself."

"I would have never thrown you out," Sunny said.

"Remember, you tried when I first got here," Judy was now in tears as well.

"Yeah, but you're still here, aren't you?" Sunny said with a half-smile this time.

He wanted to ask Judy to stay with him for the rest of his life, but she was right, he wasn't ready, and then there was Tom.

"What about you marrying Tom?" Sunny had to ask.

"I haven't given him an answer; and no, I won't marry you either," Judy said.

"Why not?" Sunny asked somewhat surprised.

"Because you're not ready," she stated plainly with a smile.

"I don't want to lose you," said Sunny.

"No matter what happens, Sunny, you won't lose me; I'll always be here for you. Now let's get dressed and have a good time tonight," Judy commanded softly.

"Judy, you may be right, but I'm not going to lose you. I'll always be here for you too," said Sunny.

"I know Sunny. Now let's go. I've got to meet Tom pretty soon," Judy said.

These were not the words Sunny wanted to hear. He finished getting dressed, wondering the whole time if he wasn't some kind of a jerk to not pull his shit together and ask Judy to marry him. Needless to say, Sunny was a little confused as he drove over to pick up Cindy. Sunny wasn't sure whether Judy still wanted him or if he had gotten his walking papers. He thought she wanted him, but boy, was he bewildered. Besides, Sunny had these feelings for Cindy and wasn't sure of where he stood with her either.

When Sunny drove up to the condo, Cindy's car was already there. Corsage in hand, Sunny walked through the door.

Sunny was hoping he was not going to be hit with any more surprises.

"Hello?" he called out.

"Sunny, is that you?" Cindy asked in return.

'Is this Deja vu?' Sunny murmured.

"Did you say something?" Cindy said, looking a little confused.

"Oh nothing, Yeah, it's me. It's good to see you," Sunny said.

Cindy came out of the master bedroom with nothing on but a pair of panties, her hair in a French braid; she was beautiful.

"You're dressed?" she asked.

Sunny was a little stunned.

"You're not and it's nice of you to notice. Don't bother finishing; I like you just as you are."

"I thought you were going to get dressed with me?" Cindy said.

They kissed and held each other for a long moment.

"What was that for, did you miss me?" asked Cindy.

"Yeah. Sorry, I had to talk to someone, so I thought I'd dress early. How ya doing?" asked Sunny.

"Just great," Cindy said.

Sunny sat on the bed while Cindy slipped on her dress.

"What are you doing after the season?" Cindy asked.

The question caught Sunny by surprise hearing it from Cindy.

"That seems to be the question of the week. I don't know," Sunny answered.

"While I was home, I got a modeling offer," Cindy said.

Sunny wasn't surprised to hear that. Cindy was truly model material.

"That's great." Sunny said.

"Yeah, that means I'll have to spend some time in New York. I know your family lives close by. I thought if you came down, we could be together," Cindy said with a smile.

Sunny looked at her for a moment she truly looked beautiful. "Aah," Sunny said.

Yeah, I'm going to stay with a friend in Manhattan," Cindy went on to explain.

Cindy didn't realize that if Sunny was going to be in Manhattan he would be working for his dad south of Houston, on Lafayette Street either on the fifth floor in the machine shop or on the loading dock. Hardly model material. What Sunny had realized was that what attracted Cindy to Sunny stopped at the Stowe border.

"What would I do in New York?" asked Sunny.

"Be with me?" Cindy said. "Sunny, I can't just leave after tomorrow and not see you again."

"Cindy, you're the most beautiful girl I know and there's nothing else 'I'd rather do than to be with you. But I just can't go and hang around New York. How would I live?" Asked Sunny

"We'll think of something," Cindy said.

"Cindy, here I'm a big fish in a little pond. I know in New York there are more guys with more things to offer you than grains of sand on a beach. When I met you, I walked through a crowd and pulled you away because of my skiing. Down there, I can't compete." Sunny explained.

Cindy looked at Sunny, leaned down and kissed him.

"You don't have to," Cindy said.

"You deserve more. I'm a ski bum. Here's what we can do, I'll go home and we'll spend time together. We have three seasons where we can see how things work out. If by the first snow fall things are not going good, we'll talk again."

"Talk about what?" Cindy said with some naiveté.

"We'll sit down and see what comes next," said Sunny.

"Okay, I love you Sunny," Cindy said.

"I love you too Cindy, let's take it one step at a time. You can't take a ski bum out of his environment too fast, he'll die," Sunny said.

Cindy finished dressing and she was truly stunning. Sunny knew in his heart he didn't stand a chance in New York. Sunny gave her flowers.

"Oh Sunny, they're beautiful," Cindy said as they kissed.

"So are you. Ready Cindy? Now let's have some fun," Sunny said.

Cindy was wearing a floor-length blue satin dressing showing her bare shoulders where it came to a satin band around her neck. Her hair was pulled back in the French braid. She was just a striking girl. They went to dinner first and she proceeded to tell Sunny the details of her modeling offer.

Sunny didn't mention Richard's offer, he knew it would upset her. When they finished dinner they drove up to the lodge at Little Spruce where the Cow Shit Cotillion was being held.

The Cow Shit Cotillion

THE PARKING LOT WAS FULL when they arrived, and Sunny could tell from driving around looking for a parking space that the guys were already there. After they found a place to park, Sunny asked Cindy,

"Do you have the invitations I gave you?"

"Yes I have them right here. You don't really think you'll need them, do you?" Cindy asked.

"You bet! That's the rule. No invitation, you leave," Sunny said.

They started to walk across the parking lot and within a few steps it was apparent they were walking in mud.

"Oh no, it's mud!" Cindy said.

Sunny reached down to the back of Cindy's legs and swept her off her feet.

"You could have driven me to the door, but this is more romantic. What about your shoes?" Cindy asked.

Sunny smiled and gave her a little kiss and said, "They're rented."

As they got to the walk way Sunny put her down.

"You're so sweet Sunny," said Cindy.

"Hey watch it, I told you. Did anybody hear you?" Sunny said with a smile.

"Sunny, the invitations are in my purse! Cindy explained.

"Don't tell me..." said Sunny.

"Yup, in the car," she said with her best apologetic smile.

Sunny looked at Cindy and looked at the car and said, "We'll fake it. Who needs an invitation anyway?"

As they walked in the door, Sunny threw back his shoulders, felt his tie and looked Gar straight in the eye.

"Good evening Gar, I believe you've met Cindy?" Sunny said unflinchingly.

"Good evening Sunny. Cindy. Enjoy the evening," Gar said with a smile.

"Why thank you Gar, you too," replied Sunny.

Sunny and Cindy walked in a few feet. The lodge was elegantly decorated, the lighting was low. There were flowers and candles at the 40 or so tables, white table cloths, and each had a beautiful table setting.

At the other end of the lodge, was a bandstand with a band playing soft dinner music. Sunny looked around the room and there was Carl standing with Alice. Sunny had never seen Carl in a tuxedo before. He looked quite handsome. Alice looked stunning in a pink formal. As Sunny looked around, everyone was appropriately attired and to his dismay, behaving accordingly.

Being a ski bum was a rich kid's version of being poor and decadent. Most ski bums came from fair to good upbringings where one learned all the social graces, only to come to Stowe and allow them to lie dormant. A formal such as this was a time to display a side which, for many of them, lay deeply dormant. If decadence meant moral decay to a truly decadent person, a formal affair would be decadence to the decadent. Anyway, things were certainly out of character for the people Sunny had been used to.

As Sunny escorted Cindy to their table, Stony and Ace were already standing there. Stony had his beard trimmed and looked quite distinguished. Ace had not only trimmed his hair, but combed it too. Not surprisingly, considering his upbringing, Ace looked right at home.

Stony's date and now partner, Sue, was dressed in a dark green sleeveless gown with her hair up. Sunny couldn't believe this beautiful feminine woman was the same person who could decimate most men on both Alpine and Nordic skis. Ace had imported a date from home, who was standing with Roger's date. Both were very attractive. It was easy to see they were at home in formal dresses. Ace introduced everyone in his formal manner.

"Sharon, June, this is Cindy and Sunny." June was Ace's date.

"Nice to meet you both, Akron has told me a lot about you," said June.

"Nothing good I hope," replied Sunny.

"Not really," Ace said with a grin.

"But he said it with great enthusiasm," June explained.

"Cindy, you look gorgeous," Ace commented

"That is nice of you. Thank you, Akron," Cindy said with a smile.

"That's enough of that guys, I'm still Ace."

Roger walked up from behind.

"Good evening ladies and gentlemen. Sunny, Cindy, I see you've met Sharon and June," Roger said.

"Good evening Roger, you look most debonair this evening. Yes, I have had that pleasure," Sunny commented with all his social graces.

Carl, now standing next to him, turned and said,

"Where did you learn to talk like that?"

"A genetic affliction."

"I believe I have that same affliction, comes with being a Wasp!" Alice explained.

"Gee, I hope I don't get it," Carl stated.

Alice looked at Carl for a moment and said, "Don't worry Carl, I think you're safe."

This was about as much social etiquette as Cindy could take in at one time from some ski bums.

"Sunny, would you get me a drink?"

"Certainly Cindy, I could use several. What would you care for?" Sunny asked.

"Champagne please," replied Cindy.

"Champagne? Good idea, why don't I get a bottle. Ladies will you join us?" asked Sunny.

"Yes please," replied June.

"That sounds nice," replied Sharon.

"Me as well," Sue said.

The Hole in the Wall Gang had just found out the cultural differences between them and their dates or vice versa.

Stony spoke up, "I'll have a beer."

"Beer," Ace followed.

"Carl, don't tell me."

Sunny and Carl both said together, "Beer."

Sunny looked around the room and said, "I'll get a waiter."

Sunny went to give their orders to a waiter. When he approached the bar, Judy stood before him. As she turned to him, the sight of her dressed in formal wear was so stunning it took his breath away. That was the first time Judy and Cindy had been in the same place at the same time. Sunny was nervous, not to mention confused.

"Good evening Sunny. You look handsome this evening," Judy said.

"You're beautiful Judy. Where's Tom?" Sunny asked nervously.

"He'll be here in a minute," Judy explained.

They were interrupted by the bartender, so Sunny gave him his order. He then looked at Judy for a long moment.

"Enjoy the evening, Judy," said Sunny.

"One dance before the evening's out?" Judy asked.

Sunny smiled, "I thought you would never ask Judy, nothing would make me happier. I'll tell Carl to sing something very special."

Sunny walked back and talked with the guys and Cindy. Most of the conversation was congratulations about their acceptance and their anticipation for the future. Of course they were all speculating on when and where they could meet and be together in the future. As he stood alone with Cindy, she commented,

"Sunny, it seems you're the only one without any immediate plans for the future."

"I have plans; I just don't know what they are yet," Sunny said with a smile.

"Really, I'm worried about you. Isn't there anything special you want to do or be?"

"I thought being rich would be nice. In fact, I might even change my name to Rich."

Cindy laughed.

"I have some ideas but Cindy, all I know for sure is that I want to race," Sunny explained.

"Then do it! You'll be great, really, and if you took it seriously and trained, you could do very well," Cindy said encouragingly.

"Thanks for your vote of confidence," Sunny said and he really did mean it.

From across the room, he could see John walking toward them.

"Sunny, I've been looking for you. Cindy, you look ravishing," John said with that giant smile of his.

"Thanks John, you look great yourself," Cindy replied.

"John?" asked Sunny.

"Cindy, may I steal Sunny for a few minutes? It's important," John asked most politely.

"Sure, John." Cindy said.

Sunny knew Cindy really didn't mind, as he could see there was a group of admiring men waiting to pounce at the first opportunity. Nothing new.

"Sunny, I want you back," said John.

"Gee John, I didn't know we broke up. I didn't know I left. I didn't even know we had a fight!" Sunny said with his Jersey humor.

"I don't want to date you, stupid; I want you back at The Baggy Knees next year," John said.

"Thanks, but…" Sunny tried to explain.

"Wait. This year we did great and I think you and the guys had a lot to do with it. I can't be there every day and night, so I'm going to need a night manager. Besides, you're skiing as good as ever. What do you say?" John asked.

"Sounds good, John, but the guys aren't going to be here. At best it would be just Carl and me. Things are changing, John," Sunny said.

"I know, but you're the King and you've always done a good job. Just keep it in mind," John continued.

"I will, John."

Sunny went back to Cindy. Needless to say, she was surrounded by a group of men. The job John had offered Sunny sounded great; it seemed to be the next logical step. Sunny should be happy, he had come a long way from pitching shingles at the dump with Ace. But had Sunny really wanted to do it? That was a great time, when nobody wanted him for anything but being a nice guy. Sunny didn't believe any one person was the King of the Mountain. If anybody actually was king, it was Ronny Biedermann. Anyone coming to Stowe to ski to forget their worries for a time was in their own right king. With each year came some young guy who could come and go as he pleased, ski when he wanted, be with whom he wanted to be with, and claim this false, fleeting title. Where would that leave him? Sunny came to Stowe because he loved skiing and Sunny was blessed with the good fortune of good friends. Sunny didn't want to sit there chasing the repeat of a year he could never duplicate.

Sunny was still hiding a secret; he had gone through the season without exposing any of his disabilities. He had avoided any of the responsibilities that resulted in his having to read or focus out of his comfort zone. Sunny knew that the next step up in all the responsibilities could result in him hitting the Peter Principle, or at least he was afraid that it would. Sunny was afraid there was nowhere to go but down from where he was.

Dinner was served and Cindy and Sunny sat through it even though they had already eaten. Sunny took the opportunity to dance several times slowly with Cindy taking advantage of the dance floor not being crowded. After dinner, dessert was Baked Alaska. Gar and John stood up to say a few words. John proposed a toast which was eloquent and appropriate.

John began, "Ladies and Gentlemen, it is nice that through all our misbehaving we can all take an evening to be ladies and gentlemen. This year seemed to have brought some special people and times to Stowe. Time passes and the good times seem fleeting, but the people who have brought the closeness to me and Stowe will always stay with all of us. So to you that stay and to you that must leave, here's to the closeness and the future."

Everyone stood and drank to John's toast.

John continued, "And with no further ado, may the festivities begin."

There were several bands scheduled to take part in the evening's entertainment. One of the bands that played was the band from The Knees. When John finished speaking, they broke out in their rendition of the Isley Brothers' song "Shout." This song was played years earlier, but it was the same song as in the movie Animal House, which was yet to come out. After a few songs by popular demand, Carl grabbed his guitar and jumped on stage, starting their skiing song; "Here Comes the Sun." Carl's version closely emulated Ritchie Havens' version. Many people at the cotillion were unaware of Carl's talent. Most didn't know he could sing, not so well at least. Needless to say, Carl was a big hit. Carl had always been a fan of older music, so the next song didn't surprise Sunny. Sunny had told him of his intentions to dance with Judy. After his ovation from singing "Here Comes the Sun", he announced,

"I'd like to dedicate this song to anyone who wanted to dance with someone they never got the chance to dance with. So everyone change partners and try this on for size."

Ace immediately took the opportunity to ask Cindy to dance. Sunny quickly looked around the room for Judy, hoping someone else didn't get there first. A short distance away Sunny caught Judy's eye. As Sunny got there she was already talking to Vinnie, shit. Then as Sunny got closer he heard:

"No thank you. I've already promised this dance to someone else."

Sunny just looked at her and took her hand. They danced over in the corner as to not be obvious.

"I guess they're playing our song," Sunny said.

The song was "Moonlight in Vermont," a very romantic, slow song. Sunny held Judy tight and she reciprocated.

"I didn't know you could dance so well or for that matter, wasn't aware you had so many refined social graces," Judy said with a smile.

Sunny grinned a little bit. "Boys Town. I learned them in juvenile hall. By the way, you dance divinely. Isn't it nice to dance in public?" Sunny said.

Judy giggled a little. "Maybe we should go public tonight."

Sunny took a deep breath. "Not a good idea, you'd ruin my date's evening."

"Who is your date and how come you haven't introduced her to me?" asked Judy.

"Ah, she is just some girl and I didn't think you'd be interested," Sunny said flippantly.

"I always want to know who my competition is," said Judy.

"You have no competition; you're in a class of your own." Sunny tried his best to get out of that one.

He wasn't really lying; Judy was in a class of her own. But then again so was Cindy. Judy and Sunny danced and held on for dear life. At the end, Sunny even managed to sneak in a kiss. The dance ended too soon.

Sunny looked at Judy and said, "Thank you Judy. The year wouldn't have been complete without that dance."

There was an overwhelming round of applause for Carl as he stepped down. Just then Tom was looking for Judy, and it wouldn't be a good idea to let him find Sunny and Judy kissing.

"I agree, thank you. I'd better find Tom," Judy said.

Sunny found Cindy and proceeded to dance to the next song, which was also slow.

"Who was that you were dancing with?" Cindy asked.

"A good friend," Sunny explained.

"Okay, you looked like you knew her pretty well," Cindy said.

"I do. Don't worry, she's getting engaged," Sunny explained.

Cindy and Sunny danced and at the end of the song, they decided to sneak out for some real Vermont moonlight and air.

"What are you thinking about? What did John want that was so important?" asked Cindy.

"He just wants me back at The Knees next year," Sunny replied.

"That's good!" Cindy said with some enthusiasm.

"Yeah, it's okay. I just think it's time to do something big."

"I don't know what you mean." said Cindy.

"Me either. Come on, let's go back in," Sunny replied.

"Well, whatever it is, you'll be good at it. Listen, go ahead, I've got to go to the ladies room and powder my nose."

Sunny went inside and saw the band was still on break. He sat down at the edge of the stage and talked to the lead singer. As Sunny was talking, he looked around the room to see if he could locate Carl and the guys. At the opposite end of the room Sunny saw Carl. His heart stopped, then Sunny got nauseated as he saw Carl was standing there with Cindy *and* Judy. Sunny didn't know whether to confront the situation or to run. Then all three turned and started walking directly towards him. Sunny could see fire in both Cindy's and Judy's eyes.

This was one of Carl's jokes and it didn't matter anymore. Sunny looked at the three of them. Just then, Tom walked over to Judy.

"I have been looking for you, there are only a few dances left." Judy looked at Tom and she left with him.

Cindy walked up to Sunny. Sunny stood there almost paralyzed with fear as to what she might say next. What had happened was Carl had been sitting on the edge of the stage with Cindy when Judy had come up to talk to him, and the three of them had gotten into a conversation. Cindy looked at Sunny.

"She's nice," said Cindy. "I had met her before at the last race. She was cheering for you."

Sunny decided it was time to tell Cindy everything. They went out on the deck, it was a full moon, they could see across the parking lot to the mountain, the snow was melting and they could feel spring in the air. To Sunny, it meant the end of the season and there was sadness to it.

"Look Cindy, I'm not who you think I am." Sunny explained. "I haven't gone to college; I don't even have a real job. I know that Richard and John have offered me good jobs, but I'm not sure I can do them. You're a gorgeous woman and you're going to be very successful. You deserve a guy who's going to be successful too. You should go to New York, I've spent a lot of my life there, but I think I should go to Idaho and be a professional skier." Sunny paused for a brief moment then continued, "That's what's got me this far and that's what I know best."

Cindy looked at Sunny for a moment and said,

"What about Judy?"

Sunny looked at Cindy.

"She deserves more; she deserves somebody who can take care of her. Would you care to dance?"

She smiled.

"I would love to".

Sunny and Cindy danced the last few dances out on the deck under the full moon. At the end of the evening, Cindy asked,

"Sunny, have you made up your mind about what you're going to do?"

Sunny smiled and looked at her.

"Yes, I'm going to Idaho."

Leaving Stowe

THE DECISION WAS MADE. SUNNY wasn't going to spend a lot of time saying goodbye. He sat with Richard and told him what he decided to do. Richard was a very competitive guy, with both football and sailing. He understood that going to a bigger mountain would help Sunny. Next stop was John, and surprisingly he understood as well. John knew that a repeat of the last year was going to be tough to make happen.

Carl knew Sunny had made up his mind, and he was headed toward Jersey. Carl thought Sunny had known what he wanted to do all along. From the time he left junior college for that race in New Hampshire, Sunny had known there was no turning back. Sunny believed that he had to move forward now. Sunny also knew that if he stayed in Stowe he would wind up only competing with himself and his own reputation. Sunny would be working at The Knees or The Horn and see Judy and Tom. He would try and do well in the ski bum races, but everyone would talk about the year before. It was time to go.

Carl knew he couldn't stop Sunny, and he was also curious about skiing a bigger mountain. Carl had made contacts back in Sussex, New Jersey to do some construction, so he left first. Sunny packed up and as usual, the only things that went were the things that could fit in the car. Sunny was driving an old '67 Chevy Impala. The thing was a land yacht. Sunny had called home to talk with his dad, knowing he could always talk things over with him. He had a long talk with his dad and told him about how well he had skied and how the end of the year went. He also talked to his father about how he felt that it was time to move on to a bigger mountain.

Sunny's dad was the one person who he knew would understand. He was the one who had been out to Sun Valley and told Sunny how he had wished he could ski with him out there. Sunny knew his dad would let him come home and work in New York and make some money to get on his feet before heading out West. With his father's support, Sunny was going to follow his dream once again.

The Road to New Jersey

SUNNY WAS PACKED AND READY to leave early in the morning, as he knew it was going to be a long day. Packing up was a little difficult since Sunny knew whatever he had with Judy would never be the same. He saw Judy standing by his car. Sunny didn't know what to say; Judy spoke first.

"Will you call?" she asked.

"Yes, if you'll answer," Sunny said.

Judy moved closer and kissed Sunny.

Sunny looked at her and smiled.

"Just make sure you answer," said Sunny. Judy was packed up as well.

"Where are you going?" asked Sunny.

"Boston."

Sunny reached down and gave her a big hug.

"Drive carefully, I don't want to lose you," he said with a smile.

Judy smiled and said, "You're a jerk Sunny."

As Sunny climbed into his car, he looked at her and said,

"Yeah I know, but I'm your jerk." And with that he headed down the road.

It wasn't too long, maybe a few hours south when Sunny started falling asleep while driving. Maybe it was all the stress of what he had been through with the transition, but it hit him all at once. Sunny had to pull over and closed his eyes for a few minutes. As soon as he had closed his eyes he was out. The next thing he was aware of was an angel shaking him and telling him to wake up. Unbelievably as Sunny opened his eyes he looked up and saw Judy standing over him.

"Sunny, wake up, are you okay?" She asked.

Sunny couldn't believe she really was his guardian angel. They talked for a few minutes. Sunny gave Judy his parents address and phone number and took her parents phone number and promised to call when he got home. All the way home, Sunny couldn't help but think about waking up and seeing Judy, and wondering if she really would be there when he needed her.

Back in New Jersey

SUNNY FINALLY GOT INTO NEW Jersey. It was good to be back in Glen Ridge, and he was extremely tired.

When Sunny got home, everybody was glad to see him. It was great to have a home cooked meal. He had been gone a long time and everybody was anxious to hear stories. Sunny got up the next morning and went for a run to start getting back in shape. It was going to be good to take a breath and see some old friends. While Sunny was off ski bumming, the friends he grew up with were busy going to college, getting married, and working. Sunny had his usual run from his house down around Brookdale Park and back. It had gotten him through many difficult times. As he ran, he replayed the season through his mind. Most importantly, he thought about Judy and Cindy and tried to motivate himself with thoughts of Sun Valley. Sunny was huffing and puffing; he was not happy with the shape he was in. Being home would be a good chance to pull himself back together.

Sunny's dad had always had place for him at the family business when he needed it. First thing Monday morning Sunny was up and in the car, on the way to work with his dad. The family owned a tool distributing business on Lafayette Street in Manhattan. Since Sunny was only going to be there a short time he would be working on the fifth floor in the machine shop and down on the loading dock. Sunny was very happy to have the opportunity to work and earn some money. One of the salesmen that worked for the George W. Warner CO. was a really good mechanic and agreed to help Sunny redo the top end of his car before he went out West. This seemed like a good idea, because it was going to be a long drive. As soon as Sunny was able to put together some money he and Bill, the salesman, started working on the car.

It wasn't long before Sunny got a call from Carl.

"Sunny, that you?" Carl asked.

"Yeah, where you been?" asked Sunny.

"I'm up in Sussex. I have a job putting roofs on some apartment buildings."

"What are you doing this weekend? I could use some help." Carl asked.

"Well I guess I'm going to Sussex to do some roofing," Sunny said.

Sussex, New Jersey wasn't too far, it was only about an hour and a half from Glen Ridge. Sunny went up early. He found Carl on the construction site. He was standing on the roof of an apartment building. It was a Saturday, and not many of the other contractors were there, but as usual, Carl was working.

Sunny was glad to see Carl. Carl was busy hustling around and he didn't have time for much small talk. He was busy carrying roofing shingles and nailing them by hand. Sunny had not done any roofing before, but that didn't stop him from trying to help. Carl looked at Sunny and said,

"Well don't just stand there, go and get a couple of bundles."

Sunny just looked at him then climbed down the ladder took a bundle of roofing shingles and climbed back up. Carl looked at Sunny and laughed.

"Are you kidding me, we will be here all day if you take one bundle at a time," Carl said.

Carl proceeded to throw one bundle on each shoulder and climb two stories to the roof. Sunny watched in amazement. Sunny was a really strong guy, but he also wasn't stupid. A few minutes passed and Carl yelled to Sunny.

"Hey what are you doing? We're never going to get done!"

Just then, Carl saw Sunny's head just coming up over the roof line. He didn't have two bundles. He had the entire pallet of roofing shingles. Sunny had found a forklift driver and paid him $20. Sunny just looked at Carl and asked,

"Where you want them?"

Carl smiled and started unloading and spreading them out over the roof. He showed Sunny how to nail roofing shingles. Before they knew it, they were done with that apartment building and they decided to grab a bite to eat.

"Hey Carl, what happened when you went home?" asked Sunny

"It wasn't good" Carl said, "My dad was pissed. He wanted me to stay and work with him doing construction. When I told him I wanted to go out West to Sun Valley, he got really mad. So, I came up here where I knew a few people and put in a bid for this contract."

Sunny felt bad and he knew Carl was passing up a lifetime opportunity to stay and work with his father. The problem was that Carl and his father didn't really see eye to eye when it came to working together.

"Carl, I know I want to go out to Sun Valley with you, but are you sure you want to?"

"No," Carl said. "But every time I work with my dad we wind up fighting. So for now I'll put some money together and figure it out later," Carl explained.

"How are things going for you at home?" Carl asked.

"Not bad," said Sunny. "I've seen some friends from high school and got drunk once or twice. I think we should get down to the shore and do some surfing."

If Carl and Sunny weren't skiing, surfing was the next best thing. They were probably as good at surfing as they were at skiing.

"Okay. Let me finish this job up and will head down to the shore some weekend."

When you're in Jersey, you don't go to the beach or the ocean, you go to the shore. Carl and Sunny usually surfed somewhere between Lafayette and Seaside. It seemed to be a good place that had good waves. Carl's parents had a place down the shore and if they couldn't stay there, they managed to find a bed to stay with some friends or just slept on the beach.

Sunny went back home and worked for a couple weeks to put some money together. He realized that if he were going to go out to Sun Valley, he would have to have some sort of job skill. Sunny believed that he would be able to get in the ski school with his skiing skills, but his other job skills consisted of working in a bar pouring beers, changing kegs, and checking ID's at the door. Sunny liked looking at the newspaper at work during lunch. One day Sunny noticed an ad for the American School of

Bartending. Sunny's dad enjoyed having lunch with Sunny. He used to have Sunny come down and cleanup so he could take him out to lunch.

During lunch Sunny asked his dad, "Hey Dad, what do you think about me going to the American School for Bartending?"

Sunny looked up from his sandwich and saw his father's eyes light up. Sunny continued,

"If I'm going out to Sun Valley, I have to have a skill that would help me get a job."

Sunny didn't think his father heard any of that, he just heard the word "school". Sunny continued, "It wouldn't interfere with my work. I could do it at night." Truthfully, it didn't take much convincing.

Sunny's dad looked at him and said,

"That's a great idea. If you go, there is just one condition. You have to finish and graduate."

"It's a deal," Sunny said.

Sunny went to the American School of Bartending. He did well and graduated with a certificate, bowtie, bartending jacket and all. Sunny would try to be on the road to success.

Surfing

THE WEATHER HAD GOTTEN HOT and Sunny was tired of hanging around when it was time to get down to the shore. He called Carl and declared,

"It's time to hit some waves."

"I couldn't agree more," Carl said. "I'll meet you down at that great donut shop on 35."

Sunny said, "Look, I'm going to leave right after work on Friday and hope to borrow the company van and see if I can hit the waves. If I'm not at the shop, I'll be in the water, you'll find me."

Sunny did just that; he emptied out all the tools from the company van, threw in his surfboard, a blanket, and his sleeping bag. He was ready to go. He drove straight down the shore to his spot. Carl was not at the donut shop, so he went straight to the water. The waves were good. The water wasn't too bad, so he just jumped into his suit and started paddling out. No surprise, Carl and Herman were already out there.

"What took you so long?" Carl said.

"Traffic."

They surfed until it got dark. Sunny and Carl hadn't lost their touch. They jumped on waves and shredded with the best of them. When they were done, they hit the beach and just sat there exhausted.

"Carl, I got to get something to eat," said Sunny.

"Yeah me too," replied Carl.

They loaded their stuff in the back of Sunny's van and grabbed a couple of slices of pie. (If you're reading this and you're not from New Jersey, pie means pizza, it doesn't mean cherry pie or apple pie.) Carl and Sunny wound up back at the beach and sat looking at the ocean with Herman and a group of other surfers. Everybody wanted to hear stories about the winter and skiing, and everyone was enthralled. Carl eventually broke out his guitar and it wound up being a beach party. Sunny had realized that once again he and Carl were the center of attention.

Sunny also realized it wasn't something he was going to put on his resume. Sunny didn't tell anybody about attending Bartending School. Somehow, being the King of the Ski Bums seemed to be more interesting.

Sunny slept in the van so he could be close to the ocean and get up early to surf. He liked being alone and being able to come and go as he wanted to. The surf was really good, so he surfed for hours Saturday and Sunday with Carl. Sunny stayed over Sunday night, and got up very early in the morning on Monday to beat the traffic. He drove straight into Manhattan and was there a half an hour before his dad got there.

"Good morning, Sunny you're up bright and early," his father said.

"Good morning Dad. Yes, it was easier to come up this morning, the traffic was much better than trying to drive Sunday night," Sunny explained.

"As long as you made it safe, Son." His father laughed. "Let's get to work."

A few weekends later Sunny met Carl down at the same surf spot. The surf was really good, and there were a lot of surfers vying for the same waves. Sunny had just finished a really good ride and was paddling out. On the way out, Sunny turned his head to the left, looked up the beach, and saw that there was nobody in the water. As he turned his head to the right the beaches were full and people were out enjoying the waves. This could only mean one thing and it wasn't good. It was low tide, so Sunny was pretty far from shore and he realized he was paddling out to a potential shark. As he came over the top of the wave he saw Carl sitting there on his board. Sunny pushed up off his board and said,

"Hey Carl, there's a shark out here; look, everybody's headed out of the water."

Carl looked at Sunny and said,

"That's alright, I'm not hungry."

Sunny continued to paddle toward his friend. Just then, as he paddled over the next swell he saw it; a fin, a really big fin. It was a shark, and not too far away. Sunny yelled to Carl,

"Holy crap, look at that."

There was no time to make wise cracks then. Both Sunny and Carl looked back and started to paddle for the next wave. They both caught the wave at the same time. Both were doing great and almost on the shore when Carl slipped and fell off his board. Sunny saw Carl fall out of the corner of his eye and pulled up to get him out of the water. Soon both Sunny and Carl were safe and standing on the beach. They looked at each other.

Sunny said, "That was a little too close for comfort."

Carl wasn't paying any attention as he was staring at the ocean; Sunny looked out as well. Carl's board was being taken out to sea with the tide. Sunny looked around and grabbed a towel to dry off. As he looked up, he saw Carl running toward the water with the lifeguard's oversized surfboard. That could only mean one thing. Without thinking, Sunny took off after him. Sunny caught up to Carl and jumped onto the surfboard with him.

As Sunny got onto the surfboard he said,

"Hey Carl, nice day for a paddle in the ocean with a shark."

Carl replied, "Yeah, well it's not like I have a lot of surfboards lying around. What you are doing here?"

As Sunny paddled, he remarked,

"Well, besides wanting a view of your ass while I was paddling, you didn't think I was going to let you have all the fun; besides, if this shark comes after us I thought I would throw you overboard and get your surfboard."

"Nice try, asshole," Carl replied.

"Yeah, but I'm your asshole," said Sunny.

Sunny and Carl retrieved his surfboard and they also managed to get an overwhelming lecture from the lifeguards. Fortunately, Sunny knew one of the lifeguards and they managed to not get kicked off the beach for the summer. Sunny would go down to the shore several more weekends and surf with Carl and Herman. He continued to work on his car to get it ready to go out west.

Carl had a white van that he managed to trade in for a Chevy Blazer.

One day, Carl showed up at Sunny's house all packed up and ready to go. Sunny's parents were sitting in the kitchen having breakfast as he looked outside and saw this brand-new Chevy Blazer pull up the driveway.

"Hey Sunny, who is that?" His father asked. Sunny looked out the window.

"It's Carl. He must've gotten a new car."

Sunny went outside.

"Holy crap Carl, where did you get that?" Sunny asked.

"I traded in my white van and with a little bit of finagling, along with the monthly payment, this is what I got. You ready to go?" Carl asked.

It was only August and Sunny didn't have nearly enough money to go. The cost of fixing up his engine really hit him hard. He looked at Carl a little stunned. Carl always did do things on his own time schedule and without warning.

"No, I'm not ready. I have to work some more and put together some more money. Come on in and grab a bite to eat."

Carl went into the house to spend the night and left early in the morning.

"Well, I'll go out there and get things set up; I'll be waiting for you. I guess I'll just head west and figure it out from there," Carl said.

Sunny looked at Carl with a smile.

"You could just stop at a truck stop and pick up a map."

"Yeah I could do that. I probably will," Carl said.

"Give me a call when you get there, will you?" Sunny said.

And with that, Carl was off.

The Calls

SUNNY WAS AT HOME ONE day sleeping up on the third floor when he heard, "You got a call. Pick up," from down stairs. He picked up the phone and could hardly hear.

"Hello, hello?" said Sunny.

"Hey, can you hear me?" Carl yelled into the phone. "I'm at a party so I have to talk fast. Man there are more pretty girls here than in Miami Beach. You got to get out here."

"Great, how will I find you?"

"Ask anyone. It's not a big town. I have to go." said Carl.

"How do I get there?

"Drive to Salt Lake and take a right. Hurry!" Carl explained and then he hung up.

That weekend, Sunny received another call.

"Are you in New Jersey yet?"

Sunny recognized the voice immediately. It was Judy and he was very glad to hear from her.

"Yep, I'm almost there," She said.

"I thought you were going to call me when you got to New Jersey."

"Well, I wasn't so sure that you wanted hear from me," Sunny replied.

"How are you doing? Where are you?" asked Sunny. Sunny actually was surprised to hear from Judy, he'd thought she would be making wedding arrangements.

"Well I'm doing okay. I'm in Boston. I thought I'd come down there and work for the summer. I'm surprised to catch you at your parent's house. I thought you'd be on your way to Idaho by now," said Judy.

"No, not yet. I needed to work some more to get the money to go out. I still need to work at least three or four more weeks before I'll have enough," Sunny explained.

"Hey Sunny, I had a thought. I am taking a little time off between my summer work and winter. How about if I ride out to Denver with you?" Judy said.

This caught Sunny by surprise. He wasn't sure this was a good idea, but it was a long ride. He sure wouldn't mind the company.

"Are you sure? Come on down, we can go out in New York before we go. It's the least I can do," Sunny said. He had spent a lot of time thinking about Judy. He wasn't sure what she was thinking about him, but Judy had always thought for herself and did what she wanted. If Judy wanted to ride from New Jersey to Denver, then that was okay with Sunny.

The Accident

Sunny spent the next couple of weeks working and making the last finishing touches on his car. When it was ready he called Judy to tell her to come on down. Sunny and Bill went out to celebrate and to see how the car rode. Unfortunately, Sunny had a little too good at celebrating. As he turned to go into a parking lot, another car hit him head on. Sunny and Bill were okay, but the entire front end of the Chevy was completely smashed. The other person was taken away in an ambulance. All Sunny remembered was that the police told him to get to the sidewalk and start walking. Sunny walked to his brother's house which was about five blocks away. The next morning, Sunny found his car at the place where they had towed it. The whole front end was totaled. Fortunately, the radiator frame and engine were still intact. Sunny looked around and there was another '57 Chevy, with the back completely totaled. Bill helped Sunny negotiate the front grill and fenders. He had his car and the new grill and fenders towed to his parent's home.

It was Saturday, so Sunny went into New York and got every tool he could into the company van, went home, and cut every piece he could off the Chevy with a torch. By 8 o'clock the next morning, it was down to the frame, radiator, and engine. Sunny called his friend Phil, who he had grown up with. He was a good mechanic and worked with Sunny and his dad at the shop.

"Hey Phil, I need your help. I was in an accident the other day and I gotta get my car ready to go out West. Could you come over and help me put some parts on?" asked Sunny. Phil only lived a couple blocks away so Sunny knew it wouldn't take him long to get there.

"Sure Sunny, I'll be over in a few minutes."

Just then the ever familiar, green Volkswagen pulled up in the driveway and he heard that unforgettable voice.

"Hey Sunny, how are you doing?" It was Judy.

Sunny looked up from underneath the Chevy.

"I've been better, but it's good to see you," he said.

Just then, the tow truck came in. Sunny met him at the curb.

"Is this the right place for this?" The driver asked.

"Yes, can you back it down the driveway?" Sunny asked.

Just as the tow truck started to back down the driveway, Phil walked up and stood next to Sunny.

"When you said put a few parts on you weren't kidding," Phil said holding his coffee.

Sunny brought Judy in to meet his parents. Both his mom and dad were delighted. Judy had more poise and grace than Sunny had, of course. They were pleased that Sunny had attracted such a beautiful, nice girl. Sunny and Phil went back out to the garage and put the front end on the Chevy. They didn't use a lot of screws, they just spot welded everything in place. The trip out west was a one-way trip for that front end; it wasn't coming off. There weren't going to be a whole lot of repairs. This accident cost Sunny a lot of the money he had saved, but he was going to go no matter what. When the guys were done, Phil left to spend time with his girlfriend. Like Judy, Phil was always there when Sunny needed him.

Sunny and Judy ate at home as everyone had a lot of questions—mostly as to why such a beautiful, poised, intelligent woman would be with Sunny. After a good night's sleep, Sunny made good on his promise and took Judy into New York. Judy was somewhat surprised to see how familiar Sunny was with New York City. Judy and Sunny had never really been anywhere outside of Stowe together. They ate at Mama Mia's in Manhattan, which was a little touristy, but it seemed like the thing to do. By this time Sunny had developed a skill of being able to drink large volumes of alcohol, and he had transitioned from beer to scotch. The decadent lifestyle was catching up to him. They saw each other in a different world and talked about their lives and their dreams. They talked about what it would be like to live together and be married. Sunny told her about going through the American School of Bartending. He knew that Judy would understand that bartending at an upscale ski resort could produce some income. After the day in the city, the two were off to Idaho.

If you had never driven cross-country, leaving from New Jersey was only exciting for about the first two hours. When you drove across Pennsylvania, you believed that Columbus was right. The world is flat, and you're going to drop off the edge of the Earth. It takes a long time just to get out of Pennsylvania, and Route 80 was the only way to go. Sunny didn't have a lot of money for motel rooms, so he was going to be driving straight through. It was not going to be a luxury trip. Sunny wasn't really sure why Judy wanted to go. Maybe this was how she brought things to an end. Maybe she thought Sunny would change his mind. Maybe she thought she would change her mind and go with him. Maybe she just wanted to take a drive to Denver. They did have a great chance to talk openly. It was early September and it was a pretty drive. They drove, laughed, talked, and even managed to make love in the Chevy.

Sunny managed to get a room one night as the drive was getting to both of them, and they were too tired to do much else but rest. It was nice just to be together. Sunny was still very much aware that Judy was more than special, and he couldn't take care of her.

He only had a couple hundred dollars in his pocket and the car was on its last legs. The most valuable items that Sunny had were his skis. Judy really did deserve more. Sunny had no idea about his future. When they reached Denver, Judy had to go straight to the airport as she had to get back east. Sunny drove Judy there and walked her to the gate. He realized that he was on his own now. Judy was not going to be there for him and he wasn't going to be there for her. As she boarded the plane, Judy looked at him and said,

"Sunny, I love you." Sunny gave her a kiss and said,

"Judy I love you too." With that she turned and walked onto the plane.

Judy flew back east and married Tom.

Denver

SUNNY DROVE INTO DENVER AND found his brother Jeff. Jeff was attending the University of Denver and was living in the basement of a house. Sunny was out of money, and needed to find a short-term job to earn some more to get out to Sun Valley. When Sunny got to his brother's house, he was glad to see him. Jeff had been doing pretty well at school, but he didn't want to live in a dorm. Jeff took Sunny for a tour of the college. He introduced him to some of the girls at school.

Sunny knew he had to find a job pretty quick if he was going to earn enough money to get out to Sun Valley. He felt confident with his new degree and bartending skills. Sunny looked in the local paper for ads for bartending. He saw an ad for a local bar that sounded pretty good, the Riviera Club. Sunny didn't have a clue which bar was which, it just sounded a little more upscale. He was anxious to try out his new skills as a bartender and avoid just slinging beers. Sunny called and arranged an interview, then put on a sports jacket and tie. When Sunny arrived at the address, he was a little confused and somewhat disappointed. It looked like an old house converted into a bar with a martini glass for a sign with one of the sides hanging off and a broken screen door. Nevertheless, he needed a job so he took off his sports jacket and went in.

In his white shirt and tie, Sunny opened the door only to find himself in the middle of some sort of a bar brawl. Directly in front of him was a pool table. Sunny really didn't want to get into a bar fight, but as soon as he walked into the bar he knew avoiding a brawl would be really difficult. He thought maybe he could hide underneath the pool table or something.

Unfortunately, the pool table went all the way to the floor and that wasn't an option. So the next option was to try and move around to the back to see if he could get through the fighting. Just then, somebody ran up to him and tried to grab him by the tie and pulled him into a punch. This was a really bad idea. First, because Sunny was wearing a clip-on tie and the tie came off, leaving the guy standing there looking a little stupid. Second, Sunny could throw a right-hand punch that could drop most anybody and he did. But he still didn't want to get into a fight and he tried to get to the back. On his way back, he grabbed some guy who started yelling,

"Don't hit me!"

Sunny looked at him and said, "I'm not going to hit you. I'm here for a job interview."

The guy looked back a little stunned, as Sunny had him pinned against the wall.

"Okay you got it."

Suddenly, Sunny felt a very sharp pain in his back. Somebody had decided to cut him with a church key, a bottle opener. Now Sunny wasn't a small guy and didn't like to fight either. But he had grown up sparring with his older stepbrother Gary. He had gotten into a few fights when he was younger and he wasn't bad at it. Growing up in New Jersey, you either got good at fighting or you got beaten up. Sunny didn't get beaten up. He turned around and wasn't able to readily identify the person who had assaulted him, but he didn't care at that moment. Sunny rarely ever got mad, but when he did you probably didn't want to be in the room. Sunny grabbed one of the pool cues and quickly emptied the room.

To Sunny, this was just another bar brawl and he'd seen a few. Maybe it was the disappointment from not being able to use his skills from Bartending School, maybe it was the frustration from not having enough money to go to Sun Valley, or maybe it was everything built up from Judy leaving. Whatever it was, it was out and so was everybody else. Sunny walked up to the bar bleeding, reached into his pocket and pulled out his resume and his bartending certificate and said quietly,

"I'll understand if you don't want to hire me."

The owner was a woman and the manager was standing next to her somewhat stunned. Sunny looked at her and said,

"I really apologize. I hate to fight and I really don't know what came over me; it won't happen again."

The owner looked at Sunny and saw that he was bleeding quite a bit.

"Are you okay?"

Sunny looked at her.

"Oh yeah, I think I'm fine. I'll probably need a new shirt." He smiled.

She looked at him again and said,

"When can you start?"

They gave Sunny money for a new shirt and pants, as his were covered in blood. Sunny went back to the university to look for his brother in the dorms. He ran into one of the girls that his brother had introduced him to.

"Hi, have you seen my brother, Jeff?" asked Sunny. "I am trying to find him."

"No," she said. "I think he is with my roommate. You're bleeding, are you okay?"

"Yes, actually I just got a job, but I think I may need a stitch or two. Tough job interview," Sunny laughed.

The girl looked at Sunny and said,

"Come in my room here and let me see if I can patch you up some."

She was really nice and was able to put a few butterflies on Sunny's back, clean him up, and give him a T-shirt. Sunny used the money he got to get stitches and bought a new shirt and pants and took her out to dinner to celebrate the new job.

The Riviera Club turned out to be a great place to work as it served Mexican food. Sunny had never had Mexican food and didn't understand a word anybody was saying when they ordered it, so he would write down what he thought they said and send it into the kitchen. Sometimes they would laugh and probably told him to go screw himself; and he wrote that down without knowing it, but Sunny really enjoyed working there. It was a great bar, and they had a live piranha in a tank behind the bar. The owner always tried to get Sunny to clean the tank and that was just too much for Sunny; he just wasn't about to go stick his hand in a tank with a piranha. When Sunny told them he was off to Sun Valley, they were sad to see him go. Needless to say, there were no more bar fights while Sunny was bartending. Sunny even got to use some of his bartending skills.

On to Sun Valley

It was October, the air was getting cold and it was time to get to Sun Valley. Sunny's best friend was out there, and he knew he had to get there. He had earned enough money to make it out to Sun Valley. Sunny looked at a map, packed up again, and headed off. He still wasn't used to the long drives of the west and the land yacht he was driving was doing great, but it wasn't wonderful. Sunny thanked his brother for all the hospitality and headed off. Sunny drove straight through from Denver to Salt Lake. It was a long push. When Sunny got to Salt Lake, he was tired. He didn't want to push it the last little bit. So he got a room, bought a six pack, grabbed a burger, filled the bathtub, and soaked. This was IT as Carl would say, *'Just one more turn and straight up to Sun Valley.'*

Sunny woke up early and grabbed some breakfast. He knew that he needed to drive from Salt Lake to Sun Valley on a full stomach since he knew there was a storm coming through. Sunny had never seen weather like there was out west, but was determined to get to Sun Valley although he didn't even have snow tires on the car.

As Sunny drove from Salt Lake up through Idaho, it seemed to go on forever. He had never seen the landscape like he saw coming up through Bellevue. It seemed flat forever at first: then all of a sudden, the mountains appeared. The road was desolate for a long time and the weather was really harsh. It snowed sideways at times. Then Sunny saw the mountains. He was in awe, and to a certain degree, overwhelmed. Most of all, he just had to find Carl or someone he knew.

Sunny drove straight into town to a gas station on the right-hand side.

He was exhausted, but he had gotten there. Sunny got out to fill up the land yacht. Just for the heck of it, he thought he'd ask the guy at the gas station,

"Hey, I'm Sunny how are you doing?"

"I'm Durg," the guy said with the most pleasant, thick Idaho accents.

"You're a long way from home, aren't yuh?" Durg asked, as he looked at Sunny's license plate.

Sunny looked at him and smiled. He loved his accent.

"Yes, I am," replied Sunny. "You wouldn't happen to know another New Jersey guy, a friend of mine named Carl would you?" Sunny asked.

"The short little Italian-looking guy driving a Chevy Blazer?" Durg asked.

"That's him. He makes quite an impression doesn't he?" Sunny said.

"Yeah, the boy is not shy," Durg commented.

"Do you mind if I use your phone to call him?" asked Sunny.

"No, not at all," Durg said.

Sunny called Carl, and Durg gave him directions to the little cabins where Carl had rented a room. Sunny was really glad to see Carl. It wasn't great, but it was a place to live and that wasn't easy to get in a ski town. Sunny knew that this was starting over in Sun Valley, Idaho.

Sun Valley, the Beginning

THE CABINS WERE ALL THEY could afford, and at least Carl and Sunny had their own room. Sunny and Carl were not able to live together very well, as they both had strong opinions about things. It was difficult if you put two alphas in the same room. The worst was agreeing on food. Carl's idea of cooking was to put everything into a frying pan, burn it and add mayo and call it breakfast or dinner. It was all the same to him.

Sunny on the other hand, had different ideas. He was actually a pretty good cook.

Carl gave Sunny a tour of the town of Ketchum. Sunny had never seen a town like Ketchum. It was an old town in the midst of a transformation by the '60s ski invasion. There were still a few holdouts, like the Alpine Bar. As Carl brought Sunny up to the door, he pointed out the sign on the door which read, "Women and College Students are Tolerated."

Sunny looked at Carl and asked, "Are they kidding?"

Carl laughed.

"Let's go in, you'll see," he said.

They went in and the sign was not kidding. It was one of the last holdouts. The bar was dark with a great mural of a nude behind it. Across the street there was another bar called The Casino. You could actually go in and see old cowboys sitting around playing cards and telling lies, even seeing some of them with side arms. The other bars in town were restaurants and bars with entertainment more geared to the ski industry. Carl drove Sunny up to the mountain named Baldy. Sunny couldn't believe it. It was more mountain than he had ever seen and he couldn't wait. This was the fresh start he was hoping for.

The next stop was the resort, Sun Valley. It was about a mile from Ketchum. You could see the difference between the town and the resort. The joke was: all the girls go to Sun Valley and all the guys go to Ketchum. Sunny now understood why his father was so impressed with Sun Valley. The Lodge was beautiful, and looking out at the mountains from the lodge was an inspiring sight. When Sunny and Carl walked through the lodge, they could see and feel the history. Sun Valley was America's first ski area. Sunny started to feel at home. There was only one problem then—both Carl and Sunny needed money, and there was no one to call for help. They were completely on their own, and they knew it. That was the risk of going out west and not knowing anyone.

If it weren't for Carl, both men would have starved to death. Carl saw a guy named Mark painting some trim. He had done that work before with his dad, so Carl put on his best suit and walked up to Mark and told him he could do that trim better. Mark hired him the next day. Carl talked Mark into hiring his friend, Sunny, to help stain the decks. Mark was a great guy. He was a Mormon who had a construction company and had gotten the contract to stain the decks in Sun Valley. The only way to do it was to roll them and to do the rails by hand. It was cold, dirty, difficult work, but it was work.

Now in New Jersey, when you worked construction, payday was on Friday. When you worked construction in Idaho and worked for a Mormon, payday was once a month. This was a problem if you were two starving kids from New Jersey and there were no advances. Mark was kind and generous and opened his home to Carl and Sunny for meals, as well as treating them like family. Both quickly understood how valuable it was to have somebody who was so kind and willing to give them work and food. Sunny and Carl worked hard and showed up on time.

The deck staining job turned out to be interesting. To gain access to some of the decks, Sunny and Carl had to go into the condos and look for the doors. Some of the condos had hidden rooms with bathrooms and libraries and their own decks. It was kind of fun to see the secret lives that people were living. Sunny never got to meet any of the people who owned those condos with the secret rooms.

Mark was very good to Sunny and Carl too, and they kept in touch for a long time after that. November was here and so was the snow, so the time for staining decks was over.

As the snow came, so did people. The town was filling up and the bars were opening. Sunny knew what to do next. He knew the bar business and he knew this was his opportunity to get back on his feet in a ski town. Sunny managed to get a job bartending in a bar called the Crazy Horse, just off Main Street. It was a small bar that used to be an auto shop. The Crazy Horse primarily sold beer, which was perfect for Sunny even though he was hoping to move up to a more affluent bar where he could practice his drink mixing skills. The bar mostly played country music and had some country bands. This was okay with Sunny. He got along well with George, the manager; they seemed to both speak the same language, bar and hustle. Sunny was back.

Carl always had his paint sprayer to pick up jobs and since he was a self-taught architectural designer, he was able to draft architectural plans. He also did construction jobs. Soon Thanksgiving came and the mountain opened.

Getting a Job on The Mountain

IT WAS TIME TO GET on the mountain. Once again, it was Carl who got Sunny and himself the introductions. Carl had managed to get a Canadian Ski Instructor Certification while he was in New Jersey. This had qualified him for a job interview. The ski school director was named Paul and he was anxious to get more Americans on the ski school. Carl introduced himself, and managed to get Paul to interview them on the mountain and watch them ski. Carl was a shoe-in with his certification, but Paul wasn't quite sure as to why Sunny was there. Sunny only had one pair of skis, and they were 210 centimeters that he had used for racing. Through Carl's certification, he had practiced doing slow technical turns to demonstrate skiing. This was not a skill Sunny was prepared to display.

Carl and Sunny caught up with Paul almost at the top of the mountain. When Paul had asked Carl where he was from, Carl had said he was from New Jersey. Paul said there weren't too many big mountains in New Jersey. Sunny didn't speak at all. Neither Sunny nor Carl mentioned that they were Nastar pacesetters nor did they mention that they had been living in Stowe for a season or two. Sunny didn't have time to mention that he went to high school in Stowe and trained out at Mount Hood. At that moment, Paul's impression was that he was looking at two boys from New Jersey.

Paul said, "Well, let's see what you can do, follow me."

Paul skied slowly, methodically, carefully, and Carl followed him precisely. Sunny had a little difficulty skiing that slow with his long skis. When Paul turned around, he saw that Sunny had some difficulty on a couple of the turns at the lower speeds.

232

Sunny, not usually nervous on a pair of skis, turned to Carl and took a line from Butch Cassidy and Sundance Kid and said, *"Can I move?"*

Carl knew exactly what he meant and just nodded his head. Paul looked at Carl and asked,

"What are you talking about?"

By this time, they were standing up at the exhibition trail and it was pretty steep. Carl looked at Paul and said, "Just a second, you'll see."

Sunny took a deep breath and took off. Maybe it was the fear of not getting on the ski school or the fact that there was a really great hill right in front of him. Sunny let it loose.

Carl turned to Paul and said, "He's better when he moves faster."

After Sunny was done ripping up one of the steepest hills on the mountain, Paul looked at Carl and said, "Okay, you guys are in. Come on down and pick up uniforms." Paul and Carl skied down. Paul came up to Sunny and said,

"You didn't learn that in New Jersey did you?"

Sunny smiled and shook his head, "No. I went to high school in Stowe and I spent some time out at Mount Hood in the summer, thank you though."

Paul looked at him and said, "That was a great run."

"Thanks again," Sunny said.

And just like that, Sunny and Carl were on the Sun Valley Ski School staff. Now That was something for Sunny to call home and tell his dad. On the ride back down into town, Sunny couldn't help thinking that he had come from skiing the streets of Glen Ridge to working at the Sun Valley Ski School. He just wondered what could be next. Carl and Sunny truly had something to celebrate.

Christmas in Sun Valley

CHRISTMAS IN SUN VALLEY WAS always beautiful, and this particular year there was a lot of snow, so it really did look like a postcard. Both Ketchum and Sun Valley were charmingly decorated. It was very different from the New England atmosphere that Sunny had grown accustomed to. In Ketchum, the streets and storefronts were lined on both sides with decorations and lights. The town was full of people who were walking around in their ski outfits and the ski shops were packed. That night, you could hear bands playing from the bars. Sun Valley was exquisitely decorated in white lights, and the town looked like something out of a Disney movie. All the shops and restaurants were full. Sun Valley had an outdoor pool where the steam bellowed up. You could see through the glass the people swimming and laughing, drinking their wine.

This was time for Sunny and Carl to work, when the tourists were there. People needed ski lessons and Sunny was in his element. For Sunny it was work all day and work all night. He wasn't complaining; he had gone from staining decks, and wondering where his next meal would come from, to getting regular pay on the mountain and also getting paid plus tips down at the Crazy Horse. By this time, being away from their families during Christmas was part of living in a ski town. It was the price to pay and not a good price either. Sunny even had to work on Christmas Day, and didn't call home until after he got off the mountain. He managed to catch up with Carl.

"Hey Carl, did you get a chance to call home?" Sunny asked.

"Yeah, I did. They're okay, how about you?" Carl asked.

"Yeah, I did too. The same as last year," Sunny said.

"But a different place and a different time."

"You have to work tonight?" Carl asked.

"No, the Crazy Horse is closed tonight. Whatta you say you and I go into town and see if we can grab a Christmas dinner."

"Sounds good to me."

Carl and Sunny went home and got changed to go into town to grab a burger.

"Hey Sunny, you haven't been out picking up any girls lately. I am worried about you," said Carl.

"It isn't like it was. I've been out with some girls at the Crazy Horse, but it's just not the same," Sunny said.

Carl could see that Sunny just wasn't himself since he left Stowe.

"This is about Cindy and Judy isn't it?" Carl asked.

"I suppose so. I just can't get the idea out of my head that I screwed up with both of them. It's not like I have a whole lot of money to do a lot of dating here, we're just getting back on our feet," Sunny explained.

"Come on Sunny, snap out of it. It's been long enough. We came out here to start over so, start over!" Carl snapped at Sunny. "I haven't seen you run or do anything to get into shape lately," he continued.

"Well there are some local races here starting after the holidays. Maybe I'll go out to the training area. There are some serious pros up there, so maybe I can start training with them. As far as women well, I don't see you on your game either," said Sunny.

"Speak for yourself. I'm doing okay."

Things were different in Sun Valley. There was no Hole in the Wall Gang, there was no condo—there was just Carl and Sunny. Carl had managed to get himself thrown out of the cabin they were in, and Sunny had moved into a double-wide trailer which was actually pretty nice. Carl got his own housing.

Not Going in the Right Direction

CHRISTMAS AND NEW YEAR'S CAME and went. Sunny had gotten into the groove in the bar scene and was partying pretty hard. He did manage to get up to the training area where some of the pros were training. There was a national Pro Tour, and the pros from Sun Valley were a league above the ones he had seen at Stowe. The only Pro who was really competitive at Stowe was Greg Bartlett.

One day in Stowe, Greg jumped into a local race, dead last, and managed to ski through ruts up to his knees on the inside and beat everybody. That was the caliber of skiers who were training. Sunny went up and followed the pros and got to know a few of them. He wasn't too far behind, but he wasn't there yet. There were some local races Sunny was able to get into, and he did pretty well.

One day Sunny was in one of the other bars with George. George had watched him race in one of the local races where he did really well. George acknowledged Sunny by saying,

"I saw your race today. I didn't even recognize it was you."

Sunny looked at George and said, "Yeah, I get that a lot from people. They don't recognize me when I'm on the Hill. I must look very different in my ski clothes. Everybody thinks I can't ski since I'm from New Jersey." George looked at Sunny and said, "Do you want to make some money?"

Sunny wasn't quite sure what George was up to, but at this point, he wasn't going to turn down the opportunity to make a little extra. George turned to one of the other guys in the bar who was working in the restaurant and said, "Sunny can you beat him?"

Sunny knew who he was and had seen him ski. He had even seen him race.

"Yeah I can beat him," Sunny said.

"By how much?"

Sunny had started a bad habit of drinking scotch, but he knew what he was doing at this point.

"How much do you want me to beat him by?" Sunny asked.

"I want you to lose the first run and then just squeak out the win on the second run," George said.

Sunny knew what George wanted to do. This wasn't a good idea, but Sunny didn't really like the guy and he got tired of people thinking he couldn't ski. George had a lot of guts pulling this off.

"Are you sure?" Sunny asked.

"The question is, are you sure you can beat him?"

"Yes. I can, but they're not gonna like it when we're done."

George called the guy over and introduced Sunny to him, and as predicted, the guy didn't recognize him. George in a boastful way started saying," I think my guy here from New Jersey can kick your ass."

These were fighting words, and in the skiing world nobody from Idaho wanted to be beaten by a New Jersey skier. Those were the people that came out on vacation who gave you a hard time.

Sunny decided to throw on a New Jersey accent and say, "Yeah, its beeyootiful here, you get the fresh air and everything. I think I can ski pretty well."

George piped right in.

"I'll put $100 on Sunny."

The guy looked at Sunny. "I've never seen you ski before, you make that $200."

The poor guy took the bait. What he didn't know was George wasn't going to wait until after the first run to double the bet, which was exactly what had happened. At the next race, Sunny took off and he did something he had never done before—he held back and tanked the race, not too much, but just by a half a second. George was waiting at the finish. Carl was also waiting at the finish and he skied over to Sunny.

"What the hell are you doing Sunny, I saw that?" said Carl.

"I don't know. I must've had a bad run," Sunny replied.

"Keep your voice down. I'll pick it up on the next run." Sunny skied by George. George quietly leaned over and said, "Don't beat him by too much."

Sunny couldn't do that on the next run; instead, he let it go and won the race by a full second. George had doubled the bet and then some. Sunny met George in the bar and Carl was with him. George was really excited. He had hustled that guy out of about $700.

Carl caught up to Sunny. "You're going to get yourself killed pulling that crap."

Sunny looked at Carl. "Yeah I know, but I just picked up $300 and it felt good."

Sunny was pretty drunk by this time and his skiing was bad, but he was getting better at drinking. He also managed to get better at introducing himself to the local female talent. Stowe was an undergraduate degree in decadence and Sun Valley was the graduate degree; Sunny was getting excellent grades.

Skiing out west was a different world than back east. People used to drive up to Stowe for the weekend and only stay for the week through the holidays. When you were in Sun Valley, people flew in and they stayed all week. A few people drove up from Boise, but by and large, it was a wealthy crowd and they came to party. They had money, drugs, and alcohol. And if they wanted a ski instructor or professional skier, that was all part of the package. What happened in Sun Valley stayed in Sun Valley. The problem was they went home, but the people who lived there didn't. Eventually it caught up to them.

One day, Sunny got a call while he was at home in his trailer. It was a familiar voice.

"Hey, what are you doing? I haven't heard from you in a long time."

It was Cindy. Sunny reached down to the side of his bed where his bottle of Johnny Walker was and took a quick sip.

"Holy crap, Cindy!" Sunny said. "What are you doing? I thought I'd never hear from you again!"

"Why not?" She said in a cheerful voice.

"I'm out here in Sun Valley. I was in town with a girlfriend and we thought we'd come out and do some skiing. I wanted to look you up."

Sunny couldn't believe it. "Where are you?" he asked.

She gave him the name of the hotel where she was staying. Sunny wasn't sure he wanted to see her, but knew he wasn't in any shape to argue at the moment. He was still skiing okay, but he was a little hung over. He remembered the night when he had met her mother and drank too much.

"Give me a few hours and I'll meet you in town." Sunny said.

Cindy knew there must have been something wrong, because usually Sunny would have been up early and on the mountain.

Sunny pulled himself together and went into town He walked into the restaurant. She looked a little older, more mature, and more beautiful. Sunny looked older and more tired. She jumped up and gave him a big hug and kiss. All the feelings he was trying to get away from flooded back.

"You look great, Cindy," Sunny said.

"You look tired Sunny! Nice to see you too." He smiled and knew she was right. He had never expected to see her out there. It was a couple of thousand miles from Stowe. Cindy was in New York modeling and she could afford to go anywhere she wanted to.

"Have you been up skiing yet?" asked Sunny.

"No, not yet. I'm going to go up tomorrow."

Cindy introduced her friend to Sunny and they sat and had dinner. After dinner, Sunny took them over to the Crazy Horse where he had to work and introduced them to everybody there. Sunny didn't want to show Cindy where he was living. A double-wide trailer is not exactly something you brag about. Cindy invited Sunny to her room after he got off work. Sunny wasn't sure how that would work with her roommate, but that was okay with him and he managed to stay sober that night. When he got to the room, Cindy was just as striking as he remembered and ready to pick up where they had left off. Her roommate had stayed with friends that lived in Ketchum. Sunny was honest with Cindy, and told her about his living arrangements and what he was doing. She told him all about her modeling in New York.

The next day they all met at the lift and Sunny managed to avoid getting assigned any ski lessons, so he was free to ski for the day. The only things

Sunny had left were his skiing and what he did. They caught up with Carl at the restaurant at the top of the mountain called the Round House 9000 (because it was at 9,000 feet). They ate lunch, sat on the deck, and looked at the beautiful view. Sunny was glad to see Cindy. He knew he was in a bit of trouble and hoped that Cindy would pull him back. After lunch, Sunny and Cindy skied like it was like old times. The magic was back and he was his old self just for a few days. Cindy did go over to Sunny's trailer. As she walked in she commented,

"This isn't so bad. This is nice."

Sunny looked at her and laughed. "For up here, this is not too bad, but still it is a shit hole. Let's not kid ourselves," Sunny said.

Sun Valley was full of high-priced housing. It wasn't cheap out there. Cindy truly didn't care. For a beautiful model, she could go with the flow and be happy where she was. But just as fast as she came into town, she left. And Sunny was left with the same hole in his heart as he had when he came into Sun Valley.

Sunny spent the next month skiing and training as much as he could with the pros that were on the Pro Tour. There was a pro-A race at Sun Valley and he managed to sign himself up and get into the race. During the qualifiers, Sunny got a reality check. He actually didn't ski too badly, but when he came up against two of the pros, Bobby Cochran (a former US Olympic team member), and Andrzej Bachleda (who had skied for Poland in the 1968 and '72 Olympics), Sunny got his ass kicked. He was up against the big boys and he knew he was not in their league. These guys were in the league of a Ron Biedermann, and Sunny had always known that there was a natural talent level above his. He wasn't that far off, but they skied so much smoother and quieter, so much more relaxed and had beaten Sunny by one and a half to two seconds on each run. Sunny knew he was close to the end of his racing career, though he continued to train and ski. Sunny also continued to drink, party, and get to know the locals and the women. By this time, Sunny could drink hard liquor all night and go home only to do it again the next day. Everyone who knew Sunny knew that he was a really good skier, but they also knew he was a better drinker.

Sunny woke up one day and decided he needed to start getting back in shape. He decided to go out for a run so he jumped into the shower, took a shot of Johnny Walker, which was in the shower, and went out for a run. It wasn't 100 yards before he threw up. He continued to run and continued to throw up. Sunny went back to his trailer and jumped in the shower, feeling as if he might have worked up a sufficient sweat to kill some of the demons—only to throw up one more time. This time it was blood. Maybe it was fate, maybe it was luck, and maybe it was someone looking over him. But just then, Carl happened to walk into the trailer.

"Sunny, you here?" Carl yelled.

Sunny was gasping for air and bent over the toilet. Carl opened the bathroom door and saw Sunny standing there with blood all over the place.

"That's it, you're coming with me." Carl said.

Carl took Sunny straight to the hospital in Sun Valley. After a quick examination, the doctor walked into Sunny's room.

"Well Sunny, you have an ulcer. You have two choices, quit drinking or die."

Carl was standing next to him and heard this. Sunny looked them and said,

"Is there a third option?"

The doctor looked at Sunny. "This isn't funny and no. Take this medication and get help; you have to stop." Carl left the hospital with Sunny. They didn't talk much. Carl turned to Sunny and said, "I'm not gonna watch you kill yourself. I don't want to be friends with somebody who throws his life away because they want to drink. You're not skiing like you used to. The only thing you've gotten better at is drinking. Pack your things, you're coming with me."

Carl was driving a big Suburban. He drove Sunny to his trailer and Sunny threw some things together.

"Where we going, Carl?" Sunny asked.

"Just pack a sleeping bag, some warm clothes. I'll get the rest. I'll be back in a half an hour."

Sunny packed his things. When Carl got back, the Suburban was loaded up with some supplies. Carl drove Sunny out of town and up the Triumph Road as far as he could go. He drove up until the four-wheel-drive Suburban couldn't go any further. He looked at Sunny and said, "This'll do."

Sunny looked at Carl. He knew what was going on. He was going to dry out. Sunny and Carl stayed out there for three days. They talked, they sat in lawn chairs, sat around the fire, ate Carl's cooking, which would've cured anybody of anything or killed them, solved the problems of the world, and talked about what was important and real.

Carl drove Sunny back in town and he waited while Sunny went to the house and threw out every bottle of liquor there was. Sunny did the next hardest thing he could do. He called his dad and told him everything. Sunny was on the first flight home the next morning. Sunny had known he was on his own when he was out there, but when it came to his health, his father wasn't going to compromise. He wanted his son home, he wanted his son safe and healthy. He didn't ask.

When Sunny arrived in Newark Airpor,t and his father saw him, he was shocked to see that Sunny had lost about 25 pounds. He looked gaunt and unhealthy. Sunny's dad was glad to see him.

Sunny looked at his dad and said, "I'm in trouble, I need your help."

His dad just looked at him and said, "Let's go home."

Sunny went home, ate healthy, and as usual, went to work the next day. Work was the best thing for Sunny to keep his head on straight. By the end of the week, Sunny was back running and started to feel strong again. You see, Sunny's family was Irish and some of them don't do so well drinking. Sunny's father understood this. Within three weeks, Sunny went to his dad and said, "I'm doing pretty good. I think it's time for me to go back." His father understood Sunny wasn't going to quit; he also understood that Sunny wasn't going to drink. He knew his son's determination. Sunny never did drink anymore after that day.

Back in Sun Valley

SUNNY GOT ON THE PLANE to fly back to Sun Valley. He was unsure as to whether he could live in the decadent ski town and not drink. It would kind of be like someone swearing off sex living in a whorehouse. He could do it, but it damn sure wouldn't be easy. Sunny had to refocus on what he was, and therefore remember what drove him there. Sunny recalled watching Bobby and Andrzej ski the course so effortlessly. All Sunny could think was: what happened to his dream? When Bobby and Andrzej skied the parallel slalom together, they looked at each other and they skied in perfect synchronization—and still beat Sunny by a wide margin during the qualifier. Sunny knew that if he were going to survive, he would have to focus on what he loved and that was skiing. He had to get back in shape, get back on the mountain, stay out of the bars and fulfill his dream to be a professional skier.

Carl was waiting for Sunny at the airport. 'You look better," Carl said with a smile. "What took you for so long?"

Sunny looked up and smiled back, "Traffic." "How are things back east?" Carl wondered.

"Well, it's still there. It was good to be back home. I was able to get back on my feet. I did my usual run around Brookdale Park. Got to get some money together working for Dad."

"They're still holding a job at the Crazy Horse. They're worried about you," Carl informed him.

"Good to know! I'm gonna need a job. Did they miss me at the ski school?" inquired Sunny, pensively.

"Not really, your Austrians grab all the lessons," Carl said with some disdain. Carl looked straight ahead while he was driving. "What are you going to do Sunny?" he asked.

Sunny knew what he meant. Without even looking over, Sunny just stated very clearly: "Option one, I'm not going to be one of those people sitting on a barstool 15 years from now."

"Good to know," Carl said.

Sunny went back to the Crazy Horse and they were all glad to see him. He simply explained that he couldn't drink. He didn't explain that he just wasn't going to—ever again.

Margaux

SUNNY WENT BACK TO WORK and went back on the mountain. He was skiing much better and his attitude had changed, but Carl could see there was something missing with Sunny. He had been through a lot, and lost everything. Carl knew he felt he had lost Judy and Cindy, as well as a lot of his skiing, but Sunny was getting his skiing back. Carl also knew that Sunny felt he wasn't the same if he couldn't be part of the bar scene. So ski bumming was out.

Sunny was at home relaxing as Carl drove up.

"Hey Sunny," he said. "I just saw the perfect cure for you."

Sunny looked at him. "A cure for what?" Sunny asked.

"A cure for Judy and Cindy."

Sunny looked at Carl; he knew what Carl was trying to say.

"Okay, I didn't know it was an illness, but I'll bite. What do you have?"

Carl looked at Sunny with a big grin. "I just saw the most amazing girl sitting in the middle of Main Street. I was talking to her and she's really nice. You gotta meet her. She's really tall and she's perfect for you."

Sunny stared at him and said, "Okay, and?" With Carl there was always "and" something else.

"Well, there is a catch," Carl began to explain.

"Yeees?" inquired Sunny.

"Well, the catch is I think she's only 19 and she's Earnest Hemingway's granddaughter," Carl confessed.

Sunny stopped staring at Carl, looked down at the ground, shook his head, grinned and said, "Are you out of your fucking mind?"

It was more of a rhetorical question.

Carl looked at Sunny and responded with the stock answer, "Well, you're not the first to notice." Carl went on to say, "When did we ever give a shit what other people thought?"

Sunny looked at Carl. Sunny couldn't help but think: WE'RE Back.

As they drove into town, Margaux was still there. She was exactly what Carl described, this wholesome, beautiful girl standing out in front of the Alpine Bar. Carl parked the car and they walked up to the door. As Carl got closer he looked at Margaux and said, "Hey, how you doing? This is my friend Sunny."

Margaux looked at Carl and said, "I think I'll call you Carlo."

It was clear that Margaux did what she wanted. She looked at Sunny and asked quite directly, "Hi, what kind of name is Sunny?"

Sunny looked at her. She had a brilliant smile, and she was just a little taller than he was.

Carl asked, "Margaux, do they let you in the Alpine?"

Margaux just said, "Sure. I've known Posey my whole life."

Sunny was a little confused as Margaux wasn't old enough to drink, but again, this was Margaux's town. And she had an air about her that said she did just exactly what she wanted. Sunny was infatuated.

Carl said, "Well let's go inside."

The Alpine bar was Margaux's kind of place. This was Margaux's town and it was for locals. Margaux was not just a local, she was THE local. She was from the town where Ernest Hemingway lived and she was a Hemingway.

Margaux, Sunny, and Carl went in and sat at the bar. Carl ordered a beer, Sunny ordered a cranberry juice, and Margaux ordered a beer as well. Sunny didn't even ask how she got served in the bar.

Margaux turned to Sunny and asked him, "You don't drink?"

Sunny knew it was going to be an issue and he wouldn't be able to avoid explaining why he didn't drink, so he just looked at her and said, "Nope, I'm not allowed to. Doctor's orders. Let's leave it at that."

Sunny was anxious to talk to her because she seemed so honest and open and nice. Sunny felt a little funny as he was five years older than Margaux. She didn't seem to care. Sunny talked about his skiing, and what he and

Carl had done in Stowe. He went on to talk about some of their adventures without adding the rated X versions. Margaux turned to Sunny and stated, "I'm going to be up on the mountain tomorrow. You want to go skiing?"

"Sure," Sunny answered.

Sunny knew that Margaux had skied all her life. They had talked about that, and they talked about Sunny's racing and being on the ski school. Sunny was very anxious to see what it would be like to ski with Margaux the next day. Most of all, they just seemed to hit it off. Sunny couldn't help but wonder why someone so tall, so beautiful, so nice and so famous, or at least potentially famous, would be so open and kind and want to ski with him. This was déjà vu all over again, as Yogi would say.

Sunny was up early, and he felt great. He was anxious to ski. It was a beautiful day. He looked at the mountain. He never could get used to the size and beauty of Mount Baldy. He still hadn't skied the entire mountain and the trails had offered everything he wanted. As he got to the lift, there were no lift lines. It was quiet. He could hear the lifts running and felt a slight breeze. It was cold but the sun was out. Sunny must've been one of the first ones at the lifts. He was surprised at how much snow there was and how long the ski season was. The difference in the weather made a tremendous difference in how you felt. Back east, the days would start out clear and about the time you got your skis on, the clouds would be blocking the sun. Not in Sun Valley, though; sunny day after sunny day, snow at night or for a few days and mostly clear skies. When Sunny got to the lift, he was excited to just let his skis run. He managed to avoid being assigned a lesson at the morning ski school, meeting lineup at Dollar Mountain by having his ski school jacket a little dirty and smelling like he had spilled a beer on it. Sunny quickly changed into a different ski jacket on the way from the lineup to Baldy.

Just as Sunny stepped into his skis, he heard a voice. "Hey Sunny. You ready to go?"

It was Margaux. Sunny had hoped to see her, but honestly, he didn't really expect her to show up. Many people had told Sunny they wanted to ski with him as a part of general conversation. Sunny knew they wouldn't really go skiing with him. The other reason was he still didn't believe Margaux would get up and want to ski with him, after meeting him, was that she was able to ski with anyone she wanted to in town. At this point, Sunny didn't really care. He was feeling good; he hadn't had a drink in a month. He was starting to ski and feel like his old self.

"Come on," Margaux gestured, as she stood by the lift ready to go.

Sunny scurried over, just in time to catch the chair. Margaux didn't seem to be too concerned about her ski fashion. She wore a nice jacket but a pair of worn ski pants. It looked like she just cared about being comfortable. Margaux didn't have to worry about looking good. She looked good no matter where she was. Sunny was surprisingly comfortable with Margaux. It might have been his new attitude. It was more Margaux. She was so easy to talk to.

Margaux talked openly about her life in Sun Valley. Sunny was enthralled. Sunny talked about his own life, and even was open about his learning issues. He told Margaux things he hadn't told hardly anybody. He wasn't quite sure why he was telling her these things; he was he only knew that Margaux was understanding and accepting.

When they skied, Margaux was a fabulous skier for a girl her size. For that matter, she was a great skier for a girl of any size; she just flowed. She was powerful and athletic. She was as uninhibited on skis as she was in her personality. She skied as she lived. Sunny and Margaux skied well together. To be able to stand on top of Baldy and look out over the snow towering mountains and the town—with the sun in your face and a woman like Margaux—the next two days were the definition of a ski dream. To be able to find somebody who had the same ability and rhythm to ski with him was not easy and didn't happen often.

Sunny and Margaux skied all morning and talked on every chair ride. When they stopped for lunch at the top of the mountain, Sunny wasn't tired at all but he was hungry. Margaux knew a lot of people and introduced Sunny as her friend to everyone she said hi to. Margaux didn't have a bad word to say about anyone. For the first time in a long time, Sunny felt relaxed and comfortable with Margaux, and Margaux seemed to be happy to be with Sunny.

After lunch, Sunny and Margaux skied some more. Margaux knew the mountains better than Sunny did. Sunny was in heaven. He had found someone who could act as his mountain guide, someone who was a great skier, someone who was tall, beautiful—and to finish things off, *genuinely nice*. Sunny and Margaux skied down to the car. They'd had a great day and Sunny didn't want it to end, but he didn't want to jump into the usual hustle. He knew Margaux had probably heard just about every line there was, and Sunny didn't want to treat Margaux like the others.

"Margaux," Sunny said, "You are great. I really liked hanging out with you today. You're a very good skier. I can't thank you enough."

Sunny bent down to take off his skis. Margaux surprised Sunny when he stood up by giving him a kiss.

"Thank you," she said. "Coming from you, that means something. You're really a good skier too."

Sunny was stunned. Without thinking, he pulled her to him and kissed her back. Then holding her close, Sunny said, "We have to do this again."

Margaux smiled and said, "Hey, would you like to come to dinner?"

Sunny thought, why not? "Sure," he replied with some reluctance.

Margaux went on to explain, "Everyone will be at home, and I'd like them to meet you."

Again Sunny was stunned. Sunny and parents—not so good. But now this was different; he would be sober. He didn't want to treat Margaux like the others. So he looked at her and asked, "How do I get to your house?"

"I just live north of town. Would 7 p.m. be okay?" Margaux asked.

"Yeah, that'll be fine," Sunny answered, trying to hide the nausea he had suddenly felt.

And with that, Margaux was gone. Sunny had a little over two hours to clean up and meet the Hemingway family. Piece of cake. A shower and a bottle or two of Pepto Bismol, and things should be ducky.

Sunny went back to his trailer and looked around for some clean clothes. Carl showed up shortly after Sunny got home.

"I saw you skiing today. You were skiing pretty good," Carl said, trying to support the Sundance Kid.

"Thanks, Carl."

"I saw Margaux skiing with you. She's not bad—not too many girls can ski like that," Carl was quick to observe.

Sunny looked at Carl. He knew what he was getting at. "Yeah I know. She is something else," Sunny said.

"Hey Carl, Margaux invited me to dinner at her house tonight," Sunny explained with a somewhat panicked look on his face.

"Holy shit Sunny, you're going to dinner with the Hemingways!" Carl stated.

Sunny looked up again. "Yep."

"You don't waste any time," Carl joked.

"Hey, it wasn't my idea. Me and parents don't get along so well, usually. The last time I went to dinner with a girl's parents, it didn't turn out so well, remember?" Sunny reminded Carl.

"You'll be okay Sunny, you're not drinking and you know all the WaspY etiquette shit; you'll be fine. Just don't tell them what you've been doing over the last two years," Carl advised.

"Oh great! What should I talk about, then?" Sunny asked sincerely, with panic in his voice.

"I don't know. What do all you Wasp people talk about when you get together?" Carl went on to ask with his Jersey insight.

"Well, I suppose I could sit around and talk about nothing for a while. Margaux told me where she lived but I don't really know where I'm going to. Do you know where it is?" Sunny asked.

"Yeah, I know where they live," Carl said. "You want me to drop you off? You might need a four-wheel-drive." Carl looked at Sunny and advised, "Try that sweater I gave you a couple of Christmases ago."

It was a good idea. Sunny looked as presentable as he was going to in that sweater.

Sunny and Carl took off in his Blazer in the cold, Idaho snow-covered night so Sunny could meet the Hemingways and have dinner with Margaux. Sunny was nervous; he wondered if they would ask him if he had ever read any of Ernest Hemingway's books, which he had not. What would he say? Also, he'd never really been received well by any girl's parents.

As they pulled up to the house, Sunny looked at Carl terrified and stated, "Make sure you answer the phone when I call."

Carl laughed. "Maybe I should come in with you."

Sunny looked at Carl and thought for a moment. "I don't think that would be a good idea. Having me for dinner is bad enough," Sunny said.

Carl just said, "Yeah, good luck. Besides, I don't speak Wasp. I'll be there."

Sunny was more than nervous. "Thanks."

Carl could see that Sunny was generally worried. It was good to see him alive again.

Sunny walked up and knocked on the door. Margaux's father, Jack, answered the door.

"Hello, come in," Jack said.

Jack had a big smile and was warm and welcoming. This was not the reception Sunny had expected or was used to getting by parents, much less from the famous parents of a beautiful famous girl. Margaux came out from the hallway and introduced Sunny to her family. Her sister Muffet (Joan) was watching a cooking show and taking notes for a cookbook. Margaux introduced Sunny to her younger sister Mariel, who Sunny could see Margaux was very close to. Mariel was just as wonderful and genuine as Margaux was. She always had a smile; she wasn't as tall as Margaux, but it was easy to see that she was going to be just as attractive. Sunny was introduced to Margaux's mother, Puck, who was a poised, kind, gentle woman.

Jack was open and welcoming all throughout dinner. It was easy to see that this was a caring, close family who lived a normal lifestyle, despite their famous heritage. Sunny managed to get through dinner without sticking his foot in his mouth, or he hoped he didn't. He was so nervous he couldn't remember everything he said. Sunny talked about his family back East, high school in Stowe, and his hopes to ski race. The Hemingways were amazing people. All Sunny could think was he was glad he wasn't drinking. Many other people could take a lesson from the Hemingways, and Margaux was more than special. She was beautiful, grounded, and famous—with a great family.

Sunny had to ask himself if he was out of his league once again.

Sunny thanked them for a lovely dinner and allowing him to be a part of it. Carl did answer the phone, and picked him up right on time.

For the next couple of days, Sunny walked around with a smile and a spring in his step. He couldn't wait to get back on the mountain and train with the pros. He went to work focused and confident. One day, when

Sunny showed up at the mountain, Margaux and Mariel spotted him in the lift line.

"Hey Sunny," Margaux called over the line of people.

Sunny was excited to see them. Sunny rode the lift with both Margaux and Mariel, and for some reason, they were excited to ski with him. Sunny was surprised to see that Mariel could ski almost as well as Margaux. She really enjoyed skiing with Sunny, too.

Sunny and the Hemingway girls skied a few runs. They knew the mountain like their backyard. They brought Sunny to trails and places that were new and fun. Both Margaux and Mariel seemed to have fun challenging Sunny. Sunny enjoyed the game. Carl once said, "He's better when he moves." When the day was done, Margaux drove Mariel home and went to meet Sunny back in town. Sunny had to go do a shift at the Crazy Horse. Margaux sat at the bar for a while and talked with Sunny as he worked. Sunny was in his element behind the bar, interacting with customers. Sunny could work the whole bar almost by himself and be the entertainment. Sunny hadn't told Margaux where he lived, and he decided he would be honest. Margaux had probably been in all the million and multimillion dollar homes in the Valley. Sunny wasn't about to bring her to his double-wide trailer. He did have *that* feeling again, and he thought she may too. Only he couldn't imagine why. Again, she was someone out of his league.

Carl came into the Crazy Horse and sat with Margaux at a table, talking. That was good, because Sunny was busy working, and bad, as there was no way of knowing what Carl was telling Margaux. Margaux left to go home, but not before giving Sunny a kiss when Sunny walked her out to her car.

"Thanks for today, Sunny," Margaux said.

"Are you kidding? Thank you. I have to watch myself. I could fall in love," Sunny said with a smile.

Sunny wasn't sure why Margaux was attracted to him. She liked hanging out with both him and Carl. Perhaps it was that she hadn't met anyone like the two of them. They did what they wanted, they picked a direction and went in it, and didn't really care what people thought. Margaux probably had a lot of people placing expectations on her, and Sunny and Carl were the antidote. Sunny and Carl just liked her and her family for who they were as people. Sunny was falling for her. He was falling in love with her beauty, her athleticism, her sincerity, and her kindness toward others.

When Sunny got off work, it wasn't too late. As he was walking out to his car, he saw Carl and Margaux heading up the street. Carl and Margaux had gone out to some of the other bars. Sunny was a little surprised to see them.

Margaux had her big smile. "We've been waiting for you."

"Okay, what have you guys been doing? Aren't you guys a little tired?" Sunny asked.

Carl groaned, "Yes I'm beat. I can't keep up with her, I'm going home."

"Come on, Sunny," Margaux said.

Sunny looked at this stunning tall blond with her hair in braids and said, "Margaux, I have to get some sleep. I have to be on the mountain by nine."

"Okay," Margaux said. "Let's go to your place."

Sunny was too tired to be in a panic. "Margaux, I told you I live in a double-wide south of town. Are you sure?"

"Sure, let's go," Margaux said.

"Okay," Sunny replied with some hesitation.

Margaux said, "Wait, I just have to call home and tell them where I am."

This was something different for Sunny, dating a girl that had to call home.

Sunny looked at Margaux, "I don't think that's a good idea," Sunny said. "I'll drive you home."

"No!" insisted Margaux. "I'll tell them I'm at a friend's house."

Sunny didn't like that. It eventually might come back to bite him in the ass, but he could see that Margaux had her mind made up so he wasn't going to argue. Sunny thought about it for a second and realized maybe Margaux had decided what she was going to do sometime earlier. Sunny had little to say about it, nor did he want to.

Sunny brought Margaux to the Château Sunny. Or as they say in Idaho terms, his double-wide. It made Sunny very aware of how badly he was doing financially. At the moment, he was focused on Margaux. Both Sunny and Margaux knew what they wanted. Margaux was so athletic, so beautiful and uninhibited in lovemaking as she was in the rest of her life. Sunny made love to Margaux with all the sincerity in his body, and Margaux responded the same way. The confidence Margaux had surpassed Sunny's. She was happy.

The next day, Sunny drove Margaux home expecting the worst. Later that day, Sunny saw Margaux with her usual big smile.

"Everything okay?" Sunny asked with some trepidation.

"Yeah, no problem, my parents trust me."

Margaux spent more nights with Sunny, and Sunny and Margaux got closer. It didn't seem to matter to Margaux whether it was a double-wide or a multimillion dollar house; she only cared who you were as a person. Sunny remembered when he was like that, and he thought that Margaux brought the best out in him. He hoped he was a positive influence on her as well.

Sunny showed up at the ski school lineup the next week to be assigned a couple of lessons. The first was a celebrity, Buddy Hackett, the famous comedian and movie star. Sunny wasn't the type of guy who was star struck. Sunny evaluated people by how they treated others. Buddy turned out to be not only really funny, but a really smart man. He wasn't the best skier, but he gave it a hell of a try. Buddy's intelligence also made him somewhat intolerant of fans that were pushy or rude; however, one day Sunny and Buddy were taking a lunch break and they ran into Mariel. Buddy was really nice He noticed Mariel had a small scar on her nose, which he offered to help her take care of. But he could see how beautiful she was and would grow to be.

Carl had gotten a celebrity ski lesson as well. He had drawn Marlon Brando and his family. He had really had his hands full.

Sunny had also been assigned a ski lesson that would change his life. He had been assigned a woman and her son. The woman had worked for some famous sports announcer as his assistant. She had retired and wanted to reconnect with her son. Neither the woman nor her son had great skiing skills, and teaching them would be a challenge. Sunny enjoyed the challenge. Little by little during the week as their skiing skills improved, their relationship improved also. They were able to find a common denominator through skiing and strengthen their relationship as mother and son. Sunny was invited to have dinner with them at the end of the week. It was a magnificent dinner. They had enjoyed each other's company and found a real common interest. Sunny realized how powerful skiing could be in strengthening relationships with families. It wasn't about skiing; it was about who you skied with. The connection you have with your family when you're on a chair lift can provide precious moments. That ski trip with your family is what you remember, which is exactly what happened to Sunny.

Sunny and Margaux continued to see each other. Sunny went to a party with Margaux and came down with a terrible stomach illness. He spent days at home sick. Margaux had gone out of town, to San Francisco. Sunny lay around the trailer and realized that Margaux needed to be Margaux Hemingway the model, or whatever she was destined to become. She shouldn't be with a guy living in a double-wide, driving a '67 Impala, no matter how good he skied or how much fun he was.

After being with Margaux at the party Sunny, saw that there were times it wasn't about how you felt about each other. Margaux needed someone who could support her fame. Sunny knew that he couldn't. When Margaux returned from San Francisco, she explained that she badly turned her ankle which was why she was there so long. Margaux and Sunny had a long talk. Sunny really did want the best for her. It was a difficult time for both of them.

Sunny skied hard and trained hard. One day it was announced that there would be a Pro-Am ski race. The Pro-Am is a big yearly event. The ski race was an event where the pros were members of the ski school, and the amateurs were people within the community. A team consisted of one woman and two other skiers. The teams would be selected during a Calcutta fundraising event. People could bid on the teams, and based on the bid prices, a handicap would be assigned. Most of the Austrians were full-time employees. There were very few Americans on the full-time ski school staff. The director of the ski school had known that Sunny and a few other skiers were skiing well—and decided to tip the odds to help the Austrians.

In 1974, the economy was bad and Americans were having a hard time finding work. There were gas lines. The director of the ski school wanted the school to have an Austrian flavor and discouraged Americans from wearing things like cowboy hats. The problem with that was Sun Valley and Sun Valley was in Idaho which was, and is, about as American as you could get. There was a lot of division between the Austrians and the Americans in the ski school. A couple of the Austrians from Stowe, who had been previous members of the Austrian Development Team, showed up in town—and Sunny knew the ski school was trying to stack the deck.

Sunny got to bed early after working so he could be fresh to train. The phone rang.

"Hello Sunny," his father said. "How are you?"

Very surprised to hear his father, Sunny answered: "I'm good, but how are you? Is it late back home?"

"Yes, I suppose it is, but I'm not there. I'm in the Lodge," his father explained. "I thought I'd come out and do some skiing."

"Dad, that's great. I can't wait to see you," Sunny said. "How about breakfast? I'll come get you at the Lodge."

Sunny couldn't wait to see his dad. He knew he wouldn't be there if it wasn't for him. Sunny met his dad at the Lodge the next morning. It was great to see his dad had done what he usually did, which was to sign up with Sunny for an all-day private lesson. He enjoyed going up to the ski school desk and requesting his son. Skiing with his dad was like old times.

"You look great Sunny," his dad acknowledged.

"You too, Dad. I'm glad you came out," Sunny said.

"Ruth tells me there's a big race, a Pro-Am, are you going to race?" his dad asked.

Ruth had been friends with Sunny's dad and the family for many years. She was the daughter of a big electric contractor back East. She would eventually go on to be the mayor of Sun Valley.

"Yes Dad, I'm going to race. I think I can do pretty well," explained Sunny.

"Ruth tells me there will be a Calcutta tonight. Sounds like fun," his dad stated with some enthusiasm.

"Yes, I'll be there," Sunny explained. "We have to be there for teams to bid on us. I don't think many people will recognize me, so I don't really expect much. I'll say this, I'm skiing pretty well. But I think they brought in some ringers."

Sunny's dad was very proud of his son. He said, "I know you're going to give them a run for their money."

Sunny just laughed. "Yes, I am, Dad," Sunny stated with a smile.

Sunny skied the rest of the day with his dad and then met him later at the Calcutta. Sunny's dad and Ruth bid on the team, but actually got outbid by another gentleman. The mood during the Calcutta was festive. There were more wealthy people there than Sunny had ever seen in one place in Sun Valley. The Austrians were hovering around the potential bidders, like dates at a prom. When the bidding was over, Sunny went with his dad and Ruth for a quick cup of coffee—and then home to get ready for the race.

The next day Sunny woke up early and tuned his skis in his kitchen. He went to the ski school locker room and saw his friend Whitey sitting on the bench in front of his locker. While he was pulling his boots on, Whitey turned to Sunny and said, "That's kind of a bad deal."

"What do you mean?" Sunny asked.

"Well, the ski school director decided that all the full-time skiers should be in the first seed," Whitey explained.

(A seed was a group of 15. So being in the first seed meant that the full-timers would have access to the best snow).

Sunny just looked at Whitey a while. "I guess we can figure out how to ski ruts," he thought for a moment. "The rules say that we're allowed to sideslip after the first seed," Sunny said.

"That would take some doing," Whitey said in his Idaho drawl.

"Yeah, well, then we can get some of the other people who aren't racing from the ski school to slip for us. All right, I'm gonna go up and see if I can get my feet underneath me," Sunny said as he left for the mountain.

Sunny was at the lift early only to see Mariel there, too. Sunny knew many of the other racers would be trying to run gates before the race, but Sunny also knew he just needed to clear his head and ski. He needed to get his feet underneath him and his rhythm back. Skiing with Mariel would be the perfect way to warm up for the race. Mariel was always positive and supportive. She helped Sunny ski and focus.

Mariel helped Sunny get ready. The race was a Giant Slalom. Sunny kept to himself during the inspections. He only talked to his training partner, Mariel Hemingway. The first run came off and the Austrians ran the first seed. The ruts weren't too bad. It looked like the entire ski school was lined on both sides of the race, watching. Right after the last Austrian had gone in the first seed, all the ski school who were watching proceeded to slide into the course and sideslip the course, gate by gate. The Austrians were furious and stood down below yelling and shaking their fists.

The Austrians had stuck together and the Americans had stuck together. What the Americans had done was perfectly legal. It just leveled the playing field and the Austrians didn't like it. Sunny ran seventh. He came out of the starting gate—3, 2, 1, go. Sunny had a strong start, and all he could think of was *round turns, smooth, look ahead*. He was running on autopilot. Sunny was skiing fast. He knew he was having a great run; he could almost see the finish—turn after turn. And then he lost his focus just for a moment. He looked at the gate and took a gate backwards. He went in the wrong way, causing himself to come to a complete stop. Sunny threw his body to the next gate and started. Sunny felt a huge rush of adrenaline, and as he lunged toward the next gate, he got back on course. Sunny had lost valuable time. He skied across the finish line upset with his mistake. He saw his dad.

"You did great, Sunny," his dad said proudly.

Sunny knew that mistake cost him valuable time. He felt having his dad there was like old times, but he didn't want to let his dad down. Just then Sunny heard,

"Sunny that was a great run. I can't believe you did what you did at that gate! We thought you were out of it." It was both Mariel and Margaux.

Carl showed up. "You did it, kid!" Carl yelled.

"Thanks, but…" Sunny didn't have to finish.

"No, I'm never seen you ski better," Carl said.

"Thank you," Sunny said, "but that really cost me."

Just then Sunny heard the announcement that he had come in second behind Boone, one of the other Americans. *Boone and Sunny had beaten all the Austrians.* Sunny had beaten them by stopping and starting again, which made it worse. Sunny had to just wait to see if his time was going to hold up. As he waited, he couldn't believe how wonderful it was to be with his dad, Carl, Margaux, Mariel, Ruth and people who had supported him so much.

It was a long wait. There had been some really good skiers. His time held up. Sunny had come in second. Then it wasn't the time to focus on the mistake *but time to celebrate*. Everybody would head off to bars, but Sunny didn't drink and his training partner certainly wasn't old enough. So Sunny, Margaux and Mariel, and his dad and everyone else went to an ice cream place and had ice cream sundaes. It was the perfect celebration. Sunny's team did really well. That was just as important. Later that night, there was an awards ceremony at the Calcutta for the race. When Sunny's name and team were called, he walked up on stage with his cowboy hat. They continued to call his name even with Sunny being on stage because they didn't recognize him. He reached out and shook the man's hand. The announcer then turned to the audience and said, "It's nice to see Americans win one and two this year."

That was not only a victory for Sunny and his team but for the Americans. Sunny was able to share his victory with his dad, Carl, Mariel, and Margaux. Sunny's dad went back to New Jersey, proud of his son. To Sunny that was The Ski Dream.

The Pro AM

Time Marches On

ONE NIGHT SUNNY WENT TO see Carl in the Sun Valley Lodge. Carl had put together a band and they were good. Carl had to play in the Duchin room for a party, for some politician. Carl was standing on stage with his old suit and a 20 X Stetson hat. Sunny loved hearing Carl entertain. He had come a long way from playing a few songs and collecting a few bucks at the door. During a break, Carl was standing on the stage. Sunny went up to talk to him. The room was loud and noisy. Just then, Margaux came up to the stage, all 6 feet of her, with her enormous smile. She was just wonderful. Margaux had very quickly grown from this girl who would wear her hair in braids to this tall, exotic woman.

As she approached the stage, she began to introduce a man in a blue pinstriped suite and wing tip shoes. Carl and Sunny recognized it immediately, the New York uniform, a bit out of place in Idaho.

"Sunny, Carl, I would like you to meet my friend, Errol," Margaux said proudly.

Errol looked a bit out of place with his New York uniform (the blue suit), expensive shoes—or maybe it was Sunny and Carl who were a bit underdressed, looking like they belonged in the Grand Old Opry. But Carl took the opportunity to see if Errol could fit in.

Margaux continued, "Carl, this is Errol."

Carl leaned down, shook his hand and introduced himself, "Darrell, how you doing?" Carl spoke with the heavy Idaho drawl.

"Errol, it's *Errol*," he corrected without cracking a smile.

Just then, Sunny decided to join the party. He reached out and shook

Errol's hand and introduced himself as Carl did. "Darrell, how you doing boy, good to see you, welcome to Idaho."

Again Errol was not amused and corrected Sunny: "It's Errol."

Carl looked at Errol, turned to Sunny and in a loud voice yelled over the music, "Boy, must be hard to hear or something, that's what I said!"

The whole conversation seemed to look like some sort of Warner Brothers cartoon with the big rooster. Sunny caught up to Margaux a little later and asked how she was doing.

"Just be careful, New York is a Different Place," Sunny defended their little introduction.

"How did you know he was from New York?" Margaux questioned.

"Remember, I grew up back there," Sunny explained.

Sunny had an uneasy feeling about a wealthy New Yorker coming into Idaho and bringing Margaux back East. Sunny was a little nervous as to whether Margaux was ready for New York. So was Carl. Ready or not, Margaux was a woman—tall, statuesque, famous. Errol was a good-looking, wealthy man from a famous family. What bothered Sunny and Carl was there was nothing either of them could do about it.

"Margaux, if you need me, give me a call. I'll be there!" Sunny stated emphatically.

"I know," Margaux nodded. "You guys are great."

The Crazy Horse

THE CRAZY HORSE WOULD REOPEN and the country bands would play. The Crazy Horse was beginning to get the reputation of having a rowdy crowd. On the weekends, some of the independent loggers would come down in the town and get a little drunk, get rowdy. Sunny's bouncer was a really nice guy, but he wasn't allowed to get into fights. Joe was a tough guy who a judge decided to make an example of some time ago—and put in prison for failure to re-register his address to the draft board. Sunny believed in second chances, so other than putting Joe—and Sunny for that matter—in a tough situation, he thought he would sit down with the other loggers and make them an offer. Sunny sat with five of the logging crew and found out that they had been through difficult times. So Sunny offered them a deal. If they would clean up, they would get a meal and some beer. To help Joe out, two of the crew would stay in the bar at all times and NO getting drunk. It turned out they were a nice group of hard-working men that just needed a break. They took the deal. Sunny asked one of the wait staff to go down to The Gold Mine Thrift Store (the local thrift store is a great place if you're living in a wealthy town) and get some clean clothes. Off to the local hair salon and then back to the Crazy Horse for a hot meal. The guys looked great, and the Crazy Horse never did have much of a problem after that.

Carl came in to the Crazy Horse with a poster he had drawn. Carl was an excellent artist. It was a cowboy sitting on a bronc, playing the fiddle. Carl had decided to organize a concert. He talked a group of local fiddle players and every local artist into signing on for the concert. Carl did a masterful job in promoting the concert. He had gone into every town and put the posters everywhere, including the back of every bathroom stall. The concert would be held in a portion of the Sun Valley Lodge.

The night of the concert, Sunny was standing in a long line waiting for the doors to open. Sunny decided he was too busy with the Crazy Horse and Carl should handle this one on his own. Sunny had always gotten stuck working the door collecting money while Carl was playing. As Sunny stood there in line, he looked up to see Carl standing on a table at the head of the line yelling Sunny's name. Sunny couldn't believe it. Sunny worked his way to the front of the line, fearing the worst.

"What's wrong Carl?" Sunny asked.

"I need your help!" Carl confessed. At that time, Carl was never one to ever ask for help. At that moment, he realized he needed what only Sunny could do. "There are a lot more people than we expected and I have no security. People are bringing in bottles and things that they're not allowed to."

He looked at Carl. He knew what he had to do. And he wasn't going to let his friend down. With a reassuring smile he replied, "I got this." Sunny stood on the same table and within a few seconds summoned his whole crew from the Crazy Horse—the loggers and some friends, *big friends*. In moments, the door and security was taken care of. Carl didn't give it a second thought. Sunny went to the stage and found Carl just to give him an update. Carl was already focused on another issue. He was looking a bit upset again. The crowd was getting restless and Carl had just broken a guitar string.

Sunny looked at Carl and sighed, "Okay what now?"

Carl was standing there with his 1920s suit and his 20 X Stetson, in his cowboy boots. He looked at Sunny, and with a confident grin stated, "No problem."

Carl did something amazing. He jumped on stage and grabbed the microphone and started strutting across the stage. With his best cowboy boots and his head thrown back, he started singing, "You just stick out your little hand with every woman-lovin' man sayin'…and Howdy do, Howdy do, Howdy do"… and then broke into a Shirley Temple song.

When he was done, the crowd went crazy. Only Carl could pull that off. The concert was a huge success. Butch and Sundance pulled off another one.

That Sunday, Carl stopped by the trailer and asked Sunny to take a ride. He took Sunny up the Triumph Road, the road Carl had taken Sunny up to dry out. This time he stopped at the Triumph Mine. The Triumph Mine was a huge mine, over 600 acres which at one time was responsible for a large portion of the state's revenue. The mine was closed sometime in the 50s.

Carl stood at the mine footings and looked at Sunny and said, "I am going to buy this, I need a couple hundred dollars."

Sunny looked at Carl and shook his head, looking somewhat in disbelief and answered him: "Carl, you're out of your mind."

Sunny gave him the money. Carl not only bought the mine footings, but the payroll building, the plumbing shop, and many years later, he bought the whole mine. Who would've thought? So much for Sunny's intuition.

Sunny Tries a New Sport

THAT NEXT WEEK BACK AT the Crazy Horse, Sunny was getting ready to open the bar. A couple of cowboys walked in and asked to speak to the manager. Being curious, Sunny spoke to them. The cowboys were selling advertising for a program for a rodeo that was being held north of town—The Devil's Bedstead Ranch Rodeo. The program sounded like it would probably be good for business and it was reasonably priced.

"Okay," Sunny blurted out quickly. "Just one catch. I want to ride."

The cowboy looked like a deer in the headlights of a car. He didn't expect Sunny to answer so quickly, and he didn't expect Sunny to *request to ride*.

"Have you ever ridden in a rodeo?' the cowboy asked.

"Nope, haven't even seen one," replied Sunny.

"And you want to ride?" The cowboy asked.

"I thought I'd like to try broncs, maybe even bulls," Sunny noted. Sunny glanced at the cowboys and explained: "I'll take a full page ad…. No ride, no ad."

"I think we can do this," the cowboys agreed.

Sunny put out his hand and shook on the deal. "Put me down for a full-page," Sunny affirmed. Sunny and the cowboy talked. Then Sunny got directions to the Devil's Bedstead Ranch. What Sunny had failed to mention to the cowboy was that he had grown up riding with his father. His father was one of the best event riders in the country at one time. He once had an offer to work with the U.S. Equestrian Team. Sunny felt that staying on a horse that bucks for a few seconds wouldn't be too much of a problem. A bull on the other hand might be, well, a bit of a challenge. Without

265

drinking, Sunny needed something to get his heart going other than pretty girls.

The day of the rodeo came and Sunny showed up with some of his friends from the Crazy Horse. As promised, Sunny was signed up to ride bareback broncs. Sunny loved the atmosphere of the rodeo and the ranch. The scenery was absolutely picturesque—the mountains of Idaho and a real working ranch. This was not a ski resort; this was the part of Idaho Sunny wanted to see. These were also the people that Sunny wanted to meet. These were not ski resort people who would fly in for the week. Sunny had spent so much time in the resort environment that he had not been able to get a real idea of Idaho living. These people represented some of the best of Idaho. They were hard working all-American people and rodeo was the quintessential American sport. Sunny was more than excited to give it a try. The cowboys who Sunny had spoken to admired Sunny's courage. To Sunny, this was just another adrenaline event, and he loved it. The cowboys gave Sunny a quick lesson in how to rig down, and Sunny stood over his bronc and got ready to ride. All Sunny heard was outside—and the gate chute flew open. Sunny knew how to ride. He held on, covered (meaning he completed his ride) his bronc for eight seconds. The cowboys couldn't believe it. He didn't have a score because he missed marking him out. Cowboys' feet have to be over a horse's shoulders when the horse touches down on his first jump. Sunny didn't do that. It didn't matter. Sunny had a good ride and the cowboys were impressed. Sunny, feeling great, couldn't wait for another adrenaline rush and volunteered immediately for a *bull ride*. Sunny had never even really seen a bull ride, so when he tried to rig down and ride a bull, it didn't really go well. He got bucked off right away and managed to get kicked pretty good. He got himself up and shook it off. The cowboys were so impressed, they got together and pitched in—and gave Sunny his first Stetson. Sunny had found his new sport. It wasn't just the riding; it was being around the culture of the sport. Sunny loved being a part of the western culture and the intense challenge and focus it took to ride broncs and bulls.

Hailey, Idaho had its own rodeo arena built by Rupert and some of the other guys. When Hailey held its rodeo on the Fourth of July, everybody in town showed up. It was a great time and Sunny couldn't wait to enter.

Sunny would go on to ride the Hailey Rodeo, learn to throw horseshoes and love the western culture and rodeos.

Sunny and Carl had come to Sun Valley. They lived their dreams but everything begins and everything ends. Sunny got a call from his dad one morning. There was a death in the family and it was time for Sunny to come home. Sunny knew he had to go back east. He knew he wouldn't be coming back for a while. Carl drove Sunny back east. When they got to New Jersey, they managed to call Margaux and meet her in New York for lunch. It was great to see her, but both Sunny and Carl were still worried about her.

Sunny went back to work for his dad while he figured out his next move. Sunny couldn't get rodeo out of his head. He looked up "rodeo" and found out that New Jersey had a rodeo in place since 1955, a Nationally Ranked rodeo. The rodeo was in Woodstown, New Jersey—known as Cowtown Rodeo. It was no joke, it was the real deal. On Friday night, Sunny would go down to his friend's house whose parents had some horses. Sunny would ride on Saturday morning and go down to Cowtown and ride on Saturday nights. Cowtown was a tough rodeo, Sunny had learned.

Sunny would go from the rodeo to the beach, surf and head up to the office on Monday. One day, Sunny was sitting in the office reading the paper. Sunny saw a big ad for a rodeo in Madison Square Garden. Sunny, with his Attention Deficit, didn't take time to read the whole ad. He just looked at the number to register and called. He was in. Sunny really didn't think things through. All Sunny could think of was riding rodeo in the Garden, which meant he didn't have to go all the way to South Jersey. The problem was Sunny never told his father he had been riding rodeo. Sunny's father was an accomplished equestrian rider. Sunny did not want to disappoint his dad. The difficulty he was faced with was that he drove to work with his dad every day. That Friday, Sunny didn't know how he was going to confront his dad with the news, as he would not be going home.

Friday came, and Sunny managed to sneak his bareback rigging, hat and clothes in the trunk. At 5 o'clock, Sunny had to face the music. He reluctantly went up to his father's office, knocked on the door.

Cowtown

"Dad, can I talk to you a moment?" Sunny asked. His dad was sitting behind his desk in his three-piece suit. Sunny could tell his father would not be happy.

"Dad, I have something to tell you," Sunny began to explain.

"Yes," his father asked, "what is it?

268

George H. Warner at Valley Forge Military Academy

Sunny began in a soft voice, "On the weekends, I've been going down to South Jersey and riding rodeo. I've been riding bareback broncs. I signed up for the rodeo at the Garden this weekend," Sunny explained. Sunny was really nervous.

There was a long pause. Hhis father just looked at Sunny for a long moment. Sunny could feel his disappointment.

"Okay" his father stated abruptly, "you will have to take the bus home." That's was all his father said. Sunny knew he was not happy.

Sunny got changed, grabbed his rigging and walked to the Prince Street subway station. Sunny sat on the subway and noticed people staring at him.

"What?!" Sunny barked at some of the staring passengers.

Then Sunny saw his reflection in the subway car window. He looked like a bad version of Midnight Cowboy. Sunny just laughed to himself and thought: *Could things get any worse?* He was sitting on the subway with a cowboy hat, cowboy boots and jeans in the village. Sunny made it up to the Garden. He was there early. Sunny walked up to the registration office, walked in and introduced himself. Sunny paid his entrance fee and was given his number. The broncs' he drew were *Crazy 8's* and *Catfish*. Then on the way of the office, Sunny took another look at the list. He almost threw up. This time, Sunny read things carefully. The Madison Square Garden Rodeo was the Winston Rodeo Finals and the other cowboys were the *top cowboys in the country*. Cowboys like Sandy Kirby, K. Kirby, and Larry Mahan who had been world champion cowboy many times over, and others. Sunny was able to enter under a local's quota.

Sunny went back into the office. "I'm sorry," he pleaded. "Look at this!" Holding up the list, he said, "I don't belong here." He continued to plead his case.

Sunny was white as a ghost. The rodeo office girl didn't even look up she just quietly told Sunny, "If you don't ride you have to pay the fine." Sunny didn't have money for a fine. He barely had money for the entrance fee.

The only thing to do was to find a quiet place to sit where he wasn't going to be noticed, so he sat in the dark, scared he was going to embarrass himself or get his ass kicked. Then Sunny started doing what he did best. He got a little pissed and started thinking what he needed to do to get through this. This wasn't the first tough spot he had been in. He thought: well, he could at least know which bronc he was going to ride first. So he went over to the pens where the horses and bulls were. It was so dark in the Garden, Sunny couldn't see the brands on the horses. Not one to give up, Sunny climbed over and down in the pens to see the horses' brands. Just then, Sunny felt someone grab him by his belt in the back and pull him out of the pens—just before a bull pushed up against the rail. It was Larry Mahan.

"Thanks," Sunny said, a bit startled.

Larry looked at him and stated the obvious, "You're new."

Sunny recognized Larry right away. Everybody who rode rodeo knew who Larry Mahan was. "How can you tell?" Sunny said with a laugh.

"Well, because I know everyone else and you really don't know what you're doing," Larry explained.

Sunny looked at Larry and said, "I thought I was hiding it so well."

Larry laughed. Larry and Sunny talked, and it turned out that Larry liked to ski and had been to Vail. Sunny promised to teach him to ski if Larry could keep him from getting killed. Larry decided he would be Sunny's rodeo partner for the day and help him rig down. Sunny didn't know whether he was one of the guys, or whether he could get them to sign autographs.

The Garden lights stayed dim and the Garden was filling up. The rodeo started with its opening parade. Then the American Flag was presentation and everyone stood for the *Star-Spangled Banner*. The lights came up, the Garden was packed. Howard Harris from South Jersey was a great shoot boss; it was his stock. When he said to do something, people did it.

Howard rode by the shoots and commanded, "Shoot one outside."

Madison Square Garden

The first rider was Sandy Kirby. His gate opened and Sandy's horse jumped so high, Sunny was stunned. He had never seen a horse jump so high in his life. Sunny was next. Larry was helping him but Sunny wasn't ready.

Just then, Larry did something that was incredible. He turned to Howard and yelled, "Go to six!" Howard rode over to the other side of the shoots and commanded, "Get ready."

Sunny was stunned once again. Nobody tells Howard to change, but Larry did and Howard did. The cowboy in shoot six got ready and did a hell of a ride. Sunny was ready.

The announcer, in a loud voice, called out over the PA system, "Ladies and Gentlemen, we have a local boy, Sunny Warner, from Glen Ridge, New Jersey."

The crowd heard New Jersey and the cheers were deafening. If you had ever been in Madison Square Garden with a full crowd and everybody yelling it is something to hear. It scared the crap out of Sunny.

Howard called in a really loud voice over the crowd, "Outside!"

Larry leaned over and spoke in Sunny's ear: "Just bear down eight seconds. Don't let go." The gate opened and Sunny hung on for dear life. Sunny couldn't hear anything but the sound of one person yelling over the others. A familiar voice. Sunny rode eight seconds but didn't mark his horse out and didn't get a score. He didn't care. Sunny stayed on and missed grabbing for the pickup man. Instead he grabbed for the metal rail and bruised his rib and slid to the arena floor. The crowd went crazy but Sunny could hear that one voice. That voice was the voice of his dad who had bought a ticket and was leaning over the rail to give his son a hug. Larry Mahan had run out into the arena and picked Sunny up, excited about his ride. Then Larry did something incredible, once again. He calmly walked back to the shoots, got down on his horse, nodded his head, rode an incredible ride and won the event.

Sunny rode the next night, and a lot of Glen Ridge were there to support him. Sunny's dad would go to many other rodeos with Sunny. Once again, Sunny's dad was there when it counted.

And so the story comes to an end, almost. Sunny would work through the summer. Eventually, he would go back to Stowe and take a job at the

Matterhorn. Sunny would ride rodeo in the summer at the Pond Hill Ranch with his childhood friend Tommy, who was living in Stowe. Sunny managed the Matterhorn in the winter. Tommy and Sunny would rack up a pile of rodeo stories of their own. Sunny would get together with Cindy one more time, before going to Canada to earn his Canadian certifications and coaching certifications. Sunny would even help promote Stowe's only rodeo with Richard, Kenny and Gars' leadership, on the Bicentennial Fourth of July, and win the bareback broncs.

Stowe Rodeo 1976

Carl would go back to Idaho and live in a house he built in Triumph. Sunny would complete his Canadian instructor and coaching certificates. He would eventually attend the University of Maine at Farmington—where he helped the team win the Division II Championships and helped the courageous Division II women's team hang on through the season. Carl would work hard and eventually buy the Triumph Mine. Through facing all the challenges in following his passion toward his ski dreams, he found the courage to complete two graduate degrees at Marist College and become a licensed professional counselor. Carl and Sunny would talk weekly, sometimes daily. So, if you ever see a guy or two guys in their 60s skiing on the mountain a little too fast, maybe *skiing a little better than they should* for their age, it could be them. But then again, there are a lot of skiers out there that have had their own ski dream and *this is just a story, nothing more.* Everybody should find their own Dream.

THE END

Together in New Jersey again, years later

CPSIA information can be obtained at www.ICGtesting.com
Printed in the USA
BVOW01s1242190115

383746BV00001B/1/P